A SHARP

CAPABLE OF
MURDER

Diane M. McPhee

BLUE FORGE PRESS
Port Orchard, Washington

Blue Forge Press is the print division of the volunteer-run, federal 501(c)3 nonprofit company, Blue Legacy, founded in 1989 and dedicated to bringing light to the shadows and voice to the silence. We strive to empower storytellers across all walks of life with our four divisions: Blue Forge Press, Blue Forge Films, Blue Forge Gaming, and Blue Forge Records. Find out more at: www.MyBlueLegacy.org

Blue Forge Press
7419 Ebbert Drive Southeast
Port Orchard, Washington 98367
blueforgepress@gmail.com
360-550-2071 ph.txt

In memory of two dear friends

I miss you

ACKNOWLEDGMENTS

Thanks to Blue Forge Press for their wonderful encouragement and support getting my novels published. Thank you to my friend Susan who spent hours proof reading and believing in my skill as a storyteller. Thanks also to my daughter Beth who was available at all hours to listen to me throw around ideas. My husband, Art, mentored me about weapons, drugs, dealers.... Being a lawyer and retired judge, he has seen it all. Thank you so much.

As a mother of five children, my fear of drugs, weapons, or any danger always worried me. There can be no denying that addiction and falling into the wrong crowd can overpower the human spirit and lead you down a terrible road. Parents, please be vigilant.

A SHARP CRIME MYSTERY

CAPABLE OF MURDER

Diane M. McPhee

THURSDAY, MAY 25TH

Detective Alan Sharp sat on a park bench in the Boston Commons and watched the tourists stroll past him on the path. The Commons is the oldest park in the country, dating back to 1634, and is the starting point of the famous Freedom Trail walking tour. It was only the end of May, and Alan was beginning to suspect there was an increasing number of visitors to the popular city. Although good for businesses and the general economy, more tourists meant more work for the police force. Unfortunately, like most American big cities, Boston had a reputation for robberies, aggravated assaults, drug abuse, and even the occasional murder. These crimes seemed to increase with the temperature in the summer months. Crime never takes a vacation, he ruminated.

A familiar voice interrupted his thoughts. "Hey, fancy meeting you here!" Sidney Miller smiled at Alan and sat down next to him.

CAPABLE OF MURDER

"I see you're still walking to work," Alan noted. His friend had made up his mind a year ago to get more exercise, and his two-mile hike into work seemed to do him some good. Sidney was trim, but now there was a glimmer of light in his brown eyes.

"What are you thinking about, Detective?"

Alan and Sidney had forged a friendship last year over rather grim circumstances. Sidney's brother, Marko, had been found murdered and left in an arson fire on St. Botolph Street in the Back Bay of Boston. Alan and Marko had worked closely together over the years trying to steer teens off drugs and into treatment, and Alan had been the lead detective in charge of the investigation. Marko's death was a loss for both Sidney and Alan. When the case closed, their friendship continued.

"I'm thinking about retiring, Sidney." Alan looked at his friend with curiosity knowing they had talked about retirement more than once. Being in their mid 60's, and officially being labeled seniors, both men questioned and were sometimes a bit daunted about what changes they might have to make. Neither felt like an old-timer and yet they had mused often about what it would take to ease into a comfortable life.

"I think we've had this conversation before, Alan. Is it melancholy this time, or are you really considering it now?" Sidney sat back on the bench and waited for his friend to respond.

Alan thought what a contrast they were, sitting there. Sidney was a handsome Black attorney dressed in an elegant suit and a crisp light blue shirt. He had on designer sunglasses and at his feet was a soft leather briefcase. Alan, on the other hand, was constantly struggling with a weight problem and wore his usual dark slacks and white shirt, both bought at Macy's. His light complexion made him a target for melanoma.

"This time I really mean it. In fact, I put in for a leave of absence so I can go visit my daughter, Lindsay, and her family in Seattle. I need some time off."

"How long do you think you'll be gone?"

"Just the summer. I want to enjoy the mild Northwest weather and not have to deal with the heat and storms that come through here. I've rented a small house on an island outside the city. It's a ferry ride away from downtown Seattle so I can easily commute whenever I feel like it."

"Good for you Alan! Maybe I'll take a vacation and visit you while you're there. I've never been to the Northwest."

Alan's spirits were immediately raised. His friendship with Sidney meant a lot to him and he didn't want to let it go, even over the summer. "Please do. Will Carla mind your going off and leaving her for a week or two?"

Carla and Sidney had met each other during the investigation of Marko's murder. She was the director of the Roxbury Teen Center in the Back Bay where Marko had worked as one of her counselors. By the time the case was solved, Sidney and Carla had begun seeing each other. Carla was a dynamic Black woman who resembled a well-known actress in looks and demeanor. Sometimes Sidney teased her and referred to her as Octavia, which she hated and liked at the same time.

Sidney laughed at the thought of Carla being upset with him. "She wants me to take some time off. I think I have about six weeks coming, and I could spend at least one week with you. I can see us doing some fishing."

"Fishing? When was the last time you even wore Dockers?" Alan chided Sidney over his formal clothes. Even on the weekends, he wore casual clothes that came straight from Nordstrom's. "But I would love to have you visit. I understand the Island is very laid back and so you can leave your handmade suits at home."

Sidney made a salute and stood up to go. "I better get to work before I join you on the bench for the day. Let me know when you decide to go on your trip, I can take you to the airport if you need a ride."

Alan nodded and wished his friend a great day. Things were looking up. The thought of having Sidney visit him on the West Coast made his decision easier. It was time to buy his airline ticket.

THURSDAY, JUNE 1ST

Lindsay Sharp was in a hurry to get her nine-year old twin sons off to school. Her father was arriving on a noon flight into SeaTac, and she wanted to be there early to pick him up. Traffic on 405 was always a mess, even mid-morning. Hopefully, she would be on time.

She hadn't seen her father in years. They spoke on the phone, of course, and she knew having him here in person was going to be wonderful, but it might be a little awkward, too. She was closer to her mother. It seemed that girls always preferred their moms, and this gave Lindsay a moment to pause and consider her two boys. Would they remember to call her when they got older?

Lindsay was a middle school teacher at a private school in Bellevue, a growing city on the east side of Lake Washington which marked the eastern border of Seattle. She was taking two days off from work to help get her father settled. She didn't often take a day off and she hoped her lesson plans were easy to follow. Worrying was part of Lindsay's DNA. At five foot three, she fretted over her weight and watched her calories. Maybe that's why she was so strict with her exercise and overall health regime. Now that she was thirty-two, she questioned if her life was going the way she planned. Sometimes she thought she should talk to someone about this before she worried herself to death. Where did that expression even come from? Could someone really do that?

With this thought, Lindsay pulled into traffic from the Kirkland exit. She and Sanjay, her husband of ten years, had moved to Kirkland after the boys were born. Their house was nestled in a development that was now aging gracefully. The schools were top rated and activities for the boys were well provided. The twins loved soccer but belonged on different teams so their competitive streaks would be spent on other kids.

Lindsay thought about her husband as she sat in the morning traffic. Sanjay Reynolds had been born in New Delhi and had arrived in Seattle with his parents when he was five years old. The family settled in Redmond where the schools were given high marks and Sanjay's father, Naveen, could be close to his work, as part of the growing Microsoft team. Being loyal to their East Indian culture, the Reynolds had become enmeshed with other Indian families living in Redmond and working for Microsoft. Sanjay had grown up in a rich environment.

Interlake High School in Redmond was where Sanjay and Lindsay met. She had noticed Sanjay around campus because he was one of the few East Indian guys who seemed an extrovert. He smiled and nodded to kids as they passed him and often raised his hand to respond in class. His long hair was wrapped in a topknot which also distinguished him. He was handsome, and seemed to have his own dress code, usually wearing khaki cargo pants and button-down shirts. In their junior year, they each found refuge in the school library during breaks and often found themselves engaged in casual conversation.

Soon they began dating. Sanjay's parents were happy to know he had a friend, a girl who was his friend, they reminded him. The Reynolds had plans for their son's future and didn't want him to be waylaid with ideas of marriage. Lindsay's mom was single and expected her daughter to get a scholarship to a local college so she could live at home and save money. She liked Sanjay but didn't want her daughter to marry young and take on the responsibilities of raising a family before she could enjoy her single years.

Sanjay and Lindsay both received scholarships to the University of Washington, known locally as the UW. It was during their senior year when Lindsay got pregnant, that they decided to marry. Both families had hoped this wouldn't happen, but also knew how dedicated the couple were to each other. Their holiday wedding was a lovely event.

Sanjay anticipated he would work at Microsoft when he graduated. His father had helped him secure contract jobs with the company to help research projects that were just getting off the ground. Sanjay enjoyed the work, as well as the teams he worked with, and knew the day would come when he was offered a full-time job. He was now the lead of a department.

Lindsay merged into the lane for the SeaTac airport and tried to remember how long it had been since she'd seen her father. Three or four years? How much had he changed in the past few years? Now she wondered if he would recognize her. She had cut her long hair several years ago and liked the several shades of blond foils her hairdresser talked her into. Lindsay also preferred the casual clothes most NW people opted to wear and seldom wore heels or dresses. Today she was wearing her usual Urban jeans and t-shirt with a light sweater thrown over her shoulders. Being comfortable was the way of life in the Seattle area.

Arriving just in time at the baggage claims of the airport, Lindsay looked through the crowd and finally saw her father. He was searching for the carousel with his flight number to retrieve his bags when she walked up and gave him a hug. Startled, Alan stood back and then grinned.

"How was your flight, Dad?"

"It was bumpy. I'm so glad to see you! Where are the boys?"

"School. They have a class picnic and didn't want to miss it. But they're really excted you're here!"

Alan looked at his daughter with delight. Her enthusiasm to see him seemed to come from a generous depth inside her. He remembered she had always been an easy child to please. As they walked to the carousal to get his bags, Lindsay put her arm through his. This was something new for him since they had never been an affectionate family. Alan had been in therapy for a year in Boston and had been persistently encouraged to reach out to people and accept their affections. This was a good start.

When they arrived at the house thirty minutes later, Lindsay fixed her dad a chicken salad sandwich and they sat down to talk about his plans for the summer.

Alan was eager to get to the Island. "I can move into the rental house this weekend, according to the realtor. From what I've read, it's a pretty laid-back little town. When was the last time you were there?"

"About a month ago. I have a good friend who lives there. You'll like her, she's an artist and her husband's a musician. They live in a charming farmhouse with their three children."

"So, you're familiar with the community?".

"Not really, but Tessa is willing to show you around. Although I need to warn you, there's not a lot to see compared to Boston. It's a country town with some great restaurants, a few wineries, a movie theater and even a museum. It's quiet though."

Lindsay reached for something on the counter. "Here's an article I saved for you about the Island. It's a little biased, but it gives you an idea of the community."

Alan took the article and read through the opinion piece. "I didn't realize the Island had so few people… 25,000 according to this article. I suppose since it's only a 35-minute ferry ride to Seattle, it attracts a lot of businesspeople."

Lindsay laughed. "The Island has its fair share of lawyers and other professionals who ride the ferry every day into the city, but it also draws writers, actors, and musicians. .

CAPABLE OF MURDER

It has the feel of a small town. My friend says that people casually speak on ferry rides or at parties about their acquaintances with well-known celebrities. And you should see the long lines of commuters each morning, coffee cups in hand, trying to capture a seat on the crowded morning runs. In fact, car commuters time their distance from home to the dock by the minute to reach the exact ferry they need or be late for work. It's all sort of a game. Bunch of commuters bursting with talk about how they almost missed the boat, or how early they had to get up that day. It's common chatter and never seems to annoy anyone."

Alan read aloud about the town of Winslow, the center of activity. "The writer says the town of Winslow is known for its 'charming atmosphere,' with several small shops and restaurants running up and down the two-lane street for three blocks. Popular local wineries offer wine tasting once a month to lure people from surrounding areas, including Seattle." Alan looked up at his daughter. "I think I'll find enough to do, and I'll have you and the boys to keep me company whenever you're free."

Lindsay smiled. "We're counting on plenty of visits."

Alan read the last part of the article to himself. '*Like many small, rural towns, teenagers on the Island are often bored. They refer to the Island as "The Rock" and complain about having nothing exciting to do. Feelings of isolation lead many teens to experiment with alcohol and drugs as early as junior high school. One recent NY Times edition featured a front-page article about this little oasis of an Island, saying that deep within its boundaries lurked drugs. Lots of drugs. When the article appeared, Island residents were up in arms refusing to accept there was a major drug problem, and claiming their children were all college bound and were taught not to use drugs. This attitude is common in many affluent communities everywhere, the belief that wealth and status keeps you immune from lower-level crimes and criminals.'*

Still, Alan found it hard to believe that the small Island community was as overwhelmed with drug problems as the big city of Boston, but he also knew that drugs weren't just a city problem.

Across Puget Sound, Island police Chief Kevin Johnson worried about the casual use of drugs infecting the Island. He grew up minutes away from the Agate Pass Bridge on the Island side and remembered when life was simpler and playing outside with friends all day was what summer was all about. His small family home had been a bike ride away from a park where his buddies met to play soccer and hang out. Now in his mid-forties, Kevin had to admit that things had changed over the years and the Island was changing, too.

Kevin had been raised by a single mother after his father decided that Island life was too stifling for him. He walked out on his family when Kevin was three. Over the years, Penny Johnson, Kevin's mom, struggled with her responsibilities and eventually gave in to soothing her anxieties with alcohol. Kevin had survived her unpredictable parenting by rushing home from school each day and helping his mother with chores, hoping she would resist her drink of choice. By the time he was in the eighth grade, a school counselor became aware of Kevin's role in the family and offered him a list of AA meetings to give to his mother. Kevin encouraged, and then demanded that she go. When he graduated from high school, his mother had stopped drinking all together. But he knew she had traded addiction for addiction. She gambled. Just over the Agate Pass Bridge was the Suquamish Casino with all the gambling opportunities and promises of a better life she hoped for.

Penny was now in her mid 60's and believed she only had a few more years to win big. She loved the sound of the slot machines and the roll of the dice. She loved the flashing lights and the never-ending glasses of soda that were delivered when you held up your hand to a waitress. She didn't need the alcohol anymore when she had the thrill of winning to keep her going. Over the years, she had won $1000, $500, and lots of $20 pots. Her best friends were gamblers, and they all clapped and yelled whenever one of them won. Even if it was only on the nickel machines. It was like one big party every time she came to play. Her gambling friends told her not to look back, just keep playing and dream about how you would spend the money

Penny didn't want to think about how much money she had spent gambling each week because that was counterproductive. But she had experienced some gambling losses over the years and had to take the equity out of her house to pay her bills. Now, to keep up, she rented her small basement to a young guy who went to the community college in Bremerton. She also worked part time at the near-by gas station convenience store on weekends to give her the extra cash she needed to keep gambling.

Weekends were her busiest days at the store. Penny always showed up for her eight-hour shift dressed in jeans and a sweatshirt Her knees were beginning to bother her due to the considerable weight she had put on once she stopped drinking. She hid a lot of it under her sweatshirt but couldn't dismiss her uncomfortable aches and pains after standing at the counter for long hours. If she could just stop eating all the junk food, she might be able to lose thirty pounds. It would be a good start.

Kevin checked in with his mother weekly. In fact, he usually tried to see her a couple times a week to make sure she was sober. He didn't like her spending so much time gambling at the casino because he was aware that booze flowed easily. But she never showed signs of drinking, only euphoria when she won a couple dollars. If she was happy, then he was.

Not surprised, Penny was pleased that her first customer of the day was Kevin. He smiled at his mother, "How's your day going?"

"I just got here, and it looks like a good one." Penny loved her son and gave him a big hug.

"I'm on my way to a soccer game," Kevin reported, "It looks like KJ will make the intermediates this year." KJ was Kevin's oldest son, named after his father. Kevin Junior liked the name KJ because it sounded like a disc jockey or a rock star. He was ten. His younger brother, Brent, was eight and didn't seem to like sports, but their five-year-old sister Lucy loved everything that KJ liked. It was nice to have a fan.

Kevin and his wife, Julia, kept a close watch on their three children. Julia worked in the office at the Middle school and heard too many stories about kids acting out and making bad choices involving drugs and drinking. As a result, she kept her kids busy with activities and made sure they were respectful and paid attention to their responsibilities. All three were good students, and Julia planned on keeping it that way.

After watching his son's soccer game, Kevin went back to work for a few hours. He had a small team of officers who patrolled the Island and worked regular hours during the week. There wasn't much crime, mainly petty thieveries and car wrecks that were sent to the local Judge Pro Tem who most often handed out community service sentences. Occasionally, there was a disruption caused by a marital dispute, aggravated assault, or drinking that Kevin had to handle himself. If it involved a serious injury, he handed the case over to the Kitsap County Court in Port Orchard. The biggest problem on the Island was DUI, and the two cells in the Island jail were used most often to hold drunks than any other reason.

Now that weed was legal, Kevin had a difficult time deciding what action to take. He sat at his desk in his quiet office and, once again, considered the options. As far as he was concerned, driving stoned was the same as driving drunk, and he wanted to treat them as the same. Maybe getting your driver's license suspended would cause Islanders to think twice before ingesting and driving. He decided to investigate what approach other jurisdictions might have on this.

He knew that Island kids found ways to get weed, drugs, and alcohol. He was also aware that shrewd dealers prowled the Island schools looking for buyers. In fact, he recently heard rumors about some of the high school athletes buying pain meds from dealers, and so Kevin planned to start looking into the athletic department for any evidence of drug activity. He made a mental note to talk to the County's Drug Squad to learn more about the potential impact and misuse of drugs on the Island, especially for teens.

Kyle Smith had always been a multi-sport star athlete on the Island. Although he liked all the school sports, his favorite was soccer, and his favorite position was central defender. His game play in that role was highly acclaimed, and he took pride in his ability to protect the ball and make just the right pass at the right time. Kyle liked being the one everyone depended on, but sometimes all sorts of problems were thrown at him, making him feel frustrated or even angry. He was expected to be the lead communicator during a game, and to remember the last thing the team needed was for him to make a mistake. On the other hand, the coach continually urged him to stay calm and be well-prepared. Sometimes he felt the pressure was taking over his whole life and he wanted to put the stress behind and just play the game. It was during the first home game of the year, that Kyle's dream of leading the team to victory ended.

Kyle remembered going airborne for a header and coming down awkwardly on his right leg. When his knee gave way, he felt an immediate surge of mind-bending pain. Lying prone, after falling to the pitch, he saw the look on his coach's face and knew... his soccer days were over.

Kyle had to have major knee surgery. Although the surgery went well, Kyle's recuperation and rehab did not. After his surgery, he was prescribed a short course of low-dose OxyContin to ease his post-operative pain. He was no stranger to drugs, and had, on occasion, smoked pot with his friends. But once he relied on OxyContin to ease his pain, he was hooked. When he asked for more meds, his doctor refused, saying he was worried about the highly addictive potential of Oxy. But Kyle didn't intend to go without Oxy and decided he would find other ways to get it.

It didn't take him long to find a source. One of his classmates told him about a guy at one of the restaurants in town who sold pills, and soon Kyle was fully addicted to the opioid. As a result, the dominos began falling and he became moody and less focused, especially at school. Kyle began to be secretive and battled with his parents when his grades began to plunge. They wanted him to talk with a counselor, but all Kyle wanted was more Oxy.

To get the "relief" he wanted, Kyle had to keep increasing the amount of Oxy he took, and that meant spending more and more money just to keep up. Drugs weren't cheap. After graduation, he planned to find a cheaper source.

FRIDAY, JUNE 2ND

L indsay told Alan he could borrow one of their cars to get around the Island. It was an old Toyota they planned on keeping for the boys when the time came. Pleased, Alan asked the boys if they wanted to ride with him for the trip to the ferry dock in Seattle. They yelled their approval and were excited to have their grandfather's attention all to themselves. They were eager to make plans for visiting him soon.

"Do you think we can fish one day?" Rani asked. "My dad said we have some fishing rods in the garage we could use. I don't think he knows how to fish."

Alan didn't either. He had grown up in the city and his only activity was learning to play tennis. But he'd try to fish if that's what they wanted to do.

"Maybe you could bring your bikes over for a weekend and we could bike around the Island. I hear there's bike trails everywhere." Alan suggested.

"We have new bikes! We can speed around because they're dirt bikes."

Alan's heart sank for a minute. Could he keep up with these two active children?

As Alan merged the car south onto I-5, he was pleasantly surprised to see Mount Rainier, looming in the distance. "The Mountain" as it's known locally, towered 14,000 feet over the surrounding area and was the centerpiece of the National Park of the same name. On clear days, such as this, the view was breathtaking.

Waiting in line at the Coleman dock to board the ferry, Alan realized that Seattle was much bigger than he expected. He knew it was a thriving city, but the amount of traffic along with the mix of skyscrapers and building cranes were still surprising. Seattle's downtown area looked a lot like other US big cities he'd visited, but unlike the old industrial cities he was used to on the East Coast, Seattle was green with trees and greenbelts. It's downtown gave way to a thriving waterfront with a breathtaking view looking west across Puget Sound to the snowcapped Olympic mountains sparkling in the distance. And unlike the narrow streets and rows of brownstones in his beloved Boston, the houses in this area were detached and set on green lots scattered with tall pine and cedar trees. From small Craftsman cottages to larger two and three-story modern McMansions, the city mixed old and new in an array of pleasant looking neighborhoods.

The ferry ride to the Island was picturesque and calming. Because Seattle lies alongside Puget Sound, an inland arm of the Pacific Ocean, people were encouraged to look for whales arcing through the waters. Alan, however, was content to watch the city in the background slowly recede against the backdrop of the snowcapped Cascade mountains. As the ferry approached their destination, the air smelled fresh thanks to the breezes from the open waters of Puget Sound, and Alan felt himself relaxing. He took a deep breath and realized how much he needed this vacation.

As they drove off the ferry and turned left into the town, Alan was pleased to see the small-town atmosphere of the Island community. The charming shops, restaurants, and stores along the three-block downtown area seemed old fashioned to Alan after living in the congested Boston area.

The boys, who were searching the town for adventure, saw a blinking pizza sign on a small restaurant door and decided it was time for lunch. "Can we have pizza, Grandpa? We're really hungry!"

"Let's see what your parents have planned for lunch. But I promise you we'll have pizza at that place when you visit. I'll try it out a few times and tell you what I think." Alan teased the two boys and appreciated their rolled eyes.

The small house he rented was located just outside of town and tucked into the first block of a development near the high school. It had a lush garden in front and Alan remembered the realtor saying there was a sprinkler system and a weekly landscape company who managed the property. That was a relief since he knew nothing about gardening. Entering the front door, Alan recognized the welcoming living room from the online advertisement. He admired the comfortable looking leather sofa and easy chair which were placed near a brick fireplace flanked by bookcases. The dining room and kitchen were open to this room and the light from the three front windows and high ceilings made everything appear much roomier than expected.

Alan smiled and turned to Lindsay, "This is perfect."

Lindsay agreed and helped carry her father's luggage to the large bedroom in the rear of the house. Decorated in pale colors, this room looked fresh and peaceful. She was beginning to envy her father's new retreat and wondered if he would exchange places with her for a weekend.

Rani and Kirin were busy looking at the second bedroom and wondering how they would share the double bed. They decided to bring sleeping bags and take turns when they slept over. Maybe their grandfather would get an air mattress.

"So, Dad, is there anything you hope to do while you're here? Write a book? Learn to speak Spanish?" Lindsay was teasing him but wondered if her father would be bored in such a quiet environment.

"Besides seeing more of you, I guess I'll just take it a day at a time. I have several books I want to read, and I promised myself to get more exercise. Daily walks and watching my diet will be a good start."

"On Sunday my friend Tessa is having a birthday party for her husband who's turning forty. We're invited and they want you to come too. Lots of Island people will be there."

"Sounds great." Alan wanted to please his daughter and get to know her friends, but he didn't think that a younger crowd would be interested in him. He would go anyway.

When he returned from getting some groceries later in the day, Alan thought about the next couple of months. If he could just slow down and relax, he might begin to see his future clearly and decide about his retirement. Opening a bottle of red wine from a local winery, he sat in the easy chair and thought about his life. Over thirty years on the police force had gone by quickly. He wondered if it was true that everyone who got to this age looked back over the years with astonishment. Marriages, children being born, careers, all added up to a life fully lived. Of course, he would have changed a few things along the way if given the opportunity, but he was thankful to be sitting where he was, enjoying a glass of wine, and not needing to be anywhere.

SATURDAY, JUNE 3RD

Alan woke up the next day to the sound of birds. When was the last time he heard this melodious singing? He really couldn't remember. But now he lay there and enjoyed it. What would he do today? This was an entertaining thought since he realized that every day would begin like this for a while. He was so used to climbing out of bed, into the shower, and then rushing off to the precinct. Years of working on reports of violence and crimes were in his blood, and he wanted to shake them loose so he could relax and enjoy his family

After finishing his emails, Alan decided to start his exercise program by walking up to town. It was probably less than half a mile and he wanted to stop at the library on the way back to catch up on Island news. He had heard they had a weekly newspaper that was filled with events and local musings. His cell phone rang as he walked past the high school.

"Hi Dad, how are you doing?"

Alan smiled to hear his daughter's voice. "I'm on a walk right now, just passing by the high school."

"Do you want to call me back?"

"No, I'm enjoying talking with you on my walk."

"I wanted to remind you about the birthday party Tessa has planned. It's tomorrow and we can pick you up on our way there."

"Sounds good. I'm looking forward to it." Alan tried to sound sincere. He would do anything for his daughter, and if she wanted to introduce him to her friends, he would go to the party.

Alan continued to stroll along the old sidewalk, peering in the windows of the shops. Galleries and wine shops were featured along with a few clothes shops. He mused how someone from the Boston area would be lost without their Starbucks and trendy clothes stores that lined their city streets for blocks. He might get used to this slower pace.

Alan was pleased to see that the Island newspaper, *The Review*, was available at the diner where he stopped for lunch. He ordered an omelet and a scone and set about reading local news. Alan read that the high school seniors graduated that afternoon. Big parties were planned. On the fifth page he noticed the police section and read through the weekly incident reports. There were three car thefts, a DUI, and several noise disturbances. It looked like a typical week in the small town.

Before he left the diner, Alan's phone rang. It was his son, Sam. "Hey! How are you doing?"

Sam had moved back in with Alan the year before,

after deciding to get some work experience before completing his master's degree. "I'm doing great! Harry and I just went for a run." Harry was the aging Golden Retriever who had lived with Alan for years. Now that Sam was around, the dog's allegiance was quickly drawn to the younger energy and he followed Sam everywhere. "How's the Island?"

"Calm. Peaceful. Small. I think I'll be able to relax here. Your sister let me borrow their extra car so I can explore. The boys want to spend time with me, so I've got to plan some fun things to do."

They spoke for a few more minutes and then rang off. Alan thought about how much progress Sam had made over the year. Once he admitted to having an addiction to Adderall and getting help, his attitude and life completely turned around. And his job at the Teen Center in Roxbury helping teens with addictions, brought out the best in his son. Alan was proud of Sam and was also proud of himself for maintaining some distance during the process.

When Alan returned to his house, he decided not to plan too far ahead and to enjoy the day. With old age retreating and advancing unpredictably over the years, Alan reminded himself to regard it as a new adventure and go with the flow. Once he removed his shoes and put his feet up on the sofa he fell into a deep sleep. Two hours later, he awoke with a start, but felt refreshed and not the least bit guilty for nodding off. He decided to make a salad for dinner and then go for another walk around town.

The evening was warm as Alan made his way along the quiet streets. He stopped at The Doc Restaurant to enjoy a glass of wine before returning home and was surprised when he heard sirens racing through town. This was obviously an unusual sound for this little town, because every customer looked up and was alarmed, needing to know what had happened. A disturbance like this, the bartender told him, was seldom heard, and it raised eyebrows. Alan understood. He finished his wine and walked back home.

SUNDAY, JUNE 4TH

Sunday, early afternoon, Lindsay and Sanjay showed up to take Alan to the party. It was a beautiful day, and they were dressed casually since it was an outdoor BBQ celebration. People were bringing their own meat to grill, and Lindsay had brought homemade frosted brownies and marinated chicken as their offering. It was an Island custom… people shared everything…books, babysitting, recipes, fruit, vegetables, and gossip.

"Did you hear about the murders last night?" This was the first thing Lindsay asked her father when he got in the car.

"No, where?"

"Here! On the Island! The news said that two teenage kids were shot! Everyone's going to be talking about it at the party."

"Sounds terrible," Alan replied, wondering how this small community would handle such a crisis.

Changing the subject, Lindsay told her father that

Tessa and Simon's old farmhouse was built in 1898 and was one of several landmarks on the Island. Alan was amused that 1898 seemed "old" to people of the west. But he kept this to himself.

When they arrived, there were several people already sitting on deck chairs with drinks in their hands or wandering around the thriving vegetable garden by the old barn. Tessa greeted them and invited them to grab something to drink and make themselves comfortable. Alan grabbed a beer and Sanjay and Lindsay each took a glass of wine. It felt like an old fashion country picnic, thought Alan, as he gazed across the open fields.

Alan asked Tessa about the history of the house, and she offered to show him around.

Beginning at the front door, she stopped at the entry. "This was probably the front room originally, you can see how small it is, probably less than 200 square feet. And the smaller room adjacent to this one was probably a bedroom. We use the small room as a TV spot for the kids." They turned around and walked into a larger light filled room with hardwood floors and a modern wood burning stove. "We know the house has been remodeled several times over the years. This addition was added in the 70's by the people who owned the house at the time."

"You must spend a lot of time in here," Alan was admiring the oak woodwork that framed the windows and doors, "I would, it's beautiful."

"We use this room for everything. When company visits or the kids want to spread out and play games or horse around, this is the biggest room in the house. It gets a lot of light, and we can see the field from here. That's where our pony is." Tessa smiled at the thought. She loved that little horse.

On the other side of the house was the kitchen which had another wood stove, and well used appliances. Tess beamed, "I think this is the best place in the house. You can imagine hundreds of meals being cooked over the years. Probably thousands. We have all our meals in the kitchen dining area where we can look out the large picture windows to the fields and linger for a while." Alan loved the old-fashioned ambiance of the room and then noticed another window over the stove that peered out to a large blooming apple tree. It was all very enchanting.

Stairs leading up from the kitchen were steep and led to four sleeping rooms and one bathroom. Once again Tessa explained that the original house only had two small bedrooms. Walking down the narrow hall, she noted how the people who added the downstairs addition also added a large bedroom and a smaller room next to it. "We're a little cramped upstairs, but it's worth it because of the rest of the house."

"All very charming," Alan smiled. He liked the farmhouse and he liked Tessa.

Returning to the group, Alan heard people talking candidly about the murders. Lindsay saw her father and insisted on introducing him to Police Chief Kevin Johnson who was there for a very short visit.

"Chief Johnson, this is my dad, Alan Sharp. He's a

Homicide Detective from Boston taking a well-earned break here on the Island for the summer."

The men shook hands, and Alan inquired about what had happened.

"It's very sad," Kevin began, "Two teens were murdered. In fact, if you look down this road, you might see police tape at the scene. It happened right there!"

Alan looked past the field and across to a red farmhouse.

"I'm on my way now, the crime scene is just behind the farmhouse." Johnson pointed to an older red shingled house with a wraparound porch. "There's a dirt path that goes into the woods quite a way. Someone heard gun shots and called us. At first, we thought it was someone hunting, even though that's illegal. So, I came out to check and found the bodies. Two teens, a boy, and a girl. I can't tell you how awful that was to find." Kevin ran his hands through his slightly greying hair.

Alan wanted to tell him about the big city homicides but held off. Instead, he asked, "Were they local kids?"

"Yes, recent graduates."

"I'm sorry to hear that. It must hit the Island hard when someone they know is killed, especially in such a manner. Did you know the kids?"

"No, my three are still in elementary school. But I do know one of the parents from soccer games. He keeps score for us when the kids are competing with other schools. Just a really nice guy."

"Do you think it had to do with drugs?" Alan

suspected he already knew the answer because drug killings were usually involved with this kind of homicide. These kids had to be into something dangerous to have it end like this.

"Probably. I don't know if you're aware of the denial here on the Island. People are afraid of drugs but unwilling to admit we have a problem and that kids are using on a regular basis. Kids aren't dumb or innocent. Drugs have always been around, along with people refusing to do anything about them. I came by the party because I know a few people here today, and I wanted to reassure them that we're doing all we can."

"Well, my best to you, Chief. I deal with drug-connected violence all the time in Boston and there's no easy answer. We just keep chipping away and trying to give kids alternatives. But the families and communities have got to help, too. Even the politicians who say they'll clean up the city just walk away after the election. It's discouraging and very, very sad."

Lindsay walked up with another person she wanted her father to meet. Maggie owned the Bed and Breakfast on the Island and immediately took Alan's arm to begin a conversation. She was in her 50's and had the energy of a grade school girl. Her smile was contagious, and she seemed to know everyone. Alan was invited to grab a plate of food and join her at a table. He was drawn to the natural optimism of this woman.

Maggie Freeman loved to meet new people. Her B&B on the Island was popular, and she delighted in spending hours listening to her customers talk about their lives while they ate her country style breakfasts. She laughed loud and had a sympathetic heart if you needed someone to care. She was also a pillar of the community. Her popular recipe book was dedicated to her friends and a percent of the profits from the sales were donated to the local schools. Maggie was a gem.

Alan was enjoying his conversation with Maggie when Police Chief Johnson sat down beside him. "I wonder if you could do me a favor, Detective," he began, "we have a town meeting coming up this week and people are going to want to hear about the murders. There should be a good crowd. Most Island people don't want to think about all the drugs and dealers their kids get involved with, but I was hoping maybe you could talk to them about kids and drugs in the big city. If they heard from you, maybe they would pay more attention to things right in front of their faces."

Alan hesitated to let this sink in, but Maggie was nudging him to say yes. "Please consider this, Alan. If things have gotten to the point where kids are killed, it's time for the Island to take notice."

"When is the meeting?" Alan was taking his time to consider all the reasons not to get involved. This was his vacation, and he wanted to make it clear that he was not interested in any investigation.

"Wednesday, at the high school."

Well, thought Alan, the high school was right next door to his house. "Okay, let me know the time and I'll prepare something."

Both Chief Johnson and Maggie were pleased.

J oel Spencer was watching the people at the party carefully. Besides his job at The Doc restaurant in town, he often took catering jobs for families around the Island. That was why he was at Tessa and Simon's house; he'd been hired to help serve the crowd and clean up afterwards. When he overheard the Boston cop being introduced, he thought again about the kids who were murdered. Chief Johnson said the investigation was looking into drugs and Joel wanted to keep a low profile. Everyone was on edge, and he hoped the old Boston cop would stay out of things.

At 28, Joel had already been fired from three jobs. Determined to clean up his act and start over, Joel moved to the Island ten months ago because of its reputation for quiet living and easy access to Seattle. He found a place to rent over the town gift store and took a job at The Doc Restaurant as a waiter. So far, all he needed to do was smile at his customers and pay his rent. No one knew about his drug problem.

Joel had grown up in a typical American family in eastern Oregon with two older brothers and a younger sister. His ADHD problem wasn't discovered until he was in fifth grade, and by that time everyone thought he was dumb. He was tall for his age, which also made kids avoid him, or fear him. When his anger boiled over as kids teased him, the resource room teachers had trouble calming him down. By the time his parents got him into treatment and on the right medication, it was too late for him to finally fit in. His reputation as a troublemaker was already cemented, and his only outlet was more drugs. Throughout middle school and into high school his dependence on drugs grew. He made easy money by doing odd jobs for neighbors and helping around the house so he could afford his drug habit. By graduation he was so reliant on the fistfuls of uppers and downers that he'd lost track of exactly what and how many he was taking. He didn't give much thought to his future.

His parents tried to talk him into going to vocational school, but Joel resisted. He finally took a job in a warehouse because the hours were good, and nobody cared when he took long breaks to have a smoke. But he was fired after six months for careless mistakes, as his drug habit became worse.

He eventually moved in with his part time girlfriend, Fran, and got another warehouse job. Because of the drugs he relied on, Joel's behavior became erratic, and he bounced from increased alertness, to restlessness, to aggression. After a while he couldn't sleep through the night and became paranoid over the smallest things. This behavior, and Fran's insistence, sent him into rehab. Joel tried his best to give up the drugs he was so dependent on, but after a year of outpatient work, he just could not. Fran finally left him, and Joel lost another job.

That was when he moved to Seattle. He heard about the warehouse work at Amazon and decided to give it a try. He rented a room in an apartment with two other guys who worked the warehouse. They were regular guys like him and spent most of their money at bars and clubs in the city. Joel wanted to put some money aside and thought about trying rehab again, but he got caught up in the "single's life" and partying. When he didn't show up for work on three occasions, he was fired. That's when he decided to take the ferry to the Island and keep a low profile.

Joel thought he was smart about drugs. He didn't buy on the Island, even though he knew there were dealers everywhere. Instead, he took the ferry to Seattle and easily bought what he needed on First Avenue right outside the Pike Place Market.

The Market served as a business place for many small farmers, craftspeople and merchants and was one of the oldest continuously operated public farmers markets in the country. Most people thought of the popular tourist destination only as a desirable place to buy fresh local fish, meat, flowers, farm products and gifts. But, in truth, drugs were bought and sold at an alarming rate in some of the shops and on the streets in and adjacent to the Market.

Joel had his favorite dealers who had his stash ready weekly. Besides his regular pills, Joel purchased some cocaine, meth and weed. He used the pills and meth to boost his energy to get through the day, at night he smoked weed to relax. He sold what he didn't use to kids around the town.

On the way home from Simon's birthday party, Alan told Lindsey and Sanjay about his decision to speak about drugs at the town meeting. They were both surprised and questioned him about getting involved.

"Dad, this is your vacation. Please tell me you're not going to get involved with an investigation!" Lindsay was adamant.

"I'm not going to get involved with anything!" Alan exclaimed. "I promise you that. This is my time to relax and doing police work is not on the agenda."

"What did you think of Maggie?" Lindsey decided that changing the subject might be a good idea.

"She certainly has a lot of energy. I imagine her B&B does a great business."

"According to Tessa, she's the life of the party wherever she goes. And it's true that her place has a waiting list, especially during the holiday months."

"She invited me to brunch tomorrow."

Lindsey smiled at her father. "I hope you're going."

"Yes, you bet!"

By the time Alan walked into his house, he was exhausted. Maybe it was from sitting out in the sun on the deck, but he thought it might also be from the conversation. He couldn't remember the last party he had gone to. Today he had purposely kept his energy at a high level so he could remember names and families. After all, it was a small island, and he would probably run into many of them at the store.

He was looking forward to seeing Maggie at her B&B in the morning. Before he turned out his light, Alan looked up Maggie's B&B on the internet.

The Island B&B was built in 1907 by a shipwright who worked at the West Blakely Mill. He and his wife had nine children and enjoyed the 5000 square foot comfortable house. It sat on a half-acre overlooking Rich Passage where they could watch the ferries go by and see the lights of distant shores in the evening. The property was converted into a B&B in 1982 and finally came into Maggie Freeman and her husband's hands in 1986. There are five guest rooms, three with private bathrooms. Over the years, many innovative updates and improvements have been made. The garden with a rustic gazebo and unstructured masses of seasonal blooms is photographed regularly by guests and tourists.

Alan was pleased with what he read.

MONDAY, JUNE 5TH

Maggie Freeman liked the Boston detective a lot. He had a gleam in his eyes and a subtle sense of humor that tickled her. She had been widowed four years ago and was left with the responsibilities of running the business and raising her teenage daughter. Carrie was now in college on the East Coast and only home on holidays. Her summers were spent catering parties with an elite company in New Haven. They had hired her immediately after learning her skills from helping her mother run the B&B. Maggie was proud of her daughter, but she missed her company.

This morning Maggie had three overnight couples for breakfast. She offered her usual homemade oatmeal, scones, muffins, and fruit as a start and then brought out her egg scramble which was the house specialty. Hot coffee and tea along with a variety of juices were available and allowed for lingering and visiting. Maggie learned that one couple was from Canada and on their way to an Alaskan cruise. The boat usually left around 4:00 from a Seattle pier and they were musing about what they would do before it left. The other two couples had attended a family wedding in Poulsbo. It was a large affair, and they were especially happy to have found Maggie's B&B, because all the nearby hotels had been filled due to the local school graduations. Maggie enjoyed listening to her customers and, yet, hoped they would move along so she could get things ready for Alan. She was making her famous quiche to go with the homemade scones and muffins.

At twelve o'clock Alan knocked on the door of the B&B. He had stopped for a minute to admire the beautiful garden in front. Obviously, someone loved to garden. Chairs and tables graced the wraparound porch of the three-story house, as an invitation to sit and enjoy the lush flowers and plants. Maggie opened the door and gave Alan a hug. This amused him, and he realized how much he enjoyed the embrace.

Alan had spent a year in therapy after his friend Marko had been murdered. At first, he thought it was because of his problems adjusting to the cascading changes aging was pushing upon him. But after a few months, his therapist, Rose, had coaxed him to acknowledge his grief over the death of his friend and to understand and confront his loneliness and fear of intimacy. This was why he had taken the leave of absence from work, to spend time on himself. And now here he was being hugged by someone he really didn't know, having brunch with her at her home, and feeling okay about it.

Maggie led Alan into the beautiful foyer of the house

and down the hall to the kitchen. The room was smaller than Alan expected, but every inch of space seemed to be dedicated to food. Muffins and scones where in baskets, bowls of fruit were set out, bread dough was rising, and appliances were evenly spaced on the counters. The atmosphere was homey and functional at the same time.

"How about a Mimosa, Alan?"

Alan wasn't a fan of champagne, but he was delighted with the offer. Maggie mixed their drinks and then led him to the dining room off the kitchen. It had a large oak round table that appeared to seat ten. As they sat next to each other on two cushioned chairs, Alan noticed the paintings of domestic landscapes and lovely gardens which hung gracefully on the walls.

Maggie saw him appraising the artwork. "The paintings are from local artists. In fact, they're for sale if someone particularly admires the work. The artists on the Island love to display their work in several businesses and shops. Which one do you like, Alan?"

Alan looked at the six paintings on display and said, "I'm partial to the garden scene in the small painting. Is it your garden?"

"Yes! I encourage several artists to use my house as a subject. We have great fun when they spend the day here."

Alan was beginning to like the Island more and more.

Maggie served her delicious quiche and promised Alan she would send the left-overs home with him. Moving to the comfortable cushioned chairs on the porch after their meal, Maggie asked Alan more about his past.

"Well, there's not much to say. Two marriages and two children over the years, and now I have two grandchildren. It all went by so quickly. My job took up so much of my time and I guess sometimes I forgot to enjoy things along the way. That's why I'm here on the Island... to relax and think about what's ahead for me."

"What made you choose the Island?"

"My daughter talked me into it. How did you meet Lindsay?"

"Tessa and I are great friends. I think the girls planned on introducing us at the party. Sneaky... but I'm glad they did. I would love to show you around the area if you like."

Alan smiled and agreed to take her up on this.

Maggie then remembered about the town hall meeting. "Are you ready for the meeting on Wednesday?"

Alan put his coffee cup down and leaned towards her. "I'm not certain what Chief Johnson hopes to have me say. I can talk about drugs in Boston and teens getting into trouble, but I'm not sure that will apply to the Island."

"Oh, yes it will!" Maggie stood up and offered Alan more coffee. "People here have their heads in the sand when it comes to drugs. When my daughter was in high school, she said all you had to do was walk to the designated smoking area and you could buy anything. Teachers seemed to ignore what was happening because they didn't want to get involved."

"With your proximity to Seattle, I would think it's common knowledge that drugs would find an outlet here. Are Islanders really that much in denial?"

"I'm afraid they are. Of course, we have a group of citizens who try to raise awareness and educate people with meetings and classes. They usually spread their messages to the younger kids in the hopes of convincing them to avoid drugs and recognize the dangers. But once kids get into middle school, all that good work seems to go to waste."

"What are the kids using… or do you know?"

"I hear about marijuana, of course, but also things like Ecstasy, Oxy, and Adderall. Kids complain that life is so confusing, and pressure is so great that they rely on drugs to cope with things."

"Well, that's universal. Kids from all over the country, probably the world, complain about the pressure. I don't think the media and video games are helping either. Our ancient times of growing up without cell phones and the internet are deep in the past." Alan smiled at Maggie. "I mean my past. You're much younger."

"Not that much!" Maggie laughed and then realized it was time to wrap things up. She looked at Alan and reassured him, "Alan, I'll be there on Wednesday to hear you speak. But if you want to call and run things by me before, please don't hesitate to call."

Alan thanked her for offering. He gathered up the quiche she had promised, noticing she had also packed him some muffins, and gave her a hug goodbye. He was proud of himself.

Kevin Johnson was concerned about too many things today. His mother had not answered her phone this morning when he called, and this always put him on edge. And he just received the final report from the ME about the autopsies of the slain teens.

The report revealed:

Kyle: Death caused by a bullet penetrating his aorta causing him to rapidly bleed out.

Shelly: One shot penetrating her brain, died instantly.

Weapon: Based on cartridge shells found at the scene, a 9mm semi-automatic handgun.

Both victims were found fully clothed and declared dead at the scene.

Toxicology tests: Revealed: amounts indicating alcohol consumption within 24 hours; marijuana in amounts indicating recent ingestion; trace amounts of MDMA (Ecstasy).

Kevin was on his way to let the grieving parents know the results. When he had spoken with them the day after the murders, they were in no shape to answer his questions. They would be hit hard with the report about drugs today.

The family of the slain teen-aged girl, Shelly Mann, lived down by Fort Ward. This older neighborhood had fallen on hard times and needed money to fix the shambled houses and roads. The Mann's house was on the edge of the neighborhood, hidden by a six-foot hedge. Walking down the path to the house, Kevin noticed a thriving vegetable garden and a rabbit hutch. He wondered why people loved to keep rabbits as pets these days.

When Kevin knocked, Mr. Mann opened the door. He was lean, with rimless glasses perched on the end of his nose. He was dressed in faded jeans and an unbuttoned worn plaid shirt over an off-white tee. He acknowledged Kevin and put out his hand. They walked into a living room which was remarkably tidy, in fact everything was so clean that the tables and floors gleamed. Kevin was impressed. Mrs. Mann was seated in a comfortable chair beside the brick fireplace, and she looked at Kevin with eyes that were blank. He knew she was still in shock.

"I'm truly sorry to be here under these circumstances," Kevin began. "I will make this as quick as I possibly can." Kevin took a seat on the faded sofa. "Can you tell me what Shelly might have been doing in the woods that night?"

Mr. Mann spoke up, "All we know is that she was going to dinner and then to the graduation party with Kyle. They left here around 6:00. She was excited to be graduating and they were both planning on going to the community college in a couple of months. We just don't know how this could have happened to our little girl." Tears were starting to fill his eyes as he walked over to put his hand on his wife's shoulder. She had begun to weep.

Kevin took a moment before asking the couple something they probably didn't want to hear. "Did you know that your daughter took drugs? I'm only asking because our toxicology tests revealed a significant amount of drugs in her system."

"No, she did not. We are positive about this." Mr. Mann looked disgusted at the thought that Shelly would even know how to buy drugs.

Kevin nodded his head as if in agreement, and then continued, "It appears that both Kyle and Shelly had taken drugs hours before their deaths. If this was the only time they had used anything, it certainly was very unfortunate."

Moving in another direction, Kevin asked, "Can you tell me who Shelly's friends were?"

Mr. Mann ran his fingers through his unwashed hair and thought for a moment. "Let's see, Mira Connelly and Jessica Sykes are her best friends. I heard they're devastated over what's happened. I don't really know who Kyle hung out with, but I guess you'll talk with his parents."

"Whose party did they attend that night?"

"It was a group party at the old hall. Parents had arranged it for the graduates and had hired a band and everything. We all contributed some money to make it special." Mr. Mann's voice trailed off and he checked to see that his wife was okay. "What do you know about who did this?"

"We're looking into everything. I appreciate your help and will leave my card with you. Call me about any concerns or questions you may have, or if you remember anything you think might help. And, again, I am truly sorry." Kevin stood to leave. He couldn't imagine how the couple would carry on. Shelly was their only child.

His next stop was to meet with Kyle's parents. They lived in the Manitou Beach area, about twelve miles north from Fort Ward. As Kevin drove there, he called his mother once more to make sure she was okay. Still no answer. He then called her at work and was told she had called in sick. He decided to go check on her after he was finished with the interview.

Mr. and Mrs. Smith lived in a charming farmhouse settled on two acres. It held a showcase of flowering gardens and bird houses of all shapes and sizes that were arranged whimsically around the property. Kevin had called beforehand to prepare them for his visit. When he drove up, Mr. Smith met him at his car.

"Thank you for coming, Chief Johnson. My wife is in no shape to talk today, so I thought we might sit out here." He pointed to a table under an umbrella. Both men sat and Kevin took out his notebook.

Kevin knew Kyle's father from soccer games and hated to give him this added information about his son. "Cody, I'm sorry to tell you that your son and Shelly both had significant amounts of drugs in their systems."

Cody shook his head. "I'm not surprised. Kyle had it in his head that drugs were easy to get everywhere, and he didn't know what the big deal was. He claimed all the kids took something, either to get high or calm down. We kept warning him about addiction and hoped he got the message."

"Did he ever tell you who the dealers were?"

"No. He had become very sullen lately. We were worried and then hoped that his dating Shelly would cheer him up. She was such a nice girl. This all makes me just sick."

"Can I look in Kyle's room today?"

"Yes. We haven't opened the door since it happened. We have two younger children and we're trying to help them cope right now."

"How old are they, sir?"

"Eleven and eight. They're very upset."

Cody led Kevin into the house and up the stairs to Kyle's bedroom. It was small, like most farmhouse rooms, and typical of a teen space. Clothes were piled on the floor, posters of video games on the walls and an unmade twin bed. The small closet was jammed with sports equipment and jerseys. Kevin knew that Kyle was a soccer player. His father kept score for the little leagues and never missed a game of Kyle's over the years.

Kevin looked in the obvious places for clues of drugs, but he knew kids fooled adults. He took Kyle's laptop and left the room.

Cody stopped him at the door, "What will happen now? Will his body be released for us to bury?"

"I'll let you know as soon as possible. Thank you for your help, and, again, I am so sorry." Kevin felt at a loss to say anything else. He shook the man's hand and walked off.

Kevin's mother lived only two miles away and so he drove over to see what she was doing. Not answering her phone was typical, but not going to work was troubling. When he got to the house, she met him at the door with her usual cigarette in her hand. "Sorry I didn't call you back. I got in so late last night, or I mean this morning, and I overslept. I'm just getting ready to go to work now."

Kevin looked carefully at his mother for signs of

alcohol but saw none. That was a relief. One of his fears was her lapsing into her old addiction. "Do you need a ride?"

"No, I'll drive. I'll have to stay late to make up my time."

Kevin gave his mother a quick hug and left.

Joel was working the early morning Monday breakfast crowd when he overheard customers discussing the murders. Speculation was that it was drug related and people worried that the Island was changing. Kids were tattooed, pieced, and flaunted wild colored hairdos these days, trying their best to antagonize their parents. That wouldn't be so bad, except their attitudes were rudely demanding. They challenged everything and seemed to have power over the rules that were made for them to follow. Yelling and talking back to parents were well known traits of growing up these days, making life miserable for most families.

Kyle Smith had worked a couple days a week at the restaurant. Joel often went out of his way to help him, but he was an arrogant kid who liked to goof around when business was slow. Joel wondered if the kid had ADHD like he did, or something, because he constantly made mistakes with the orders. Rumor had it he was going to be fired soon.

"Hey, Joel, what's on the menu today?" Joel smiled at Deputy Sheriff, Lana Clark.

"The usual excellent food, deputy." Joel took her to her favorite booth and handed her the menu.

"I'm really sorry to hear about Kyle," Joel said quietly,

"this has got to be hard on everyone."

"The Island is grieving, Joel. Shelly and Kyle were both liked around here. Especially Shelly. She was an excellent student and had plans for college. It's so sad."

Joel left her table to wait on his other customers. If the rumors were true that drugs were involved, he thought it best to stay clear of his visits to Seattle for a while. He had enough stuff at home to hold him. In the meantime, he wanted to keep his eyes and ears open to how the investigation was going.

Joel had a record. Not for drugs, but for DUI and larceny. In his early twenties he had stolen a car from one of his friends. It probably wouldn't have been that bad except he was driving drunk when he was arrested. His public defender got him off with a fine and probation, but it still went on his record. Something like that just kept following you around. He was lucky that restaurants didn't require a criminal background check.

Deputy Lana Clark was 34, single, and had moved from San Diego one year earlier after splitting with her boyfriend. They had been together for five years and still hadn't agreed on anything. Because of the high cost of living in southern California, Lana had tried to keep the relationship together and save as much money as she could. When the time came to move out, her excuse was taking a job in Washington State. They both agreed it was over and wished each other luck.

Lana's earlier years in police work had been as a traffic officer. She was a fully trained and sworn-in member of the police force, but instead of dealing with crime, she had been assigned to traffic investigations, specifically traffic accidents and fatalities. The traffic division where she worked had been created to help police patrols manage roadside problems, assist drivers in trouble, close roads, and direct traffic away from accidents. Lana had liked her job but wanted to move up from paperwork to investigations. After 2 years she finally worked her way onto the accident investigation team. At the same time, she started taking classes for the Detective's exam. She was ready to move into criminal investigations.

The job on the Island was a promotion for her. Kevin had a limited team of officers and needed a deputy who also had a background in administration. He had interviewed several people and liked Lana's qualifications the best. Her familiarity with the administrative side of things was a plus because he needed to hire someone to tackle the paperwork and organize the office. He had unfortunately inherited years of neglected and disorganized files from the much-loved retired chief. Hiring an outside person to reorganize the clutter was probably a good political move for Kevin.

Lana's investigative experience in traffic and her detective courses were an added plus in a small department where all his deputies had to multi-task. Kevin also wanted some diversity to reflect the slowly changing population on the Island. Lana was Black. Kevin's wife, Julia, was half Hispanic and constantly complained about the lack of diversity on the Island. Hiring Lana had given him points at home.

Over the months, Lana had done an excellent job getting police reports in order and was praised for her work on several traffic related problems. New street signs were posted, and a current map of the Island was in place. She continued her detective course work and training and felt ready to take on more responsibility and get involved in complex cases and investigations.

Kevin understood her ambition but reminded her that the Island wasn't a mecca for serious crime. What they saw mostly were problems like drugs, a few burglaries, and larceny which were overtaking the pristine reputation of the community daily. However, with the terrible murders of these two teens, Lana was perfectly positioned to get more involved. Kevin asked her to interview Mira and Jessica, the friends of the deceased teen, Shelly Mann.

Alan decided to stop by the library on his way home from Maggie's. He wanted to review past issues of the local paper and get an idea of the Island community and its members. The library took up a corner of the block on Madison Avenue and appeared to be recently remodeled. Alan first noticed the bulletin board in the library entrance that was filled with offers for classes and meetings. Catering to the Island needs and people, everything from Tarot Card readings to piano lessons were listed. Alan stood for ten minutes looking over all the messages. If he had to choose, he might take a class in mosaics offered at the art museum. He always liked glass art and wondered how mosaic artists created such beautiful work.

Entering the main library, Alan noticed the artwork on the walls. Maggie had told him that Island artists displayed their creations locally, and he suspected this was the case as he looked around. He stopped to admire the work of one artist who featured a yellow boat in his painting. Very clever, he thought, and striking. He would remember to ask Maggie about this artist.

Alan walked over to the librarian's desk and asked where the newspaper section was. The librarian, probably in her early sixties, looked over her frameless glasses and told him that the past issues were on the computers. She pointed to the desktops that lined the wall.

Alan felt embarrassed that he hadn't thought of this.

Although he had his laptop at the house, he decided to use the library computers anyway, in case he wanted to print something. Looking through the past months of Island news, Alan had to admit that leaving Boston for a while was a good idea. This kind of news was colloquial and charming, highlighted with local sports, summer camps and art events. On the other hand, since school was over this week, Alan wondered what teens did to keep busy. There couldn't be enough summer jobs for everyone. For a lot of kids, too much free time without responsibility of any kind is never a good idea. That's when trouble starts.

The current edition of the newspaper focused on the murder of the two teenagers. He read their names and the reaction of several Islanders. Apparently, it was true what Maggie said about the community's denial. Several quotes were from residents who criticized the belief that the Island was infested with drugs. Others were claiming that rampant drug use on the Island was getting so out of control that kids called it 'Drug Island." It seemed the consensus was for more communication and engagement with the drug issue and better police involvement, which meant that Chief Johnson was taking some heat. Alan understood. People wanted to blame the system and not take responsibility. It was universal.

Alan had to consider his talk to the community carefully. He didn't want to overwhelm them with drug scenarios, but he did want to warn them, or wake them up to the dangers that teens face. Parents needed to be more vigilant because teens were remarkably savvy. He wanted everyone to pay closer attention to the signs of drug use. One way to start was to consider the innocent items lying around the house, especially if they suspected their teen was using.

The unfortunate truth was that kids could go online and get help finding drug concealment options. A simple highlighter could be transformed into a pipe and a straw might be used to snort cocaine. Teens were known to hollow out anything, soda cans, lip balm, deodorant sticks, to hide their stuff. Cars were common places to hide drugs because weed concealed in tea bags could be taped anywhere inside the car. Candy mint tins were great concealment devices, belt buckles and even posters on the wall might be hiding drugs behind them. Books, stuffed animals, and light switches were all used. If parents became aware of these hiding places, they might be able to at least begin a conversation with their kids.

After an hour looking through articles, Alan decided to get some more exercise and walk around town. He'd promised the boys they could visit on Friday, and he wanted to see what activities were available. Wandering down by the water, he remembered the boys wanted to go fishing. The marina had several boats, but they appeared to be privately owned. Even if he could rent a boat, Alan had no idea how to fish. Maybe they would be just as happy visiting one of the many parks and practicing their soccer. Satisfied with his walk through the town, Alan noticed it was after five and he needed to get home and write down some thoughts for his talk on Wednesday.

TUESDAY , JUNE 6TH

While Alan was drinking his coffee and savoring the delicious muffins from Maggie, he wondered how long he would have to speak to the Islanders on Wednesday. Would he have to stay for questions? He decided to call Chief Johnson.

"Hello, Alan." Kevin was glad to hear from him. "I was about to call and let you know the meeting on Wednesday is scheduled for 7:00."

"That's one reason I'm calling. I also needed to know how long you wanted me to talk and if you thought there would be a lot of questions."

"Talk as long as you want, the more you can say about drugs, the better. I'm sure there'll be questions, but because you're not involved with the investigation, the questions will be aimed at me."

"How's the case going? Do you have any leads?"

"Not yet. We're talking with the families and friends

this week. I'm hoping your talk will encourage every parent to take a more active role understanding the drug problem we have. By the way, do you have time today or tomorrow to look over the crime scene? I'd like your opinion on a few things."

"I'm free today. Where should we meet?"

"I'll pick you up. Text me your address and I'll be there around 3:00."

Alan questioned if he should really help, but since he was free this afternoon, he could at least offer his two cents worth. After thirty-five years of police work, Alan felt he had seen it all. Drug homicides were frequent in the city of Boston, and he had witnessed teens dying or getting injured as a result. Law enforcement officers who were committed to serving and protecting the public, knew that the toxic combination of drug trafficking and widely available firearms had overwhelmed the system. Drugs and violence were two sides of the same coin, leaving families devastated. The Island was experiencing this right now.

Maybe he would talk about addiction on Wednesday, too. Most teens start out with casual, recreational use which can lead quickly to addiction. Alan knew that experimentation could become a full disorder, especially when you don't even realize it's happening at the time. It's no different than with alcohol. Addiction comes on way too fast.

Kevin picked up Alan right on time. The drive to the crime scene was a short ten minutes away, just like everything else on the Island. The two men talked easily about Island news, without mentioning the crime. When they passed Tessa and Simon's farmhouse, Kevin said the couple saw their house filmed several times on the local news. Apparently, the idea that a murder could take place in such a rural setting was part of the media drama.

Kevin parked his car next to the little red farmhouse that had been surrounded with police tape. When Alan got out of the car he looked around and asked, "Who heard the shots?"

"The driver of a passing car reported hearing gun shots. The neighbors across the street were out for the evening, but we asked the older lady across from the Tessa and Simon's if she heard anything. She's hard of hearing and said she didn't hear a thing. Nice lady."

"What kind of access does the crime scene have from this road?"

"There are three paths leading to the scene. Behind this house is a narrow path, but there's easier access on the upper road. The third way in is at the corner, but it's through some overgrown plants and bushes."

"Where do you want to go first?" Alan asked.

"Let's start here." Kevin pointed to a path starting at the back of the farmhouse that led away from it into the trees.

The path was narrow but led directly to an open area that looked like a campground. There was a fire pit, and several logs were gathered around it. Alan expected the forensic team to have cleared every item of interest away for evidence. Curious, he decided to walk further into the wooded area and look around. The light caught a branch in a tree and when Alan looked up, he noticed something that was leaning against the branch. When he got closer, he realized it was a platform that had been built in the tree. Almost like a lookout.

"Chief Johnson, can you come see this?"

Kevin walked through the wood and saw Alan pointing to a tree.

"Well, I'll be darned. I'm wondering how someone got up there or if it's used at all." Both men decided it was close to ten feet off the ground.

Kevin reached for his phone and called his colleague at the fire department. "Kelly, I need a ladder at the crime scene on Oddfellow Road. It should reach at least ten feet. How soon can you get here?"

Alan had wandered off in another direction to scan the area. He saw the path leading up the hill to the road above and followed it carefully in case there was something the police had missed. Halfway up he saw some broken bushes where it looked like someone had fallen. At least that was his thought. When he looked closer, he saw a cigarette lighter. Alan called out to Kevin, "Chief, this may be something."

Kevin found Alan and quickly responded, "Please, call me Kevin. What do you have here?"

"Well, it looks like someone may have been pushed into these bushes. There's a lighter here that you might want to give to your team."

Kevin took out his cell phone and took a picture of the lighter before putting on a pair of surgical gloves, retrieving the lighter and placing it in an evidence bag. They both continued up the path to the road.

"Did your team find drug paraphernalia at the scene?"

68

"The usual things thrown around, a couple roach clips, some tin foil, short plastic straws and some candy bags."

"Who knew about this hangout?"

"Apparently a few Island kids, but nobody's talking. We're checking for fingerprints, but if it's kids, we won't be lucky matching any."

"What about the neighbors around here? Haven't they heard noise from parties?"

"The people who own the little farmhouse by the path only use it occasionally. They're from Vancouver and are thinking about selling it. It's a family property. And the people across the street probably don't pay attention. We've had to go there for family disputes a lot. They both have a drinking problem and things get out of hand sometimes."

"What about Tessa and Simon?"

"It's too far from their place to hear anything. And if kids access from the road above, they wouldn't know they were even there."

Kevin turned when he saw the fire truck come down the road. When Kelly got out of the truck, the men talked over the best approach with the ladder. They decided to enter from the lower road and carry the ladder in. With Kelly was a young hefty junior fireman.

Alan watched as the ladder was placed under the tree, joking with Kevin when they both admitted being nervous with heights as Kelly climbed the ladder.

The platform was a sturdily built wood floor about six by six, without any means of support except for the nearby branches that hung close enough for security. Kelly took a video around the platform, filming burn marks from cigarettes along with carved graffiti. He then turned the video to the surrounding areas where he could see the water of Rich Passage.

"I think I got everything up here," he yelled down to Kevin.

"Okay, be careful getting down."

Kelly told Kevin that the platform could have been a deer stand.

"A what?" Alan was curious. What in the world was a deer stand?

Kelly turned to Alan and explained. "It's for hunting. A deer stand is a lookout that keeps hunters hidden and blocks their scent from deer. Usually, they're more comfortable than a platform like that one. They can be as high as 12 feet and about four feet wide. Most of them have a shooting rail, which this platform doesn't. But the one here is big enough to hold a couple of guys with folding chairs."

Alan was amazed. "The idea that you want to be comfortable while hunting deer is almost amusing. I always thought of it as being a challenging pastime."

Kelly nodded, "Challenging and sometimes boring."

Kevin thanked Kelly for his help and promised to let him know if they found anything interesting. Kelly waved to his junior helper and took off.

Alan studied the surroundings again and then wondered, "Who owns this property?"

"We're trying to find out. I think it's an older lady who's been buying land over the years with the hope of making a big profit one day."

On the drive back, Alan questioned Kevin, "Who would want to kill those two kids? And why? Have you found anyone who might be involved?"

"We have found nothing. Maybe forensics will come up with something, but right now we're stuck."

"What about the gun?"

"The bullet casings we found were from a 9mm semi-automatic. A lot of people around here own a gun like that for self-defense."

Alan thought for a minute. "I always look for what doesn't fit. What would you say doesn't fit here?"

"Let me think about that," Kevin said. "We know Kyle was a drug user, weed and some uppers, but Shelly didn't do drugs according to her friends and parents. She was a quiet, studious kid. So that doesn't fit. Why did she have drugs in her system?"

"That's a good question. You might want to start with that and see where it leads." Alan hesitated and then decided. "Let me know if you want to run things by me. Not in an official capacity, of course. My experience tells me that the more eyes and ears on an investigation, the better."

Kevin thanked him.

Lana was meeting two of Shelly's friends at the Pegasus Coffee Shop by the marina. Her plan was to make this as easy as possible, being more concerned for their feelings than prying information out. They were only eighteen and she didn't want them to think she was accusing them in any way.

Mira Connelly was a classic beauty. Her auburn hair was long and twisted into a braid down her back. She wore shorts, a Seattle Storm sweatshirt and walked athletically in new Converse shoes. She removed her sunglasses and then replaced them with black framed glasses that gave her a more studious and serious look. It didn't distract from her good looks.

Jessica Sykes was short and dressed in torn jeans and a Seahawk t-shirt. Her hair was shorn on one side, dyed purple and her makeup was dramatic. Lana tried her best not to stare at the difference these girls portrayed as she offered to buy them coffee.

"I'll just have water," Mira said.

"If you're buying, can I get a mocha frap?" Jessica almost smiled.

Lana ordered herself a drip coffee, the water and frap, and sat back down with the girls. They both looked nervous.

"I'm very sorry about your friend, Shelly." Lana watched the girls' expressions. Mira looked down at her hands and Jessica stared at Lana expressionless. "I understand you were both good friends with her."

Jessica kept staring and said, "Do you think we know who did this? Is that why we're here?"

Lana took this as an opening, "Do you know?"

Mira looked up, "Of course we don't know! Why would anyone kill her? She didn't bother anyone! You should blame it on Kyle... he was the one into drugs!"

"Why would you say that?" Lana reached for her coffee and stirred in some sugar and cream.

"Everyone knew that Kyle liked to smoke weed and take Oxy... or pain killers. He needed pills for his soccer injury at first, and then he just kept experimenting." Mira took a sip of water and a deep breath.

"When was the last time you saw Shelly?" Lana asked both girls.

They looked at each other for a second. Jessica spoke first, "I guess it was at graduation. After that we all had family stuff to do until the party."

Mira agreed.

"How was Shelly at graduation?"

Jessica made a face, like her answer was obvious. "We were all just happy to be leaving the Island for good. That's about all we talked about."

"Where are you planning to go?" Lana was interested.

"I've got a sister in San Diego I'm going to stay with. It's my gap year before college."

Lana looked at Mira, "And where are you going?"

Mira shrugged her shoulders, "I've got a job at the bookstore this summer and then I'm going to the community college. Just to get my credits to transfer to the UW."

Lana thought she would push a little harder. "Did you know of anyone who maybe wanted to hurt Kyle or Shelly? Anyone who didn't like them?"

Both girls shook their heads. Jessica spoke up, "We're all shocked! Everyone! I'm just glad to be getting off the Island in case it's a serial killer or something."

Mira gave Jessica a push, "That's great! Just leave me here to be killed!"

Lana assured both girls that it didn't look like there was a serial killer at large. "Did either of you have classes with Shelly?"

Mira spoke up, "I'm in drama and I saw her there. She and Kyle worked on the sets and so they were always around when we rehearsed."

"What was the last play?" Lana loved the theater.

"Clue... you know, like the game?"

"That must have been fun. Who did it in your play?"

"The mistress, with the dagger in the library." Mira smiled at the thought. "I played the mistress. It was great."

Lana looked at Jessica, "Are you in drama, too?"

"No way. But I did go to see this one. Mira was great." She gave her friend a shoulder push.

"Who else did Shelly hang out with?" Lana thought the mood had changed and she could probe a little more.

Mira looked at Jessica and shrugged. "I don't know. We all just hang around together. Especially the drama people. Otherwise, we go to school, jobs, activities, and home."

"No parties or entertainment?" Lana searched their faces to see if they were holding back or were worried about something.

"Occasionally, there might be a party if someone has a reason. The Island is suffocating, and everybody is just waiting to leave." Mira looked at Jessica for help or, maybe, confirmation.

"I don't hang out much," said her friend, "I only turn out for track... I ran the Island marathon and came in tenth."

She put up a fist in celebration.

"Nice," Lana liked this girl. She seemed to be grounded and older than Mira. Sometimes that's from having to grow up too fast because of family pressure or responsibility, and she wondered what her story was. "Thank you both for talking with me." She gave both girls her card and stood to leave.

"What do you want us to do now?" Jessica asked as she looked at the card. "Is this where you tell us to call if we think of something that's important?"

Lana smiled. "Yes, if it's important." She now had some free time and decided to check out where the girls lived. Mira's address was in the trendy Rolling Hills neighborhood. The houses ran along the shore, some boasting three stories which meant fabulous views. Mira's family home was a modest two-story house with a beautifully landscaped yard. It was set back from the road and had a Seahawk flag out front. Lana next drove to Jessica's house which was further up the road next to the small shopping mall across from the popular Bay Hay and Feed store. Her house was not as charming. It needed paint and the yard looked shabby due to the overgrown weeds and the three old pickup trucks parked out front. Lana thought about Jessica running track and wondered if more running was in her future.

Checking her watch, Lana decided to return to the station. Kevin was at his desk when she walked into the building. "Anything new from the scene?" Lana remembered he had asked the Boston cop for his opinion on the crime scene.

"As a matter of fact, we might have something. We found a platform, what looks like a deer stand, built up in a tree not far from the crime scene. I have forensics looking for prints or evidence that might be helpful."

"Up in a tree? How high was it?"

"About ten feet off the ground. I had Kelly bring a ladder to the site and climb up to take some photos. I'm just looking at them now."

Lana walked over to his desk to view the photos. They showed the graffiti and carvings and what looked like drawings or maybe a map of some kind. It could also be idle doodling with a knife. "How could someone without a ladder get up there?"

"I think they climb up. You know kids today; they take rope climbing classes at school and then do the rock climbing at the gym. They can climb just about anything."

"Can you see anything when you get up there?"

"A view of Rich Passage and then just the immediate area. A lot of trees block the view of the murder scene."

"Do you think this has something to do with the murders?"

"Anything is possible. How did it go with the girls?"

"Fine. They didn't give me any new information. They both seemed like nice kids. I drove by their homes afterwards, just to check things out."

"Any ideas?"

"I think Jessica might know something because she informed me that she was leaving town soon to go live with her sister in California. Maybe I should talk with her again before she goes."

"Probably a good idea."

Kevin seemed distracted as he rifled through the reports he had been reading and finally realized that Lana was staring at him.

"What do you want me to do now?"

Kevin tapped his pencil on the table several times and then said, "Why don't you call the drama teacher at the high school. Maybe he knows something the girls aren't saying."

WEDNESDAY, JUNE 7TH

Alan decided to have lunch at the diner on Wednesday. He heard their homemade bread and soups were legendary and he wanted to eat a hearty lunch before his meeting at the high school in the evening. He still worried about how relevant it was to compare the drug abuse in the city of Boston to this Island. Alan recognized that life was complicated everywhere, and a lot of people used some sort of addiction to accept what they couldn't handle or change. But he didn't know anything about the habits or opinions of the Island.

As Alan sat by the window eating, he saw Joel walk past. He remembered meeting him at Tessa's party and questioned to himself why a single guy wanted to work on a quiet Island, when most young people wanted to run the other way. The Island seemed to have many conflicting nuances.

Joel was returning from his weekly Seattle venture to

Pike Place Market to let his dealer know he wouldn't be back for a couple of weeks. Word was out that the two teens who were murdered had drugs in their systems and he wanted no attention to land on him. He wanted to keep a low profile and mind his own business.

When he arrived at the restaurant, the manager said the police chief had called and wanted to speak with the staff. He would be there tomorrow at 10:00 and everyone had to attend the meeting. Joel knew the police would eventually ask the restaurant employees about drugs. Unfortunately, he had sold some weed and pills to Kyle and a few kids off and on but didn't think anyone would talk. He hoped.

Alan hadn't spoken with Kevin since their trip to the crime scene. Out of curiosity he had looked up the yearly crime report on the Island. According to the FBI, the total crime rate was 68% lower than the Washington State total crime rate. That meant someone had a one in 2500 chance of being a victim of a violent crime each year. In fact, there was a one in 110 chance of being a victim of a property crime. It seemed that the Island was a safe and secure place to live. Alan was impressed. But it didn't distract from the fact that serious crime could be pervasive, even in a tight little community.

When he got home, he reminded himself to call Lindsay. The boys were coming to visit on Friday, and he wanted to be prepared with snacks and movies. He was surprised when his phone suddenly rang.

"Alan, it's Maggie."

"Oh, Maggie! Good to hear from you. What's up?"

"I wanted to know if you're ready for tonight and if there's anything you want me to do." Alan smiled at the offer. "I think I'm all set. But how about going out for a glass of wine afterwards?"

"You might be mobbed with questions. Let me bring a bottle of wine and some dessert with me and we can go back to your place. What do you think?"

"Sounds perfect. I'll see you there."

Alan looked around his house to see if it was presentable for a visitor. He wasn't a sloppy guy, but he did notice some clutter in the kitchen that needed to be cleaned up. He was trying his best to keep on top of things. Usually, he spent so much time at work that cleaning his house was far down his list of things to get done...behind laundry and groceries. His job had taken over a huge part of his life and he knew he had let things slide.

By 6:45, the high school auditorium was crowded. Kevin met him at the entrance to the building and explained that they had to move everyone to this larger space because of the big turnout. He didn't seem annoyed, in fact, he was pleased that so many people wanted to learn more about drugs and addictions.

Kevin introduced Lana to Alan. Her firm handshake and level gaze appeared confident and reassuring. Knowing how racially diverse the Island didn't seem to be, Alan was pleased to meet a Black officer. Lana was standing next to a Hispanic woman who gave Alan a lovely smile and held out her hand. "I'm Julia, Kevin's wife and much better half." Alan immediately liked both women.

At exactly 7:00 Kevin walked onto the stage and asked for quiet. The noise that filled the room was hushed and he began by stating the facts of the murder. He offered condolences to both families and acknowledged them in the front row. He told them he was working and would not stop working until he found who did this. Kevin mentioned the probable connection to drug use, and then introduced Alan.

Alan didn't expect applause, but the room seemed to thunder with it. He raised his hand for quiet and began. "I'm on vacation, visiting family, and already understand why you like to live on this lovely Island. I've enjoyed dining at wonderful restaurants, strolling through the town and meeting charming people. I can only imagine what a shock it must be to have this horrible crime committed in this warm inviting community."

Shifting his gaze around the room, Alan explained how being a big city cop had given him more experience than he'd ever expected with the connection between drugs and violence. Pointing out how much money the illegal drug trade produced, he noted that dealers were always looking for new markets, which is likely why the trade had moved onto the Island. He then went right into the facts about drugs, relating how and where teens hide drugs from parents. He reviewed the common drugs among teens and how each drug led to addiction and the need for more. Alan wanted the people to know that it's difficult to admit a problem and that rehab doesn't always work the first time. Dealers know this, too. They wait for addicts to believe they're clean, and then tempt them repeatedly until they are back to addiction. It's a cycle you don't want anyone to get involved with, especially your children.

Alan paused and was met with silence. "We all have our expectations of bright futures for our kids. But sometimes you should step back and realize how much pressure you may be putting on them. If not you, then pressure from the media or any outside source that they believe is on their side. Please be vigilant. Take a minute and talk with your kids without judging them. Get them help if they need it. But do not deny the fact that drugs are everywhere. Even here."

After talking for 45 minutes, Alan stepped aside and deferred to Kevin. The silence in the room was profound. As Alan walked off the stage, he heard Kevin ask for questions and hands went up in the air. He would let the police chief take over and return home. As he walked out of the building, he heard Maggie's voice.

"You did a great job!"

"I guess I might have gotten a little preachy in there."

"No, absolutely not! People needed to hear what you said. Maybe they'll finally wake up and talk to their kids."

Alan appreciated her support and was looking forward to wine and dessert.

THURSDAY , JUNE 8TH

Lana contacted the drama high school teacher and was meeting him at 9:00 that morning. He said he would be busy with report cards and storing equipment all day. When Lana walked backstage, she found him on a ladder changing a light.

"Mr. Waters, I'm Deputy Clark."

After climbing down to meet her, he said, "Please call me David. We can sit over here if you'd like." He pointed to a sofa and chair from one of the sets. Lana sat on the chair and pulled out her notebook.

"I understand that both Kyle and Shelly worked on the sets for many of the plays."

"Yes, they were wonderful. I've been so upset to know what happened to them. They were both such nice kids." He shook his head and looked around the stage. "They loved working behind the scenes. And they were talented, too. As far as I knew, Shelly wanted to continue in drama, the creative visual side, doing sets."

"Do you know of anyone who didn't like them, or maybe had a grudge?"

David shook his head. "Teachers don't know anything. We can surmise, but it's only speculation."

"What did you surmise?"

"Well, I guess I never thought they were a great couple. Shelly was on the road to higher pursuits, and Kyle was limited to a job and maybe vocational school."

"I thought they were both going to Olympic Community College in the fall?"

"That was the plan. But Kyle didn't sign up for classes on time and so I heard he took a job at the restaurant full time."

"Our information is that both kids were into drugs. Do you know anything about this?"

"There's no way that Shelly did drugs. She wasn't in the same group as Kyle. I heard that he did drugs, but I wouldn't know what kind. I only know this because I have a daughter who's a freshman and she said everyone knew Kyle was on drugs."

"So, you never noticed a change of behavior or other signs of drug use by either one?"

"No, I didn't. But this is drama, Deputy. Kids are always acting up and goofing off. I give several warmup exercises to get them back to work because they can get pretty wild."

"Besides Mira and Jessica, who else did Shelly hang around with?"

"I don't really know. They were a threesome for sure, but I can't think of anyone else who they hung out with. Did you talk with the girls?

"Yes. How about Kyle? Who did he hang out with?"

"Well, being a soccer player, he had those guys around him. Even after his accident on the field, they all stayed friends. I can't say one in particular… maybe Tom Richardson. I think their families are friends, too."

"How long have you taught here, David?"

"This is my tenth year. I'm from Arizona and think about returning every year, especially when the rain here never seems to end." He smiled and raised his eyebrows. "How do you like the rain?"

"Getting used to standing in the rain sometimes. Let me know if you think of anything that might help the case."

Lana gave her card to the teacher and walked slowly to her car. There was something about this guy she didn't like. He seemed phony in a way that only actors get when they are in a role they can't seem to carry off. She wondered if he would stay on the Island.

Kevin was still at the station when Lana returned. She related her interview with the teacher and asked what the next steps in the investigation would be. Kevin said that since Alan's talk, several emails and phone messages had come in about the case. As usual, they had to be followed up and he wanted her to do this. He was on his way to speak with the restaurant staff.

Larry Truman, the owner of The Doc restaurant, had wished he never gave Kyle a job. He'd been a terrible employee and was going to be fired sooner or later. That didn't mean Truman hadn't felt sorry about what happened to the kid. He thought about the other teens who worked for him, and didn't think any of them were involved with the crime. Before this happened, they had complained loudly about Kyle's work ethics. Except Joel, who seemed to stay uninvolved with most things. But then, he was older.

Kevin saw Truman talking with his staff when he entered the restaurant. He always liked this guy and the food at the restaurant, too. Truman had played football throughout college and was built like a tight end. He spoke with a no-nonsense voice but had a ready smile that assumed confidence.

"Good morning, Larry, how's everything?"

"Fine, Kevin. We're just having a short staff meeting. Go ahead and ask questions, we're ready."

Kevin looked at the ten employees and realized for the first time how young they were. "How many of you went to school or socialized with Kyle Smith?" Five hands went up. That's what Kevin thought. "Okay, I'll want to have a word with you before I leave." All five, two girls and three boys, lowered their hands and looked at each other nervously. "Don't worry, it's just procedure."

"We're looking for contacts that both Kyle and Shelly had on the Island to try and understand who might want to hurt them or want them dead. Because Kyle worked here, maybe you noticed a customer who was giving him trouble or someone Kyle was afraid or anxious about. It could be nothing, but we're following up on all leads. I'll leave my card with each of you. Questions?"

No one raised their hand, which Kevin expected. Getting involved with an investigation was the last thing most young people wanted to do. The media made most citizens wary of speaking to police these days.

"Can I speak with the ones who knew Kyle at school?" As the other people left the room, Kevin noticed Joel. He had seen him at the birthday party for Simon and was impressed how easily he moved around so many people. It seemed odd that a guy his age would be working as a waiter, and Kevin wondered what his story was.

Interviewing the teens who knew Kyle got him nowhere. They all said he was a nice guy, but they didn't hang out with him. One of the girls finally said, "He was a showoff. I stayed away from him because he thought it was funny to make fun of people. He would talk about customers and listen in on their conversations. We reported him to Mr. Truman."

"Good to know, thanks." Kevin made a note to ask Truman about Kyle's work habits. He let the teens get back to work and pulled Truman aside.

"Did Kyle get into trouble with any of the customers?"

"I was going to let him go because he annoyed people. He had two sides of his personality, one okay and friendly, and the other mean and sarcastic. I think he was one confused kid."

"Anyone mad at him?"

"I don't know. Teen angst is beyond me."

"Okay, if something comes to mind just let me know."

Lana was organizing the phone messages when Kevin got back to the office. She looked up hopefully, "Anything interesting?"

"No. Well, maybe. One of the girls said that Kyle was mean, and Truman said he seemed to have two sides to his personality. He could be charming and then obnoxious. He also listened to customer's conversations and repeated them while laughing. Doesn't sound like he was well liked."

"Where do we go from here?" Lana hoped she could get out of the office and do something more constructive.

"Kyle's best friend is a kid named Tom Richardson. Let's go see if he's at home."

After the police chief left the restaurant, Joel asked for the next few days off. He told Truman he was going to visit his sister in Chehalis, but he had secretly rented a cabin in Winthrop, which was in the opposite direction. He needed to get out of town and away from the investigation to keep a low profile. If he was out of sight, maybe the police would forget about him. His drug sales to Kyle, if found out, would be a big problem.

The early lunch crowd was beginning to show up and Joel had three tables already. One table was with four women who he knew had a monthly lunch together. The pretty dark-haired lady who smiled a lot was the police chief's wife, Julia.

"Joel, how are you today?" Julia smiled at him expecting his usual greeting.

"Good as can be," he smiled back. "What can I get you lovely ladies?"

Charmed as always with this waiter, the ladies ordered their lite lunches and iced tea. He tempted them with homemade chocolate frosted brownies, but they declined. When he watched them leave, he hoped they all forgot they saw him today. He wanted to stay out of everyone's radar.

Kevin and Lana approached Tom Richardson's one-story rambler and waited for the large barking dog who came running forward to quiet down. They weren't afraid of dogs but hoped someone would call the dog off. Just as they opened their car doors, they heard a loud whistle for the dog who went tearing back inside. As the police walked forward, a teenager stood at the door, with his arms folded around his chest.

"Are you Tom?" asked Kevin.

"Yeah… what's this about?"

"We'd like to talk with you about Kyle Smith. We're told you and he were friends."

"Yeah… we were."

"Can we come in for a few minutes and ask you some questions?"

"I suppose. My parents aren't home right now."

"That's okay. We just need some information about Kyle and thought you might want to help."

Tom led them into the cluttered living room. Looking around for a chair, Kevin pulled two from the dinette set, one for Lana, and sat. Tom flopped on the sofa.

Kevin nodded to Lana to start asking questions

"We're very sorry about what happened to your friend Kyle. Right now, we're talking with his close friends to find out if they know any reason at all why he was killed. Can you think of anyone who might want to harm him or anyone who was angry at him?"

Tom shook his head and kept quiet.

"When was the last time you saw Kyle?"

"On graduation day." Crossing his arms and sinking lower into the sofa, Tom stared back at Lana. It didn't appear that Tom was going to cooperate.

Lana switched gears, "Are you a soccer player like Kyle was?"

"Yeah."

"Were you playing the game when Kyle got hurt?"

Kevin wondered where Lana was going with this question.

"Yeah... I had kicked him the ball and he ran into the other team's captain and went down. We were all shocked by how bad it looked."

"I imagine. It sounds like it ended Kyle's soccer playing. He must have felt upset by this."

Tom began to relax. "He was at first, but then he got into drama class and started working at the restaurant."

"Can you think of anyone who wanted to hurt Kyle? Anyone who maybe held a grudge or talked about hurting him?"

"No. Kyle could be a creep sometimes, but he wasn't that bad."

Lana questioned this, "How was he a creep sometimes?"

Tom's eyes drifted around the room and then back to Lana. "He could be mean. I just think he was insecure or something like that."

"Can you give us an example?"

"No... I don't want to say anything bad about him."

Lana took out her card and handed it to Tom. "If you change your mind, let us know. Or if you hear anything about what happened, call us. Okay?"

Kevin handed Tom his card, too, and they stood to leave. The large dog also stood up to escort them back to their car.

"Nice job bringing up soccer," Kevin said. "I guess now we talk with the soccer coach and see what his take was on Kyle."

Alan's grandsons were arriving the next day and he had to get to the store and stock up. Lindsay told him that both boys ate a lot of cereal and Mac and Cheese, along with chips, popcorn, and pizza. Alan's only kitchen specialty was pancakes, so he shopped for everything he needed and more. They would be with him until Sunday afternoon, which meant plenty of eating.

He had liked spending time with Maggie after the town hall meeting. Besides the bottle of Pino Gris, she also brought peach cobbler that was unbelievably delicious. Alan was surprised how easy Maggie was to talk to and thought her sense of humor was engaging. She seemed to have lived an adventurous life, traveling, bartending, acting, even going to psychics. He laughed when she told him the crazy things the readings revealed. "I was told my brother was really my father in the 17th Century, and my daughter was my grandmother from long ago."

Alan had never been to a psychic and had no desire to ever go to one. He believed that people automatically gave clues to the reader by how they dressed and spoke. If you weren't wearing a wedding ring, you probably had issues with relationships. If it looked like you were dressed for work, you might not like your job. People only went to psychics when they were unhappy, Alan thought. So, it had to be job, love life or illness. But Maggie made it sound like a wonderful experience, not to be taken too seriously.

Off and on Alan thought about the investigation. He wondered if he should call Kevin and see if there was any progress since the meeting last night. People were known to come forward after a gathering like that with lots of information they think might help. Because there was a limited number of officers on the Island, Kevin would be overtaxed with details to investigate. That always made the case slow down.

Just as Alan was considering his grocery list, his cell phone rang.

"Alan here."

"Alan! How are your lazy days relaxing treating you?"

Alan smiled hearing his friend Sidney's voice. "Very well! I'm just taking it one day at a time. And how are you doing in the big city?"

"Ready for a break, my friend. Everyday seems overwhelming with all the political crap and bogus social justice items coming through. There are so many idiots talking nonsense and people suing right and left. Did you hear about the latest scandal?"

Sidney related the Boston news to Alan and then came to the point of his call. "I think I'll take you up on visiting if the offer's still there."

"Please come anytime!"

"How about the end of next week? I have some time free, and Carla is visiting her family in Colorado, so I thought I would take off and get away. Will that work?"

"I'm free all week…and the next week…etcetera." Alan laughed at the thought. He still had weeks on the Island and spending time with his friend would be a bonus.

"Let me know your flight number and I'll pick you up. I have my daughter's old beater car; you'll love it."

"Okay, sounds good. If there's anything I can bring you from here, let me know."

Alan hung up the phone and sat down at the dining table. Having a guest was a new concept for him. Even though it was Sidney, living under the same roof would be interesting. He would call Maggie and see what activities she recommended to her B&B visitors visiting the area for the first time and if she had time to go on an excursion with them one day. Life was getting more interesting.

Alan's cell rang again. "Alan, this is Kevin Johnson, do you have a minute"

"Sure, what's happening?"

"I just received an anonymous phone call. You know the waiter at The Doc, the older one named Joel? Someone says that he sold drugs to Kyle. Do you have a minute to talk to him with me? I'd like your input."

"Okay, when are you thinking?"

"I believe he's at his apartment right now. It's right in town. How about ten minutes."

"Text me the address and I'll meet you there."

Alan waited for the text and wondered why Kevin needed him for this interview. He didn't know Joel, except at the restaurant and thought he was friendly and good at his job. Hopefully, this would be a mistake, and someone was trying to set him up.

Kevin was waiting in his car when Alan arrived. They joined forces and walked up the side stairs over a gift shop to Joel's apartment. When they arrived, they knocked quietly. At first there was no response, but when they knocked louder, they heard footsteps.

"Chief Johnson, why are you here?" Joel looked alarmed.

"Can we come in? This is Detective Sharp; I hope you don't mind if he sits in? He's visiting from back East and has been observing our departments procedures."

Joel nodded and opened the door for the two men. The apartment was sparsely decorated with an old sofa and 52" TV. Off to the side there was an old round oak dining table with four chairs and Kevin motioned for both men to have a seat.

"Joel, we just need to ask a few questions. You

worked with Kyle Smith at The Doc, right?"

Joel nervously nodded. "Off and on, we didn't always have the same schedules."

"I'll get to the point; I had a call today from somebody saying that you sold drugs to Kyle."

Joel stared at Kevin, dropped his head, and then took a deep breath. "Who said that"

"I'm not at liberty to say. I'm just here informally to ask you if it's true."

"Do I need a lawyer?"

"You can get one if you feel you need to, but this is just an informal conversation."

"Kyle took drugs. I don't know where he got them." Joel decided that a denial was best, at least until he could figure out who was talking and how much the cops actually knew. Because he also sold to other kids on the Island, he had to think fast and figure out his next step.

Kevin considered Joel's response and decided to end the discussion. "If you hear anything about where Kyle might have purchased the drugs, let us know." Kevin dropped his card on the table and stood to leave.

Alan spoke up, "How long have you lived on the Island, Joel?"

"About a year. I'm from Oregon."

"There's not much to do on an isolated Island like this. How do you manage?"

"Besides the restaurant, I get odd jobs. You know, like the one at Tessa's and Simon's."

"Do you spend time in Seattle? It seems to be better

suited for a single guy."

"Sometimes. I'm just trying to decide what my next step is, and I like living here where it's quiet."

Alan nodded his head in agreement. He thought Joel was sincere in this conversation. As Kevin and Alan walked to their cars, Alan asked him what his take was on Joel.

"I looked up his police profile and he doesn't have much of a record. A DUI and taking a friend's car without permission. If he's selling drugs he's keeping a low profile, and I don't think any of the kids are going to want to talk about it. The call we got didn't give any specifics, it might just be someone with a grudge or a red herring. What do you think?"

"I think he's hiding something. Asking about needing a lawyer that way tells me he knows he might have a problem. I would check to see how often he goes into Seattle. If he's getting his supply there, it must be on a regular basis. Does he have a car?"

"I don't think so."

"So, if he walks on the ferry, where would he go to buy?"

Kevin thought for a minute. "He could buy drugs anywhere in Seattle. The ferry dock isn't far from the Pike Place Market area which has an active drug trade, especially in the evenings after the Market closes. I know a cop who's assigned to that beat. I'll make some inquiries. To tell you the truth, I'm beginning to be frustrated with the lack of leads we have so far on this case."

Alan understood how frustrating it was to be stalled. Because the Island was so small, the pressure on Kevin was great, and people wanted the case solved quickly so they could return to their safe existence.

The men shook hands and departed.

Joel was in a panic. Who called the police about the drugs? He only sold to kids he knew and didn't think any of them would give up their source. He had to get out of town. He decided to rent a car in Seattle and then drive to the cabin in Winthrop that night. Nobody knew where he was going, and besides, he had nothing to do with the murder of those kids.

Joel called his boss and asked to work the late shift that night after all. He was relieved he had already told them he would be taking a few days off. No one would be suspicious. After work tonight, he would be on the late ferry to Seattle.

Kevin called his friend, Curt Newman, a patrol officer with the Seattle Police assigned to the waterfront area. Kevin had forwarded a photo of Joel and asked Newman to check around and see if anyone recognized him. He explained about potential drug dealing and that he thought this guy might be buying in Seattle and bringing drugs back to the Island to sell. Newman said he would ask around and keep a look out for him. If the guy was a ferry walk-on, it would be easy to tail him.

Kevin's next interview was with the soccer coach for the high school team. Doug Houser had been around since Kevin was a student. He was a great old guy, but if you got him started, he would talk for hours about all the players he thought should have made the big leagues. Doug was waiting in the gym at the school when Kevin arrived.

"Coach Houser, nice to see you again." Kevin held out his hand.

Houser took off his baseball cap and grinned. Shaking hands, he looked with pride on Kevin, "Chief Johnson. You're still in the same great shape you were in school."

Kevin smiled, knowing this wasn't the case, and walked to the bleachers to sit and talk. "Coach, unfortunately, I'm here on business. You heard about the kids who were murdered…I wondered if you could tell me a little about Kyle Smith. I know you coached him in soccer."

Houser shook his head and let out a sigh. "Kyle, rest in peace, was a showoff. He had a lot of spunk, but not the kind of talent he bragged about. When he hurt his knee, it was his own darn fault. I felt bad for the kid, but I was also a bit relieved that his smart mouth was finally off the field. I hate to say anything negative about the kid; you know I do. But I want to be honest here."

"Can you think of anyone who wanted to hurt him?"

"Not really. I've thought about that and just don't believe any of the kids would do such a thing. Is it true that Kyle used drugs? Because that might explain why his behavior was so on and off."

"We've confirmed that he did take drugs. We're trying to find his dealer. Did you hear Detective Sharp speak the other night?"

"Yes, I did. Great message to these families who think

their kids are angels. I try and keep an eye on kid's behaviors, but they're so clever these days that I often can't tell if they're drugging or not. It isn't like when you went to school here."

"I know. I've got three in elementary school and can hardly keep up. Here's my card, Coach, if you think of anything give me a call."

Houser put on his cap and nodded. "Will do."

Kevin returned to the station, no wiser than before.

FRIDAY, JUNE 9TH

It was after midnight when Joel walked onto the ferry. He had called ahead for an Uber to take him to the car rental place that was open all night. His tips from the evening crowd at the restaurant were better than ever and he had a good feeling about his decision to take some time off.

It was 2 a.m. when Joel finally arrived at the cabin in Winthrop. The owner had left the key in the mailbox, and when Joel opened the door, he eyed the queen bed and collapsed into it.

Kevin got to work early that morning to complete some reports. He'd had a restless night, thinking about where the investigation would go from here. So far, there wasn't much to go on. By the time Lana showed up at 9:00, he'd decided to follow up again with Joel. If it was true that he was selling drugs to kids, he needed to find out who Joel's supplier was and if there were contacts on the Island.

"I guess I can see how Joel might be involved with drug sales, but I really don't think he would have anything to do with the murders." Lana took a sip from her coffee mug and shook her head. "What do we know about him?"

"He has a record for DUI and stealing a car from a friend. He got fined and did some community service. That's it. He grew up in eastern Oregon. The only problem he's had is keeping a job. He's been let go from three warehouse jobs so far."

Lana thought about it. "How old is he?"

"28."

"So, moving to the Island may just be a stopover. I wonder how long he plans to stay."

"I think I'll have another talk with him. Do you want to come?"

"Sure." Lana wanted to be involved with every part of this investigation and wouldn't miss a chance to see where any lead took them.

Larry Truman was at the restaurant setting up for the day. They would open in an hour and always had a good lunch crowd, especially in the summer. "Chief, how can I help?"

"We're just here to talk with Joel. Is he here?"

"No, he worked a double shift yesterday and then wanted a couple days off. He said he was going to visit his sister in Chehalis. My guess is he's probably leaving today because he didn't get out of here until close to midnight."

"Okay, thanks Larry. We just want to clarify something with him. Do you have his number?"

Larry looked through his log of employees and gave them the number. He even had Joel's sister's number as a contact.

As they walked out the door Lana asked, "Are you going to call him?"

"It's odd that he decided to leave for a few days now. I think I'll call his sister first and see if she's expecting him."

Kevin made the phone call as soon as they got back to the station. Joel's sister said she hadn't heard from Joel in months. Kevin assured her that everything was fine, and this was just a friendly call to follow up on an Island investigation.

"So, he's not going to his sister's." Kevin thought out loud for a minute. "He doesn't have a car, but he could have rented one. And if he took the ferry last night or this morning, my guess is he used a rental in Seattle. Look to see which place is open 24-7 in the downtown area."

Kevin then called his SPD friend Curt and asked if he had been able to find any information on Joel.

"Yeah, one of the guys said he's a regular on First Avenue around Pike Place. They were watching him because they suspected he was regularly buying from one of the local dealers but didn't have proof yet. Do you want us to detain him?"

"My guess is that he's suddenly gone missing. We think he was dealing to kids on the Island and decided to take off because of the murders."

"I'll still keep a look out."

"Thanks."

Kevin looked at Lana and then decided. "I think we

better check out Joel's apartment. If he's not there, I can ask his landlady for the key. She owns the gift shop below."

The town square, where the gift shop was located, was one of a cluster of unique stores including a bakery, toy store, dress shop and deli. The bakery was already filled with customers, many who wanted to buy their breakfast before getting on the ferry. Kevin hoped their presence wouldn't arouse too much suspicion as they walked around the building to the side stairs.

After knocking several times on Joel's apartment door, they became concerned, especially because of the information Kevin had about Joel's buying drugs in Seattle. "We better go talk with Della." Kevin said.

The owner of the gift shop, Della Carmine, was an Island fixture. Her bright red hair, eccentric clothes, and equally colorful makeup surprised customers because she was an astute connoisseur of the many sophisticated items within her shop. The shelves were beautifully displayed with collections of exotic and expensive furnishings including hand painted rugs, glass blown vases, and even colorful quilted jackets. Della was surprised to see the officer.

"Is there something going on I should know about?" Della's voice reached a high note of worry.

Kevin hesitated and then asked, "When was the last time you saw your tenant, Joel Spencer?"

"Well, let me see… I guess it was yesterday. He was on his way to work. Why?"

"We just want to ask him some questions. I guess he's not home right now. Did he indicate he was going on a trip, or might be away for a while? Was he carrying any luggage, or an overnight bag when you saw him?"

"No, nothing like that. I remember he had a big hiker's backpack when he moved in, but I don't think he had it with him yesterday. Now you have me worried. Would you like to check to see if he took it with him?" Della opened a small drawer under the cash register, retrieved a master key and handed it to the Chief. "You can go up and check, just make sure the door's locked when you leave."

The small apartment was empty. There didn't appear to be anything suspicious, but when Lana searched the bedroom for the suitcase, she called out to Kevin. "Chief, you better come look at this."

On the floor of the closet, wrapped in a pillowcase, was a Glock 9mm semi-automatic.

"We need to put out an APB on him right now."

J oel woke up to pounding on the cabin door. His first reaction was hoping whoever it was would just go away. But then he heard voices, "Open up, police."

By 6:00 that evening, Joel was booked into the Port Orchard Corrections facility charged with suspicion of drug trafficking and possession of a firearm. He was also named as a suspect in the murders of Shelly Mann and Kyle Smith. Joel asked for a lawyer and was told he would meet one in the morning. He said he didn't want to make a phone call.

At the Island precinct, Kevin was waiting to hear from the ballistics lab to see if the gun they found in Joel's apartment matched the bullet casings found at the crime scene and the slugs taken from the bodies. The last thing he heard, Joel was denying any knowledge of a gun and claimed he never owned one in his life.

Earlier that same day, Alan stood at the ferry terminal waiting for his grandsons to walk from the passenger's deck. Lindsay had been nervous letting them ride the ferry alone, but she knew her father would meet them on the other side. When the ferry landed, both boys ran through the crowd and found their grandfather anxiously waiting for them. "Hey guys, slow down!" They both hugged him at once and told him they were hungry.

"Let's get back to the house and drop off your things before we get something to eat. In fact, I've got plenty of food at home if you want to relax and make plans for what we can do today."

When they walked through the door of the house, the boys claimed their beds and asked Alan if he had Mac and Cheese. Putting the pot on to boil the macaroni, Alan took out a notebook to read them the list of activities he had written down.

"I really want to practice soccer," Kirin began, "Because I'm going to soccer camp next week."

Rani shook his head, "I'm not going to that camp, I'm going to basketball camp."

Alan looked at both boys. "So maybe we should make plans to go to the park so you both can practice. I saw a park with a field and a basketball hoop."

"And we really want to go to a movie. There's the new

Addams Family movie. Or we could go see the James Bond movie." They both looked at a skeptical Alan.

"I'm not taking you to a Bond movie. Even though your Uncle Sam and I never miss one, you two are way too young to see a movie like that. There's also a bowling alley in town if you want to bowl."

Both boys agreed on bowling. Alan continued to read from his list of activities, "I think tomorrow we'll explore some of the Island. I'm glad you guys are here because I haven't had time to look around a lot. I know there's an Indian reservation over the bridge that could be interesting.

The boys were excited about all these ideas. They were staying until Sunday afternoon, and now they had more than enough to choose from.

SATURDAY, JUNE 10TH

Alan woke up exhausted. The day before had been a marathon of running on the beach and in the park. They even went to the art museum and looked around. Alan was pleased with their interest in the art and bought each of them an Island t-shirt. The boys had been up until midnight playing video games, even though they were sent to bed at ten. He kept reminding them to go to sleep, but didn't want to lean too heavily on them right away. Maybe if he kept them busy today, they would be tired out by evening. His job this morning was making pancakes.

At nine o'clock he heard one of the boys rushing to the bathroom. Good sign. Alan didn't want them to sleep late and ruin his plans for an early bedtime. "Who's awake?" Alan shouted.

Kirin yelled back from the room, "We both are."

Alan smiled and yelled back, "Anyone hungry for pancakes?"

Both boys came running to the kitchen. They were fraternal twins, Rani looked East Indian and even had Sanjay's mannerisms, and Kirin had more of Lindsay's coloring and features. Their smiles were contagious. The boys were lucky to have each other and all the privileges of a secure and happy home life. "Who wants chocolate chips in their pancakes?" This brought hands raised and eyes popping.

As they ate, Alan laid out a plan for the day. "Let's go to the park this morning and get some exercise. After that we'll drive to the reservation and have a look around. Then we'll have some lunch, and you choose... movie or bowling."

They both answered at once. Bowling won.

Kevin and Lana arrived at the Kitsap County Jail around 10:00 that morning. They met the public defender, who had already spoken to Joel and advised him on his decision to speak with the police. "He still wants to talk with you," the young lawyer told them.

Joel stood up when they entered the interview room. He was dressed in a jail jumpsuit that was too short for his tall frame. He looked like he hadn't slept.

"Joel, we're here to give you a chance to tell us what you know about the gun we found in your apartment." Kevin looked with a little sympathy to Joel, hoping he would confess or at least admit to having the gun.

Joel looked at Kevin and then met Lana's eyes. His voice was raspy when he said, "It's not my gun. I don't have a gun. Someone must have put it there."

"Have you ever owned a gun, Joel?"

"No. I'm anti-gun and wouldn't have one around me."

"Were you selling drugs to Kyle Smith?"

Joel looked at his lawyer and whispered something. "No comment."

"Were you selling drugs to other teens on the Island?"

"No comment."

"You know, Joel, this will be easier if you tell us the truth. We're investigating two murders and right now you're our only suspect."

Joel teared up, then looked down at the table and said, "I didn't kill anyone."

Lana spoke for the first time. "If not you, Joel, please tell us what you know. Even if it's just the name of a dealer on the Island.""

Joel looked at Lana, hoping she would believe him. "I didn't kill anyone," he repeated.

The interview ended and Joel was led back to his cell. They could hear him say that someone had set him up.

On the drive back to the Island, Lana asked Kevin if he really thought Joel was capable of murder. "He just doesn't seem the type."

"I can't think of any type who would shoot two kids like that. I don't know if he has it in him to kill, but I do know that anyone can be pushed to the edge. Let's see if we received results from the lab on the crime scene. That platform in the tree was weird. I'm also waiting for the results on the lighter we found to come in."

"In the meantime, what else can I do?"

"Keep looking through the emails and text messages for leads. If someone did plant the gun, they will want to let us know where to look or see if we found it."

Kevin was on the phone when Alan walked in with two young boys. He finished his call and approached the trio, "Alan, who are your friends?"

"These are my grandsons. Chief Johnson, this is Kirin, and this is Rani."

Both boys shook hands with Kevin and then spoke at once.

"What kind of gun is that?"

"Are you a good shot?"

Kevin smiled and said, "Yes, I'm a good shot. What are you boys up to today?"

"We're going bowling," they both said at once.

Kevin asked Alan if he had a minute. Alan looked at the boys and told them to have a seat while he talked with the Chief.

Alone in his office, Kevin began, "We have Joel Spencer in custody. We found the suspected murder weapon in his apartment Friday."

Alan was surprised. "What does he say?"

"That it was planted. But get this, he was in Winthrop, that's about 100 miles away, last night. It looked like he was making a run."

"So, what was his motive do you think?"

"I don't know. There were no fingerprints on the gun and Joel was at work the day after the murders. He didn't seem upset at Simon's birthday because we saw him there. And Lana saw him at work on Monday and he seemed concerned about the murders."

"Do you think he'll get bail?"

"Bail hearing's coming up, but I doubt he'll get it. He refuses to talk with us about dealing drugs. We have a lead from the Seattle PD that says Joel's been seen, on more than one occasion, talking to a suspected drug dealer in the vicinity of a known drug trafficking area. They believe Joel is a regular customer on the street and at the Market for buying. And, as you know, we got an anonymous tip that he deals to kids on the Island. So, we're following up on all this right now."

"I have the boys until Sunday, but after that I'm available if you want to run things by me."

"I appreciate that. I just wanted to bring you up to date right now."

Alan returned to get the boys who were talking with Lana. "Okay boys, your grandfather has returned. Have a good day." She smiled at Alan and then rolled her eyes. "They're a handful," she whispered.

The noise in the bowling alley helped to distract Alan from any thoughts about Joel being in custody. He would have to think about it later and just concentrate on the boys until they left on Sunday.

Lana still had a difficult time believing Joel had murdered the two kids. He seemed his regular self when she saw him at the restaurant on Monday. She suggested to Kevin that they should interview the staff again at the restaurant.

Kevin gave it some thought. "Right now, I'm thinking about going into Seattle and speaking with the beat cops who ID'd Joel. Maybe they can give us some more info on who he was buying from. Finding out who supplied him with drugs would be a clue to all of this."

"Do you want me to go with you?"

"Not this time. Stay here and take calls. I imagine people are going to want answers now that someone's been arrested."

Kevin was on the next ferry to Seattle. Saturdays were just as crowded as any workday for the ferry runs, but his police car and uniform got him boarding priority. When he reached the waterfront, he called his contact, Curt, and arranged to meet him at the lower entrance to the Pike Place Market. Maneuvering around the traffic, Kevin marveled at the shoppers' tenacity for finding parking and then shopping the busy stalls of fresh fruits, vegetables, flowers, fish, and meats at the trendy open market. It was a Seattle landmark and was often featured on TV ads, especially during football season. The real estate in the area was probably among the most expensive in the city, Kevin thought.

Curt met Kevin and walked him through the shops on the lower level. He said he had an informant who had observed Joel several times over the months. They believed his contact worked at one of the jewelry shops that sold mostly gold chain necklaces along with watches and clocks. Apparently, the owner was willing to cooperate.

Both policemen entered the shop and asked the young employee for the manager.

"He's at lunch." The kid nonchalantly pointed to the restaurant across the aisle.

Curt knew what the guy looked like and easily spotted

him at a table.

"Can we talk for a minute?"

The guy nodded and pointed to the chairs. He was in his sixties and looked worn out. His shop was a family business, but he barely made enough for the enormous rents. "How can I help you, officers?"

"We understand you do business with this guy," Kevin showed him the photo of Joel.

"Yeah, he comes in sometimes."

"We know he doesn't buy necklaces or watches. What does he buy?"

"I don't know. I just tell him to wait and then I make a phone call. Then he leaves and I don't see him again."

"Who do you call?"

"Some guy who helps pay my rent. I don't know who he is, but I need the money, or I'll lose my shop."

"Is this the only guy who you do this for?" Pointing to the photo.

"No, there's others."

"How many?"

"Maybe ten, sometimes more."

"Do they have some kind of code they give you?"

"They just hand me a card. It says, 'Have a Great Day" on it."

"Do you have a card with you?"

"No."

"Do you know what this exchange is about?"

"No."

"What's the number?"

"It's different every week. I get a notice in the mail on Mondays."

"Do you have the last number?"

"I didn't get one this week."

Handing his card to the old guy Curt said, "If you get a notice, call me immediately."

When they left the restaurant, Kevin asked him why he didn't arrest the guy.

"We already know it's all about drugs. Just about everyone with a shop or stall here has help from sources that are questionable. We think it's organized crime and we hand it over to the big guys. I'll let them know about this one."

Kevin caught the next ferry back to the Island. On the way, he called Lana, "It looks for certain that Joel was involved with dealers although there's no hard evidence. This investigation may take on a bigger scale than we think. If a dealer from Seattle is involved, Kyle and Shelly may just have been at the wrong place and saw something they shouldn't have."

Lana reported that nothing new had happened, but Jessica, one of Shelly's friends, wanted to talk with Lana again. "She seemed spooked about something. We decided to meet at a coffee shop in Poulsbo, away from anyone on the Island spotting us I hope."

"What time?"

"In about an hour."

Jessica was worried. She knew Shelly had started doing drugs in her senior year because of the pressure her parents put on her to excel. At first it was only Adderall, but then she experimented with ecstasy off and on for fun. Her parents ignored the fact that her moods were up and down thinking it was just teenage hormones. Kyle knew she took drugs and encouraged her, especially when they worked on sets and spent so much time together.

Talking with a police officer now was probably being a snitch, but Jessica was leaving in a few days for her sister's house and needed to get this off her chest. Jessica didn't take the hard drugs like a lot of the kids, but she did smoke weed. She hoped that wouldn't come up when she spoke to the officer.

Lana parked a block away from the café and sat in her car. She was fifteen minutes early and didn't feel like walking around in this town. Known for its Swedish heritage, Lana felt racial tension whenever she visited, which wasn't often. The racism was subtle, but there. When she walked into a store, even the popular bakery, everyone stopped talking and looked in other directions. What did Maya Angelou say? "When someone shows you who they are, believe them the first time." She believed Poulsbo was a racist town.

Lana saw Jessica walking up the street and decided to call out. "Jessica?"

Jessica swung around and was glad to see it was the police officer and not someone from the Island. She gave a little wave and then walked towards her.

"Do you want to go inside or sit on one of the benches

by the water?" Lana was hoping she would want the benches, because sometimes people relaxed more when they were in an open environment.

"Oh, okay, let's go sit on a bench. Sounds better than sitting inside anyway."

Finding a secluded bench with a great view of Liberty Bay, Lana began the conversation. "You understand that this is just a chat. If you have some information that will help us with our investigation, we would appreciate hearing about it."

Jessica wavered, "Will I have to meet with you again? It's just because I'm taking off for my sister's in San Diego in a couple of days."

"If you give me your number, I can always reach you. How does that sound?"

"Okay, that's a relief."

"What do you want to tell me?"

"Shelly was taking drugs."

"What kind of drugs?"

"Ecstasy and sometimes Adderall. She started taking it to boost her grades... or that's what she said. But when she met Kyle, she decided to try some other drugs. Only a few of us knew, but I'm surprised no one guessed. She could be really moody."

"Where was she getting the drugs?"

"Kyle mostly."

"That's important information for our case. Thank you for telling me about this. From talking with her parents, I believe they hadn't a clue."

"Nobody's parents know! Kids get away with... I

almost said murder… they get away with everything. That's why I want to leave the Island. Maybe people in a bigger city are more aware."

Lana put her hand on Jessica's. "You're a brave girl. I'll keep your name out of the investigation as far as I can. Trust me. I'm pretty good at this."

Jessica wiped a tear off her face and stood to leave. She nodded a quick goodbye and walked quickly down the street. Lana hoped Jessica's sister would give her more confidence and help her move forward.

SUNDAY, JUNE 11TH

Kevin took Sundays off to be with his family. After a big family breakfast, the three kids were free to play with friends. This gave Julia and Kevin time to talk and enjoy a second cup of coffee. The June day was going to be in the 70's so they sat in comfortable lawn chairs out on the porch.

"I just cannot believe Joel would kill anyone," Julia repeated for the third time. "I can see the drug part, but never murder."

Kevin liked his wife to have an opinion, especially when he reviewed cases with her. He agreed this time. "We're looking at his motivation and, quite frankly, I can't see any. Means and opportunity are there, but why would he kill anybody?"

"What's your next step?"

"Lana just confirmed that Shelly was using drugs even though everyone wants to deny it. If that's true, we need to find out where both kids were getting them. I think the lead in Seattle is our best one, but if so, that means we might be dealing with a bigger syndicate."

"It all worries me," Julia reached out to hold her husband's hand. "Be careful. Maybe that nice detective from Boston will help you."

Kevin smiled at his wife and kissed her hand. "That's what I hope, too."

Alan's arm hurt from yesterday's bowling. He had lost three games and tried not to complain about the pain. When the boys wanted to stay longer, Alan suggested pizza and they happily agreed they were hungry... again. They also decided to rent a movie and settle down for the evening. After arguing over what movie to rent from Redbox, Alan let them choose two, just to be fair. He remembered dozing off after the first thirty minutes of "How to Train Your Dragon" and didn't know when the boys finally went to bed. He was pleased to see them sound asleep in their room when he stumbled into bed at midnight.

Today Lindsay was picking up the boys on the noon ferry. He loved his weekend with them and now appreciated his daughter even more. He imagined their lifestyle was filled with the same energy he experienced, but he believed Lindsay knew how to create order out of chaos. Was that a gift, or mere survival?

At 9:30 Alan called the boys to wake up for breakfast.

Rani yawned as he walked into the kitchen. "Can we have pancakes again?"

"Sure, and how about some eggs and fruit? We'll have a hearty meal before you two need to pack up for home."

"Today? I thought we had another day?" Rani looked unhappy.

"If you remember, you start soccer... or basketball... camp tomorrow."

"Oh, yeah, I forgot." Rani ran into the bedroom shouting to his brother to wake up.

Both boys ate everything offered. Alan always appreciated good appetites and ate along with them. His walk onto the ferry and back would be his exercise for the day.

Y ou have a visitor." Joel looked up from his cell cot and questioned the guard.

"Me? Who is it?"

"Come on, you can find out for yourself." The guard led him down the hall, unlocked the outer door and took him to a waiting room.

"Dad?" Joel was surprised to see his father standing there. Although they hadn't spoken since the holidays, he wondered how his father heard he was in jail. "How did you know I was here?"

Leo Spencer sat at the table and waited until Joel also sat. "Your sister called us. Apparently, the police called her to see where you were because you told your boss you were visiting her. She got upset and called us and so we called the Island police."

Joel hung his head. "I didn't want to get you involved."

"We want to help, Joel. We're family. Tell me what this is all about."

"At first it was a drug charge... but now they suspect me of killing two teenagers! I didn't do it! They said they found a gun in my apartment! I've never owned a gun in my life!" Joel let his head drop to the table. He was exhausted with fear that whoever was setting him up would get away with it.

Leo reached out and put his hand on his son's head. "We'll try to figure this out. Did you talk with a public defender?"

"Yes. He seems okay... a little young... but he's trying to get me bail."

"Okay, let me find out what I can. Your mom sends her love. Try and be patient while I investigate things. I put some money into an account for you to make phone calls. You can call me anytime." Leo stood up and reached out to take Joel's hand. He knew that hugs were not allowed.

When Joel returned to his cell, he was overwhelmed with gratitude for his father. Knowing he had disappointed his parents several times before, he wanted them to believe he had finally turned a corner. But he knew he was just fooling himself. He dealt drugs. The police would probably get him on that anyway.

Leo stood beside his car outside of the police station. It was raining, which was known to happen during early summer months, but he didn't seem to notice the steady drops. He was thinking about Joel and the other time he got into trouble. The public defender they used had been good, and Joel didn't have to do jail time. But this sounded serious.

Leo had the name of Joel's PD and decided to give him a call.

Waiting for the PD to call him back, Leo decided it was time to call his wife and let her know what was happening.

Kate answered her cell phone immediately, "Leo, did you see Joel?"

"Yes, he's doing okay for now. He's scared, as you can imagine. But I need to talk with you about hiring a lawyer for him. They have him on serious charges and I don't think he'll get bail. Should I look up a lawyer?"

"Will a private lawyer help more?"

"Well, the way I understand it, a criminal defense lawyer is what he needs, someone to advise him of his rights, protect his interests and let him know what he's faced with."

"How are you going to find one?"

"I was thinking about calling Rob at work. He's got a brother who practices law in Seattle and maybe he can recommend somebody."

"Good idea. I like Rob and I know he'll keep this confidential. What's going to happen, Leo?"

"I wish I knew, Kate. They're holding him on a drug charge, but apparently, they also suspect him of murder. Joel denies any part of it. They found a gun in his apartment and say it's the murder weapon. Joel has never owned a gun, we both know that, and he's always been anti-gun."

"Do you want me to drive up?"

"Not right now. I'm going to get a hotel in Port Orchard...they have a Comfort Inn...and then make these phone calls."

"Let me know what I can do here. Should I call

the kids?"

"It's up to you. There's not much they can do."

When Leo hung up the phone he drove to the hotel. The Comfort Inn was on the main street of the small town. Port Orchard was three blocks of small stores including one tavern, a couple antique shops and several bail bonds places. The town faced the Bremerton Naval base located across Puget Sound and had a foot ferry that took passengers across to that side. Leo was glad the town was so quiet. He paid for three nights at the hotel and decided to get something to eat before retreating to his room. Looking down the street, he saw a Kentucky Fried Chicken, which was always good. Once he was back in his room, he called Rob.

Rob's brother was a Tort Lawyer in a big firm in Seattle. Rob gave Leo his brother's personal cell number. Thirty minutes later, the lawyer returned Leo's call. After listening to the trouble Joel was in, Leo was given the number of an older lawyer on the Island who dealt with criminal law. Leo appreciated the help and called the second lawyer.

Carson Bowen was thinking about retiring. He'd been a lawyer for over thirty years and was tired of all the paperwork. Although he preferred high end cases, this also meant being followed around by reporters and having the media chase him for a good story. Living on the Island had kept him a safe distance from the reporters who covered the courthouse and crime in the city. It also kept him off the hook from having to attend all the extra-curricular events that most lawyers relished. Carson was a quiet man and enjoyed his secluded life.

Keeping up with Island news, Carson took the time to attend the recent town hall meeting to hear Detective Sharp give his talk. Carson liked what the detective said and hoped their paths would cross sometime. Like everyone else, he had been shocked by the graduation night murders and wondered how the investigation was going. Through the Island grapevine, he heard that someone local was now in custody. Still, when Joel Spencer's father called him for representation, Carson was taken aback.

"I'm not sure I can help, Mr. Spencer. Being so close to people on the Island puts me in a rather awkward position."

"What do you advise me to do Mr. Bowen? I don't think my son is guilty and these are serious charges."

Carson understood the man's concerns. "I could talk with him, I guess. That of course would be pro bono and then I could advise him of his rights. When do you want me to meet with him?"

Leo thanked Bowen and they agreed to meet at the jail tomorrow morning.

Alan called Maggie after he dropped off the boys, had a nap, and settled in with a glass of wine. He had enough left-over food to last the week, having bought an abundance for the boys. Now he just wanted to relax.

"How did it go with the twins?" Maggie had been busy all weekend and wanted to hear stories about the boys.

"Well, let's just say I'm not a very good bowler but I

make great pancakes."

Maggie laughed. "I'm sure they had a great time. What are your next plans?"

"I have a friend coming to visit next week. Sidney's a lawyer in Boston and wants to get away and relax. I was hoping you could steer us in the right direction for things to do. In fact, I was hoping you would join us for a few events."

"I would love to! You know my schedule, busy on the weekends, but free from Monday afternoon thru Thursday. So, let's plan some fun."

"In the meantime, did you hear that Joel Spencer's been arrested?"

"Yes! I don't believe it!"

"I don't know the details, but it looks very serious. Do you know anything about him?"

Maggie sounded concerned. "Just that he's been here for less than a year and works at the restaurant. I like him. I can't imagine he would kill anyone."

"I talked with Chief Johnson only briefly. I hope Joel gets a good lawyer."

Maggie and Alan talked for a while longer and then agreed to have dinner on Tuesday evening.

MONDAY, JUNE 12TH

Lana usually had Monday's off, but Kevin had called her in for a meeting. Joel's arrest was foremost on his mind, and he wanted to be certain their reports were in order.

"I imagine he has a lawyer by now. At least I hope he does." Kevin shook his head. He was still in disbelief that Joel was the killer.

Lana riffled through her notes. "I'll write up my reports right now. I suppose the prosecutor needs to see everything we have so far."

"We'll let the County Prosecutor deal with the lawyer, but you're right, we need to be prepared to present our case to the prosecutor's office. We'll have to have a detailed file if they're really going to charge Joel with drug trafficking. And we'll need to lay out what evidence we have for suspecting him of the double homicide, forensic evidence, witness statements and affidavits, as well as our theory of the case...

the whole shebang. Let's be prepared. I wonder if there's anyone else we need to talk with." At this point his cell rang. After listening to the caller, he looked at Lana.

"Well, that's interesting. My mother works at the little gas station in Rolling Bay, and she said that Tom Richardson, the friend of Kyle's, came in and she overheard him talking on his cell about Kyle. She said that he sounded worried about a gun. Let's go see what's worrying him."

Tom worked part time with a landscaping company popular on the Island. He had been hired part-time two years ago and planned to work full time now that he had graduated. Most of the jobs were trimming and mowing for the expensive houses that had glorious views of Seattle. The work was year-round because wealthy people liked to have full gardens blooming in every season. He was surprised to see Chief Johnson and his deputy walking up the lane where he was working.

"Tom, can we have a few minutes?" Kevin raised his hand to show they were friendly.

"Okay...I guess." Tom put down his weed whacker and looked worried.

"Do you know anything about a gun, maybe a 9mm semi-automatic that was stolen?" Kevin moved closer to the teen, but in a friendly manner.

"What do you mean? Why would I know about a gun?" Tom shifted on his feet and looked from Kevin to Lana. "Who said I knew something?"

"You were heard talking on the phone with someone about a gun. Who were you talking to?"

Tom felt his heartbeat in his ears. It must have been when he was in the gas station store. Did that old lady hear him? Why would she call the police?

"Look, Tom, we're following up on every lead we have. If you know something about a gun that worries you, we need to know about it. Now, who were you talking to?"

"I called my uncle. He has a gun vault and I heard someone had broken in and taken some guns a while back. I wanted to warn him."

"What's your uncle's name and where does he live?"

"He lives in Kingston. Jack Richardson. I didn't think he'd heard about the murders, and I knew about the robbery of his stuff. He was glad I called."

"Thanks, Tom. We'll follow up on this. Don't worry about it, okay?"

"Should I call my uncle?"

"No, we'll just make a routine call about the robbery. We won't mention you."

They shook hands and let Tom get back to work.

"I believe him," said Lana. "Poor kid was just worried about his uncle."

"Seems that way. Let's follow up on that robbery and see how it was reported."

When they returned to the precinct, Kevin called the Kingston sheriff and found out that the robbery had been reported in early June. They didn't have any suspects, but there was a 9mm semi-automatic handgun that was stolen. The sheriff would email the report.

Kevin let out a long breath, "Well, this is getting

interesting. We may have more information about the gun now."

Carson Bowen drove up to the Port Orchard jail in his white sport Mercedes. He was still considered an attractive man even in his sixties. His thick grey hair and 6'3" frame made him look like he stepped out of a film. He had called ahead to make an appointment to see Joel and informed the supervisor he was considering Joel as a client. The guards at the jail knew Carson's reputation and were surprised he wanted to be involved. Eyebrows were raised as he stepped into the entrance foyer.

Leo Spencer approached Carson with his hand out. He had seen his profile photo and knew him immediately.

"Thank you for doing this," Leo said.

"No problem, let's go talk with your son."

Joel was led into an interview room and was surprised to see his father along with the tall attorney. Even Joel knew who Carson Bowen was. His reputation on the Island was that of a lady's man even though everyone knew he was a confirmed bachelor. Island people liked to be intrigued by local gossip and unfounded stories which often got out of hand. Carson was the perfect subject for them.

"Mr. Bowen, thank you for being here." Joel shook hands and then sat at the table. Leo patted Joel's shoulder and then also sat down across from him.

"Joel, where were you the evening of the murders?" Carson got right to the point.

"I was at home. It was my night off."

"Were you alone?"

"Yes, unfortunately."

"When did you hear about the murders?"

"I heard the sirens go through town and I wondered what had happened. But it wasn't until the next day that I heard what happened?"

"Who told you?"

"I heard at work. No...wait...I went to get coffee at the bakery and then I heard two people were killed."

"Did you work that day at the restaurant?"

"No, I had a job to help cater at a birthday party. There was talk about it being two teenagers. I was worried that I might know them and listened for the names."

"Okay, so Joel, you're saying that you were home on Saturday, alone, and then on Sunday you had a job catering. Did you talk with anyone Saturday evening?"

"No. I just watched some basketball and played video games. I was tired, I guess."

"What about the gun that was found at your apartment?"

Joel raised his voice to another level, "I have no idea how that got there! I hate guns! Ask my father..."

Leo nodded his head, "He always has...we're not a gun family."

Carson thought for a minute. "Do you have any enemies who would set you up like this?"

"I can't think of anyone. But...can I speak with you alone?" Joel was ready to confess his dealing drugs to teens on the Island. He didn't want his father to hear.

Leo got up from his chair and left the room. He agreed it was best if he was unaware of what Joel had to tell the lawyer.

"What is it?" Carson was ready for some information. "If it's about the murders, I want you to not tell me."

"No, it's about dealing. Can I tell you this because it will probably come out at some point?"

"Okay, let's hear it."

"I sold drugs to Kyle. Not all the time, but occasionally when he was out."

"What kind of drugs?"

"Pills. He needed Adderall and sometimes Oxy because of his soccer injury. Sometimes weed, too."

"Where do you get your supply?"

"Do I have to tell you?"

"No. But this puts you in a very precarious position, Joel. Selling to kids is going to get you jail time."

"I know."

"Did you sell to other kids too?"

"Yeah... a few."

"Do you think one of them got mad at you and set you up with the gun?"

"I've been trying to figure that out. I can't think of anyone who would."

"This is my advice. Don't talk with anyone, especially not anyone in this place, about your charges, drugs, or anything else. It doesn't matter if it's a deputy, inmate, or staff. No one! Remember, anything you say will be used in court against you. If you have questions then call me, I'll leave my number at the desk. When you're arraigned, my guess is that you won't get bail." Carson stopped and let this sink in. It was a lot for Joel to think about.

"Now," Carson continued, "I want you to remember what you did, and who you talked to every minute of that week. Don't write anything down. The staff can search your cell and your body at any time. And other inmates will gladly trade any info you give them to get a break on their own cases. You'll have plenty of opportunity to write it out if you need to, but it'll be while I'm with you and I'll take whatever you write with me when I leave. Got it?"

Joel seemed to be working through all the possible scenarios and heaved a sigh.

"Are you going to be my attorney?"

"Maybe. I'll get back with you."

Carson didn't waste any more time. He stood up quickly, shook Joel's hand and walked out of the room. Leo looked up expecting to hear an explanation but got none. "What do you think?" he asked Carson.

"Mr. Spencer, I'll call you later today. I have some people I need to talk with before I can decide on my next step."

Leo watched Carson drive off in his sporty car. All he could do now was call Kate and wait at the hotel.

Kevin had tried to get ahold of Jack Richardson but with no luck. He and Lana decided to take a drive to Kingston with the hope of catching him at home. The drive was only thirty minutes and the rain had stopped and a bright sun broke through the few remaining clouds, so they both put on their sunglasses.

Kingston was a small unincorporated community situated on the shores of Puget Sound. It was a short forty-minute ferry ride from the Kingston dock to Edmonds on the mainland where charming main streets with shops and restaurants attracted tourists from both sides. Besides being a pleasant place to visit, in the tight housing market, Kingston had become an affordable real estate market for commuters.

Richardson's modest home was located outside the town and had a tiny view of the water. Kevin rang the bell and waited. A teenage boy answered and was surprised to see police at the door. "Is everything okay?" he asked in a quiet tone.

"Yes, don't worry," Lana reassured him. "Is your father at home?"

At this point they heard footsteps and Jack Richardson appeared. "What's happened?"

Kevin answered first, "Mr. Richardson, we're from the Island and just following up on the burglary of your guns this month."

"Oh...you worried me...I thought maybe something had happened to one of my family. Come in."

Kevin and Lana were led to a comfortable family kitchen and invited to sit down at the table. Kevin pulled some papers out of a folder and began. "We have the report of your home burglary and wanted to know if any guns have been returned."

"No, I haven't heard back from the sheriff at this

point. Why?"

"We believe that one of your guns may have been used in two murders we are investigating. We have the description of that gun here."

Kevin showed Jack the report. "Who had it?" he asked.

"Well, that's an ongoing investigation. How did the burglar get into your gun safe?"

"It was supposed to be locked. As far as I know it was. But someone found the key and opened it. The key was under my laptop...you know...so I wouldn't lose it. Stupid me... everyone knows that trick."

"Do you have a clue who did this?"

"We were away for the weekend. We have relatives who have a cabin on Mason Lake, and we spent the time there. Anyone could have been here. We don't have many robberies in the area, but after that I bought a security system. I just don't know why someone would target this house." Jack felt that he was rambling and stopped to take a breath.

"We're looking into teenagers doing drug deals and wonder if you suspect anyone like this targeting you or your family?"

"No...but I'm always the last to know. It could be kids...probably is. My two teens are not involved." He shook his head to make this point.

Lana didn't want to contradict that thought, but she wondered what his teens would say about their friends. "Can we speak to your kids?"

Jack looked at them and then called his son. "Sean, do you know of any kids who would need guns to deal drugs?"

"No! My friends are all good. Why?" Sean entered the kitchen and looked worried. He was a big kid, around six feet already, dressed in a school jersey and sweats.

"These officers are trying to find out who stole my guns. That's all. Thanks... you can go back to your game."

Lana noticed the nervous look on Sean's face and wondered if he knew more than he wanted to admit. Secrets always create tension, especially those you don't want to accept.

Kevin left his card with Richardson and wondered if they should speak to the local sheriff. Looking at the time, it was already six o'clock, they decided to get back to the Island. It had been a long day.

TUESDAY, JUNE 13TH

The Island had an interesting governing structure. It's a non-charter code city with a council/manager form of government. The City Council members were elected and could set public policy by enacting ordinances or establishing budgetary policies. They also had the authority to define the functions, powers and duties of city officers and employees. The mayor was the chairperson of the council meetings and if there was a time of public danger, she/he would take over the command of the police, maintain law, and enforce order. The Island mayor's name was Pamela Ross.

Kevin saw the mayor's car parked out front of his office when he drove up. He gave a long deep sigh and sat in his car to compose himself. Mayor Ross was a loud and somewhat obnoxious presence who overstepped her authority many times. He was not looking forward to talking with her.

Mayor Ross was dressed in her usual navy business

suit which stretched tightly across her hips and shoulders. Her dyed blond hair was pulled back into a short braid and her red lipstick matched the scarlet nail polish on the nails she used to tap out her annoyance on the large bag she was carrying. "Chief Johnson, I need to talk with you."

"Nice to see you, too, Pamela. Let's go into my office." Kevin was not going to be put off by the mayor's abruptness. He knew how far her authority stretched and why she was there.

"I want to know how this murder case is going and how I can relieve the fear that the community is feeling right now."

"I'm not sure I understand…what fear are people feeling?"

"You know what I'm talking about. You had that Boston detective talk at the town hall meeting while I was away. That's something you should have run past me and the city council. Now people think you're accusing kids on the Island of being drug addicts. We do not have a reputation as a drug community!" The mayor's voice took a louder pitch and was heard by Lana who was just walking in the door.

"Good morning, Chief, anything I can do?" Lana stood at the door of Kevin's office with a slight smirk on her face. The mayor was not one of her favorite people.

Mayor Ross turned to look at the deputy and nodded. "We just have some business to attend to, you can go on with your own obligations."

Lana stared at her for just a moment and then smiled. Rolling her eyes as she left the room, she knew that Kevin had his hands full. Nobody in the office cared for the mayor's officious manner. She had six more months before another election and Lana hoped that someone more qualified and educated in the field of diplomacy would run for the office.

Kevin wanted to defend his position for calling the town meeting and cautioning the Islanders about the problem of their children using drugs. "Perhaps you heard about the attendance at the meeting last Wednesday. We had to move the crowd to the auditorium. People wanted to hear what Detective Sharp had to say and as far as I know the response has been positive."

"My sources say you have someone arrested at this time. Who?"

"True. We have someone in custody, but we're not certain if he's the one who committed the crime. I understand he's talked with a lawyer."

"Who is it?"

"Joel Spencer."

"The waiter at The Doc?" The mayor was visibly shocked. Her mouth hung open for more than a second and then she gasped. "Really? I can't believe it!"

"Like I said, he has a lawyer. We'll know more later today, or tomorrow."

Kevin very seldom saw the mayor speechless. After at least a minute, the mayor stood up and hurried out of the room. Lana watched her slam the door and then hurried into Kevin's office. "What was that all about?"

"She thinks the Islanders are all upset about being told their kids use drugs. We know who she represents, her elite chums who have sterling resumés typed up for their kids. Did you see the guest editorial in the paper today?"

"Not yet... what was it about?"

"One of the council members wrote three long paragraphs denying the idea of drugs on the Island. It was petty and harsh. This person signed the piece 'Concerned citizen' but I know who it was. He went after Detective Sharp, basically telling him to get off the Island."

"Oh no... have you spoken to him about it?"

"No, I'm going to call him right now."

At that very moment Alan was walking into town and passing by the police precinct. When his phone rang, he saw it was the chief. "Chief Johnson, I'm right in front of your building."

Kevin asked him to step in and Alan was happy to oblige. He liked Kevin and was wondering how the investigation was going.

The two men shook hands and Kevin asked Alan into his office. "Have you read *The Review* this week?"

"No, what day does it come out?"

"Today. There's an editorial in it that's not very favorable to the idea that drugs are being sold and used on the Island. It mentions you and your talk last Wednesday. I just wanted to be sure you didn't take it personally."

"Now I'm interested." Alan mused. "Do you have a copy?"

Kevin brought out the paper and turned to the editorials. Alan read the one referred to him and sighed. "So, some of the Island community wants to remain in denial."

"But not everyone. We have groups teaching kids about drugs and the damage they do, and we have programs set up for those in drug trouble. The mayor was just in and was complaining that her 'group' of friends did not appreciate your talk either. There are some of the wealthy and entitled 'citizens' on the Island who are very protective of the image of the community."

"It's too bad. Drugs are everywhere in the world. Denying it won't make them go away. For those with addictions it's a disease. I'm sorry to hear this."

"Well, it's nothing you did wrong. Please don't think less of the good people here. We want you to enjoy your visit. Do you have any plans this week?"

"Maggie Freeman and I are going to dinner tonight." Alan smiled at the thought.

"Good! I like Maggie. She'll keep you positive about the Island."

Alan left the precinct and wandered along in town. He was looking forward to dinner. Maggie said she had a gift certificate to the museum Tuesday night dinners, and she would love to use it. He would talk with her about the editorial.

Ted Macdonald, the county prosecutor, arrived at the precinct at 3:00 to speak with Kevin about the case. Kevin admired the young prosecutor who had the reputation for being thorough and understanding the community's need. He was also known for possessing effective communication skills.

Looking through his reports, Kevin decided to be honest with Ted. "I hope Joel Spencer finds good representation. I just don't think he's capable of murder, especially one this gruesome. I believe he does have drug problems, and this is according to some kids, but that doesn't mean he would kill someone."

The prosecutor looked concerned. "Any new evidence on the case?"

"You know we found a gun at Joel's place, but there were no prints or DNA. Now we have evidence that the gun was stolen from a guy in Kingston who had been robbed earlier this month. We're just running some tests now to match the gun with the murders."

Macdonald wrote this down. "Well, that's something. I understand that Joel denies the gun is his or that he even owned a gun."

Kevin nodded. "Another thing, after the search of Joel's place, no forensic evidence was found to connect him to the scene of the murders."

The prosecutor glanced at his notebook and said, "I've met with Leo Spencer, Joel's father, and he's distraught about all of this. He wants to help."

Kevin was relieved to know this. "Good. I'm glad Joel's family will support him. What should we be doing now?"

"If you don't think Joel is the murderer, then you have to find the pipeline the gun took from the original owner to his apartment."

"We're working on that already."

The two men spoke a few minutes longer and then

Macdonald departed. Lana stuck her head in Kevin's office and wanted an update.

The Island Art Museum was located steps away from the ferry dock. Opened in 2013, the beautiful museum focused on artists and collections from the Puget Sound region. Besides the museum gallery, it had an auditorium, Bistro, and plaza that welcomed Islanders and ferry riders who spend the day exploring the Island. On Tuesday evenings, the Bistro chef prepared a special dinner for members only which included soup, entrée, and dessert.

Alan had been to the museum with the boys, but the evening glow of soft lights on the artwork along with the sun setting on the view of the water was spectacular. He had dressed casually, as Maggie had suggested, and smiled when he saw her approach in a long floral sundress with a light pink shawl around her shoulders.

"You look lovely," he said.

"Thank you, kind sir," Maggie smiled. "And you look very relaxed. I bet you slept well after a weekend with the twins."

"That I did," Alan said. He was surprised and pleased how well he was sleeping since he arrived at the Island. Sleeping had always been a series of naps when he lived in Boston. He blamed his highly stressful job for keeping him awake at all hours. Now he had nothing to worry about.

Alan and Maggie walked around to view the art. "This museum is terrific, and the artwork is impressive. I heard most of it's local." Alan was admiring a sculpture of a bronze mythical beast.

"Yes, local talent, and the people who work here are all volunteers. That's why it's free to the public. I've watched it all happen, the time it took to get grants and money, and the dedication of the people who believed it would happen. I think everyone on the Island feels they had a part in building this."

When they retreated to the Bistro, Alan ordered a bottle of white wine since they were told the entrée was fish. Toasting the museum when the wine was poured, Alan looked to Maggie to begin the conversation because she appeared to be exploding with news.

"Did you see *The Review*?" Maggie was talking just above a whisper.

"Yes, I did... Kevin showed me the editorial this morning. Too bad. I hope I don't get exiled off the Island."

"Well, it made me mad! Whoever wrote that nasty piece should at least sign it so we can all judge them. I told you the Island was in denial. Have you heard anything else about Joel?"

"Kevin said his father's here and wanting to help."

"I'm so glad about that. Does he have a lawyer?"

"A public defender now. But Kevin heard that a lawyer from here might take the case."

"Did he say who?"

"No, but I wouldn't know who it was anyway. What have you heard?"

They were talking in whispers since other people might hear them at the next tables. "Only that the gun was found at Joel's. It just doesn't make sense! We saw him the day after the murders at Tessa and Simon's. If he had done this horrible thing, he would have been acting guilty, don't you think?"

"Yes, good point. Other people saw him too. How many lawyers are on the Island?"

Maggie let out a loud laugh. "If the ferry broke down, people joke that you could walk to Seattle on the top of the lawyers' cars driving around."

"Wow! I had no idea. So, it's anybody's guess who might be interested in taking the case."

Maggie looked over at a table set off to the side. She nodded her head and gave a little wave. "There's a lawyer over there. His reputation is widely known for taking on big cases. He works in Seattle and reporters like to follow him around. If a crime is newsworthy, he's there."

Alan looked to see the older man with the attractive younger woman at the table. "Is that his daughter with him?"

Maggie laughed again. "Probably his latest girlfriend. He's a lady's man if there ever was one."

When their dessert was served and the wine was gone, Alan saw the lawyer approach their table. "Maggie, it's a pleasure. I came over to introduce myself to Detective Sharp. I heard you speak last Wednesday, and I wanted to tell you how impressed I was."

The men shook hands and Alan asked Carson, "Did you happen to see the editorial in *The Review* today? I guess not everyone was impressed."

Carson nodded. "There's always something that

someone can complain about. Sorry, you were the target this time. But I wouldn't worry too much about it. I'm happy to see you've met our lovely Maggie." Carson winked at Maggie and then turned to leave.

"Do you think he's the lawyer for Joel?" Alan asked.

"I hope so." Maggie said.

WEDNESDAY, JUNE 14TH

L indsay didn't want to bother her father, but she hadn't heard from him since Sunday and wondered how he was keeping busy. She decided to call him.

"Hi, Dad, what are you up to?"

Alan was having his second cup of coffee and thinking about taking a tour of the Island. "I'm great! Today I'm going to drive around and look at some things. There's a beautiful garden here on the Island that I want to visit. Do you think it's going to rain?"

"I don't know about your weather, but it looks like sprinkles today over here."

"Is that what you call it...sprinkles? It sounds like something you put on cakes." Alan let out a short laugh. He supposed that rain had many forms in this area. Listening to weather reports each morning amused him. Percentages were given about sun, rain, wind...so nobody was on the spot to get the unpredictable weather wrong.

"Dad, Tessa and Simon attended your talk at the high school last week. They said it was terrific but knowing the Island's reputation, they didn't think it would make a difference. Has there been any response yet?"

"Apparently someone wrote a guest editorial about it this week in *The Review*. Chief Johnson said not to pay attention to it, but it was an indication of some of the sentiments here. I'm going to keep a low profile."

"Well, just be careful. How's Maggie?"

"She's a lot of fun to be with. We had dinner at the museum last night. I met Carson Bowen there. Maggie says he's almost a movie star around here."

Lindsay laughed. "He's got a reputation for sure. What about the murders? Tessa said that someone was arrested."

"That's right. Joel Spencer who works at The Doc Restaurant. Do you know him?"

"Just by name. But he was at the birthday party the day after those kids were murdered. I hope he has a good lawyer."

"Maggie wondered if Carson Bowen would take Joel as a client, but don't spread that around. It's just a thought."

"He'll have good representation if Carson does take it." Lindsay decided to change the subject, "When do you want to get together with us again?"

"I'm free. You let me know."

"The boys have their sports camps all week so I'm thinking about having you over Saturday, you could stay overnight. We would love to take you around and show you some Seattle sights."

"Sounds wonderful. Do you want to pick me up at the ferry Saturday?"

"Sure. I'll text you the time. Love you."

"Love you too."

Alan hung up. He was pleased with the idea of spending more time with Lindsay and her family. So far, his days had been filled with events that seemed to comfort him in a way he hadn't felt in a very long time. He opened his laptop to find information on, and directions to, the Botanical Gardens.

An hour later and pointing his car in the direction of the gardens, Alan passed a sign marking an exit for Port Orchard. He thought about Joel. Alan didn't really know anything about him except from what Maggie had said, but he didn't seem the type to violently hurt anyone. But if he was selling drugs, especially to kids, he was in trouble. People like Joel who casually got into the drug business had no idea how much trouble they were headed for. Drug dealers and addicts could never be trusted, and they lied even when the truth would work.

Alan arrived at the Gardens and visited the little gatehouse shop near the entrance where he was handed a map to the well-maintained two-mile trail. As he began his walk, he noticed there were several places to stop and take photos, but he had forgotten his camera. He could use his phone, but it was old and wouldn't do the scenery justice. To call the scenes 'breathtaking' was probably an understatement. Alan made himself a promise to return with his camera another day.

Shelly Mann's father entered the police station with a heavy bag under his arm. "I need to talk with Chief Johnson," he said as he placed the bag on the counter. Lana looked at the bag and then called out to Kevin. Without hesitation, Kevin invited the man into his office and shut the door. "What do you have there?" He asked calmly.

"I heard the talk the Detective gave last week, and I decided to search through Shelly's room and see what I missed. I could swear to you my daughter didn't take drugs, but I found these things in her room." He opened the bag and took out a jewelry box containing pill bottles, rolling paper, roach clips and a filtration device along with a marijuana-laced candy assortment. "I found it hidden in the back of her dresser drawer."

Kevin nodded his head, he felt sorry for this man who had been so certain his daughter did not do drugs. "Thank you for bringing it in. I'm sorry your daughter was caught up with this problem. Can I take this off your hands?"

"I didn't tell her mother. She's grieving and I don't want to upset her anymore."

"I understand. Do you have any idea at all who gave Shelly drugs?"

"Kyle."

"We're looking into his use. If they were dating and working together, you're probably right. But let us find out who the original source is for both kids. We're looking for a dealer."

Both men stood and shook hands. Kevin watched as

the stricken father shuffled out the door. This case was hurting a lot of good people.

C arson Bowen conferred with his partners and still hadn't made the decision to take the Island case. He wanted to believe Joel had been set up, but the fact that the gun had been stolen was an indication there was something else at stake. Carson was on his way to the jail to meet with Joel's father and discuss some details, as well as to talk with Joel once more.

Leo had spoken to Kate the night before and wondered what they would do if Carson said no to defending Joel. Kate had looked up Carson's profile and was impressed with his successful career. A lawyer like this would be expensive, and she admitted to Leo that she was angry that Joel had found himself in such a mess. Parents were never aware of what choices their adult children made once they left home. But they still prayed they would never get into trouble with the law.

Carson met Leo outside the corrections building to talk briefly about the stolen gun. He said he was still undecided about taking the case but would let Leo know in a day or two. In the meantime, Carson had some questions for Joel. They were escorted into an interview room and a few minutes later Joel was led in by a guard. When his handcuffs were removed, he collapsed onto the metal chair, looking exhausted and worried.

Carson began, "Joel, they found out whose gun it was. Apparently, there was a robbery in Kingston and a man named

Jack Richardson had several guns stolen. Do you know this guy?"

"No."

"Well, one of the stolen guns is the one recovered from your apartment and has been confirmed as the murder weapon. I need to know who your dealer was and who you sold to on the Island."

Joel stared blankly at the attorney. His dealer was in Seattle and the kids he sold to would be in trouble because of him. "I don't want to get anyone in trouble, sir."

"You're already in trouble...I know you're trying to protect the kids, but they'll have to deal with it. In fact, this may help them get into treatment if that's what's called for. Have you tried treatment?"

"It didn't work. But I'm not feeling too good right now and it's because my pills have been cut off."

"What were you taking."

"Oxy sometimes, but mostly Adderall and weed...it just depended." Joel looked at his father with remorse. He had let him down over the years, but this was by far the cruelest time. Leo just nodded his head.

Carson looked at Joel and thought for a few minutes. He had defended several cases where the dealer was never found, and his client lost. Joel seemed like a small-town seller and was going to be charged with murder if he didn't come clean. "Joel, this is serious, you may have to reveal everything or else be charged with two murders you say you didn't do."

Joel hung his head and gripped his hands so tightly he winced in pain. "I didn't murder anyone. I never owned a gun.

Yes, I sold to some kids. That's it."

Carson nodded his head. "Okay. Let me work on this. The arraignment is Friday morning. The judge will probably not grant bail, and even if he or she does it will be too much." He looked at Leo with the understanding that he knew the Spencer family couldn't pay the ten percent bail fee that would be required.

"So, I'll stay in jail, right?" Joel looked depressed at the thought.

"Yes. You can call me anytime to see how things are going. Call your family too for their support. I'm going to ask your parents and siblings to write a letter to the judge saying you're a responsible guy. If you can give me the names of friends or a boss who will also stand up for you, let me know."

"Thank you. I'll call you."

At this point Carson stood to leave. Leo asked if he could stay a few more minutes and it was granted.

"Joel, I've spoken to your mother and siblings. They all want to help. We don't want you to think we're abandoning you. This is a mess, but we know you would never hurt anyone, and we also know your feelings about guns."

"I am so sorry, Dad. I really messed up."

"Well, don't give up. Call me. I'm going to be here for the arraignment and then I'll go back home. But I'll come back when you need me." Leo reached out to take his son's hand. "Don't give up."

Joel nodded. "I won't, Dad."

CAPABLE OF MURDER

Carson Bowen sat in his car brooding. He was in a quandary. If he took Joel's case, he might make enemies on the Island. He had been strict about not getting involved with Island politics or legal problems. That was why he could move around so easily and enjoy his privacy. His partners in Seattle questioned why he lived in such an out of the way location, because they relished the easy access to the office and all the entertainment city life provided. Carson did not. He liked the low-key environment of living away from the city.

Carson had grown up in Quincy, Massachusetts, the oldest of three children. His father was a judge, and his mother was the executive director of a large non-profit corporation. Being the first born, Carson felt he had to live up to his parents' expectations even as a young child. There was no question that he would follow his father's legacy to Harvard and go into law. His sister was also expected to achieve, and to marry well. So far, she had accomplished the first by being an executive banker, but she had never married. Now in her late fifties, the idea of marriage was never mentioned. Carson's brother, younger by five years, was a free spirit. Not caring what his parents wanted from him, he had married his childhood sweetheart and moved to a farm in Vermont. They had raised four children who were nurtured with love. Carson envied his brother.

Moving to Washington State was the only disappointment he gave his parents. Carson never thought he would stay long with the Seattle law practice, just enough time to earn a junior partnership and then move back to the

East Coast. But as time went by, he began to appreciate all Seattle offered and when his name came up for a full partnership with his law firm, he decided to stay on the West Coast.

He purchased an older home on the south end of the Island ten years ago. Wealthy Seattle people had built summer estates on this part of the Island before there were public ferries to take them across Puget Sound. When the public ferry system was finally sailing, this part of the Island became very elitist and remained more remote, having its own country club and parties. Over the years, the houses were sold to investors or, like Carson, to someone who wanted to be away from the noise of the city.

Carson's house was not palatial but had a country charm on five acres. The three-story home had four large bedrooms and a well-maintained family kitchen with tall windows that overlooked Seattle and Mount Rainier. It was an outstanding view. Carson took advantage of the sweeping view by making the kitchen area his sanctuary.

He was still ruminating that evening as he sat in his easy chair, taking in the spectacular view, and sipping a glass of Merlot. He had to consider the politics of taking the case. He was hosting a board meeting of the city planners tomorrow night and would ask some members how the Island community was dealing with the murders. It might help him decide what to do about Joel.

THURSDAY, JUNE 15TH

Kevin needed to speak with Kyle's father again. If Kyle had been using and sharing drugs at school, there must be some clue to where he was getting them. Even though Kevin had looked through Kyle's room, he hadn't done a thorough search. He decided to call Alan to see if he could come with him.

"Good morning, Chief." Alan was already awake and having some yogurt. He thought he was losing some weight, staying away from all the fast food he usually gulped down on the job in Boston. "What's the news?"

"Are you free around 12:30? I want to go through Kyle Smith's bedroom again and see if I missed something. You're the expert on hidden drugs and I thought you could help."

"Sure. Do you want to pick me up?"

"Okay." Kevin rang off and went to talk with Lana.

"Good morning, Chief, what's our day look like?" Lana glanced up from her computer and waited for the answer.

Kevin reached for his notebook to verify a few items on his list. "We need to identify any other high schoolers who were buying drugs. Do you think Shelly's other friend, Mira, might come through with names of kids who were into drugs?"

"I'm not certain, but I'll talk with her again. This time, alone. Maybe that will make a difference with how much she wants to tell."

"Good. Detective Sharp and I are going to Kyle's to take a closer look at his bedroom. I might have missed something. Let's meet back here after lunch and review what we find out."

Mira Connelly was nervous about talking with the deputy. Her part-time job at the bookstore started in an hour but she agreed to meet Lana at Pegasus Coffee again. Mira didn't want to get involved with the investigation and she didn't know why she was called again. If being someone's friend made you a suspect, it wasn't fair. She hadn't told her parents, either.

Lana met Mira outside the coffee shop. "Do you want to go inside, or talk out here?" Lana pointed to the bench that overlooked the marina.

Looking around to see if there were others nearby, Mira pointed to the bench. "Why do you want to talk with me?"

"I just need to ask you a few more questions. Don't worry, you're not in trouble, but you might be able to help us understand Shelly a bit better."

Mira nodded slightly and sat. "What do you want to know?"

"We found drug paraphernalia in Shelly's room. Did you know she was doing drugs?"

"I suspected it."

"Why? Who gave them to her?"

"Kyle. He always had enough for anyone who wanted it."

"Who else got drugs from him?"

"Just the guys. But they probably wanted some for their girlfriends. The stuff's everywhere."

"What guys?"

"I don't want to name names." Mira started to stand up, wanting to end the conversation.

"Mira, this is important. We need to find out who deals drugs on the Island. Are you worried because you buy drugs from someone you're protecting?"

Mira stared at Lana, letting out a slow breath, and dragging out the moment, not wanting to tell the truth. "No comment."

Lana understood. "Okay, I get that some kids are sharing with their friends. But the kids doing the sharing have to get them from somewhere. We're looking for who is supplying those friends in the first place. Do you know who's selling to them?

"Lots of kids buy from each other. I know that guy from the restaurant, Joel, sold to Kyle and some other kids who work there."

"That really helps me, Mira. Listen, you're a smart girl

and have your future ahead of you. Try and be safe about the whole drug business. We're going to find out who killed your friend and make sure it doesn't happen again." Lana hoped her sincerity about drugs was getting through to Mira. "You can call me anytime, even just to talk. Okay?"

Mira nodded. "I've got to get to work."

Like most teens, Lana knew that Mira wouldn't easily betray a confidence. She decided her next step was to get the names of all the kids who worked at The Doc Restaurant.

Kevin and Alan arrived at the Smith house and met Kyle's father at the door. He mentioned again that his wife was not speaking to anyone. She was taking care of their other children and that was enough. He led them into Kyle's room.

"We haven't moved anything. It's just as our son left it."

Kevin nodded, "You can stay if you want. We just want a thorough look around."

"No, I'll let you do what you need to do." They watched him walk down the hall.

"Okay, Alan, where should we start?"

Alan once again explained to Kevin all the hiding places kids used to stash drugs. They began the search and found the first bag of weed taped to the back of a picture frame hanging on the wall. Several pills were found in a mint container, a match box, and hidden in the lining of his letterman jacket. Kyle had gone to a lot of trouble to appear clean. If he thought he was being clever, he was only fooling himself.

"Have you gone through his phone and laptop yet?" Alan asked.

"We didn't find anything. If it's true that Joel was selling to Kyle, they didn't have to leave any messages...they worked together." Kevin took photos of the locations of the drugs. He bagged the drugs and left the room.

"Did you find anything?" Kyle's father was waiting by the police car.

"Yes, we did. Thank you for letting us have a look. This will help. I understand the memorial service is Saturday. I'll be there." The men shook hands.

Alan's phone rang as he walked into his house. He was pleased to see it was Maggie.

"Hi, Alan, I'm wondering if you'd like to accompany me to a city council board meeting this evening."

Alan was surprised to be asked, especially after the critical editorial in the paper.

Sensing the hesitation, Maggie continued, "It's at Carson Bowen's house and this is our annual end of the year dinner. So, it's more of a social gathering."

Alan thought twice, "I wonder if my presence might make some people uncomfortable."

"I doubt it, Alan. You can trust me...this group cares about the Island and wants to see a change. You'll enjoy the conversations."

"Okay, I guess. Should we go together, or will I meet you there?"

"Be at my place at 5:00 and we can go together."

Alan hung up the phone and wondered again if this was a good idea. Working closely with Kevin may put him in a rather precarious position. Of course, he wouldn't talk about the investigation, but what if he overheard something that Kevin should be aware of. Alan would have to be careful.

Carson met Maggie and Alan at the door in an apron that read "The Grill Father." He had a glass of red wine in his hand and offered one to them as they walked through to the kitchen.

"Your home is very impressive," Alan remarked.

"Thanks, I've been here for quite a few years and still enjoy it. Of course, the view can't be beat." Both men looked out the window to the majestic mountain. "Have you ever climbed Mount Rainier?" Alan asked.

"No. I'm not that adventurous. I've been to the lodge several times. Out of town clients enjoy driving there and taking photos. How about you? Are you a mountain climber?"

Alan laughed at the thought and took a sip of wine. "Climbing stairs is about it. Since you work in Seattle, I'm wondering how you manage the commute."

"I got used to it. The ferry is reasonably reliable, and I don't have anyone waiting for me at home, so I keep an open schedule. Please have a seat." Carson indicated the easy chairs and a soft leather sofa that faced the windows. Alan smiled and continued to enjoy the outstanding view.

Other council members and their wives were beginning to arrive. As Alan listened to the conversations around him, he heard Carson speaking with an older man.

"I'm considering taking Joel Spencer's case. My conflict is the Island and the widespread denial that drugs are a problem. What's your opinion on how to handle denial such as this in a community that pretends to be clean?" Carson was anxious to hear the other man's opinion.

"Well, it's a problem here, that's for sure. Denial can sometimes distort reality. It's used as a way of protection, so you don't have to see or deal with the truth. I'd say it's simply a way to ignore problems." The older man shook his head and rattled the ice that was in his glass of whiskey.

Carson noticed Alan standing nearby and introduced the two men.

"Did you hear Detective Sharp speak the other night at the high school?"

"No, unfortunately I was away. But I heard about it, and I want to thank you for bringing your wisdom to our small community. Our Island remains very isolated."

"I was happy to be asked to speak. Drinking and substance abuse are just as common here as anywhere, but most people have learned to minimize the role it plays in their lives. Mainly, I believe, because most drug abusers are still capable of carrying on their usual responsibilities."

The older man agreed. "I always love the excuses of blaming parents or rationalizing and comparing yourself to someone who's worse off. It's universal. Tell me, Carson, why would you want to take this case?"

"Twofold. One is that I don't think Joel is guilty. Second is because it may be my best opportunity to expose how truly widespread the problem is and motivate people to seek help more actively for the community. We need resources. Therapists, support groups and programs to get people some help."

"What would you suggest then?" The man looked at Alan.

"Off the top of my head, I think you should continue with town meeting discussions, bring in some experts and get the conversation rolling. I was impressed by the number of people who showed up at the town meeting." At this point, Alan saw Maggie waving him over to join her group. He excused himself from the two men and gladly walked away. He hoped to avoid any more conversations about Joel, the murders, and the investigation.

FRIDAY, JUNE 16TH

Lana had all the names of The Doc Restaurant employees and wanted to discuss with Kevin how to approach each person. The owner had reluctantly handed over these names because he didn't want to have a warrant thrust into his hands. He cared about his employees and hoped they would cooperate and not give the Chief a hard time.

Kevin looked over the list of fifteen people. He knew a few of them because they had worked at the restaurant for years and were fixtures in the community. Kevin wanted to find the dealer, and he would make that clear, someone besides Joel. Whoever murdered Shelly and Kyle, so brutally, was probably not even on this list. His hunch was that it was someone off the Island and the two teens had just been at the wrong place.

"Let's split up the names. It's easier if they come in here to be interviewed and we don't have to go traipsing around to find them. When you call, tell them we'll be here all day or they can make an appointment, sooner rather than later."

Lana liked the idea. She began her calls.

Joel wasn't eating. He knew he was having withdrawal symptoms from the drugs he'd been taking and would have to work through it. He had asked for caffeine and was thankful he was given coffee whenever he wanted it. That helped. His cell was cold, but maybe that was the withdrawal too. He kept a thin blanket around his shoulders all day.

Carson Bowen had asked him to come up with a list of people he sold drugs to, but he still hadn't done this. Why would he get those kids in trouble? He could just say he didn't know their names, but because some of them worked for the restaurant, the police were probably talking to them already. Joel was creating a mental tally of everything that could go wrong.

"Your lawyer's here." A guard was rattling the keys and opening the cell door. "Come on...leave the blanket here."

Joel put out his arms for the handcuffs and was led down the hall. Carson was waiting and stood up when Joel entered the interview room. "Hello Joel. Have a seat."

Joel sat on the cold metal chair and asked, "Are you going to take my case?"

"Yes. We have some things to talk over. I understand the police chief is interviewing the other employees of the restaurant today. If you sold drugs to any of them, my guess is they will give you as a source. This puts you at the top of the list for the murders because of the gun that was also found. We also know that you were seen in Seattle on First Avenue and in the Pike Place Market several times, visiting a shop that's associated with dealing drugs. How does this sound so far?"

"Okay. Not good." Joel began rubbing his arms as if they were cold.

"So, in order for me to take your case, I need to know who your dealer was and how you contacted him."

Joel sagged back in his chair and let his arms fall to his sides. "I didn't know the dealer. It was a slick and easy operation I thought. All I did was show a card to the guy at a jewelry shop and then he made a phone call. I met with some guy out on the corner of Elliot who handed me my stuff. I gave him cash."

"How much did you buy each time?"

Joel sat up straight and brought his hands together as if to steady himself. "It depended. I got my own stuff and then I bought whatever I thought I could sell to a few others quickly. I didn't want to be caught holding a large amount if I could avoid it. It was just pills and weed. I never got anything heavy. If anyone says I did, they're wrong."

"Do you think there's a dealer on the Island?"

"I know there is! Kids tell me they're buying heroin and ecstasy all the time. Where are they getting it?"

"Okay, now I want you to listen closely. The arraignment is in an hour. I just need you to stand by me in front of the judge and plead not guilty. Because you're also a suspect in the double murder, the judge will not grant bail. Your father is still here and will be present."

"That's all I do? Just say that?"

"Yes. And then I'll get back to see you before I go." Carson stood up and watched Joel being led back down the hall. He believed everything Joel said.

D
o you think Carson will take the case?" Maggie was on the phone with Alan again. He had told her about overhearing Carson's conversation.

"I'm pretty sure. He said it's time for people to open their eyes and come to grips with the drug problem, especially about kids. He seemed determined. I guess Joel gets arraigned today."

"I still don't think he did it," Maggie said. "We would have noticed something that day at the birthday party. If you murdered two people, you certainly would have been unnerved or showing signs of fear of being discovered."

"I don't know Joel, but he sure looked innocent to me. Hey, I'm spending the weekend with Lindsay and the family. I thought we might get together on Monday for dinner. You can hear all about my adventures."

"Sure. Tell Lindsay hello from me. I've got a full house of guests this weekend."

Alan rang off and smiled at the thought of seeing Maggie again.

Kevin and Lana had been successful talking with the employees from The Doc Restaurant. Five had admitted buying drugs from Joel and each one swore it was only pills and weed. They said that Joel didn't have access to anything else. They all liked Joel and didn't think he would ever kill anyone.

Lana had a question when the interviews were over. "We're going after the drugs, but why aren't we focused on the weapon? That's what killed the teens."

"You're right, but I keep thinking it's all involved with drugs. My theory is that someone was high and got mad about something, or it was a random gang shooting. We don't have gangs on the Island that I know of, but that doesn't mean some gang wouldn't show up."

"So, where do we go from here? Did you get the report about the platform at the crime scene? Any clues?"

"There's nothing. The weather erased any prints, and the graffiti didn't make any sense. Same with the lighter we found later at the scene. It was clean of prints. So far, there are no clues to help with the case."

"Who else knew about that place? Have any of the kids talked about being there that night? Or hanging out there?"

"As far as we know, only Shelly and Kyle were there that night. But you know kids, they wouldn't admit to anything, especially if it involved being caught with drugs. Let's go over to the Deli where Shelly and Kyle had dinner. Maybe someone remembers what they were talking about, or how they were behaving."

The Deli Restaurant was on the south end of the Island. It was a popular coffeehouse and delicatessen that served a wide variety of food. Kevin and Lana were not surprised by the number of people milling around, because both locals and visitors knew the food and ambiance of this casual dining spot were great. Lana noticed that some customers were still wearing lightweight jackets because the weather was beginning to cloud up. But they didn't seem to mind the possibility of rain as they sipped their afternoon tea or wine under the colorful umbrellas that graced the round tables on the outside lanai.

The owner of the restaurant was Andy Adams. His reputation as a star athlete at the high school was still legendary. Although Kevin was older, he had known about the bullying Adams did in school and how he got away with it because of his parents. They had pressured the principals in the schools to look the other way when teachers and students complained about their son. Their family money and community involvement seemed to have sway and so Andy continued to dominate the sports fields and harass his teammates. Kevin hoped he had settled down.

Andy Adams met them at the entrance of the restaurant. He offered them something to eat or drink and escorted them to a back table. Refusing the refreshments and being seated in the comfortable wicker chairs, Kevin began, "I know you're aware of the two Island kids who were murdered. Did you know them?"

Andy's desire to help contradicted his worry about the

possible repercussions of being involved with any investigation. He decided to remain neutral. "Yes, I did. Shelly lives close by and had even filled out an application to work here this summer. She was a sweetheart and we thought we could use her for the lunch crowds. We're all broken up about what happened. Do you have any idea?"

Kevin only stared back and then smiled briefly. "We're working on it. We understand they stopped here that day before they were supposed to go to the graduation party. I wanted to know if you heard anything or noticed something when they were here. Did anyone mention overhearing them talking?"

"I worked that day, and they were both in pretty good spirits. If I knew them better, I would say they were on a high…laughing, joking, and lots of hand holding. I imagined they were just happy to be graduating and getting on with things."

"Did they say anything unusual to you or to anyone?"

"No, just the usual. They ate and then they left. I knew about the graduation party at the old hall, and I asked them if they were going. They said yes, but they had things to do first. They didn't say what it was."

"What time did they leave?"

"Around 6:30 or so. I was busy and didn't really pay attention.

"Do you know if any of your employees talked with them?"

"All of my graduating kids had the day off. But I don't get involved with all that friendship drama. If you know what I mean." Andy tilted his head and raised his eyebrows.

Kevin looked at Lana to see if she had any questions. "When you say they were acting high, did you assume they were on something?"

Andy looked taken aback at the deputy's question. "No! I just meant they were happy. Kyle, maybe, was a little wasted, but Shelly doesn't do drugs as far as I heard."

Lana nodded. Once again, she wished people would open their eyes and educate themselves on drugs. There was something about Andy she didn't like, although she couldn't name it now. She wondered what kind of a boss he was.

When they left the Deli, Kevin suggested they check out the crime scene since it was just down the road. It appeared the firepit at the scene had been disturbed after it had been processed for evidence because there was garbage lying around including rain-soaked matchbooks. The remains of a fire had left ugly mounds of charred wood and blackened rocks behind. Kevin and Lana both searched for anything that might help the investigation.

"Over here." Kevin called from the path leading to the road above.

"What in the world..." Lana got out an evidence bag.

SATURDAY, JUNE 17TH

Saturday was Kyle's funeral. St. Madeline's Episcopal Church, just a few blocks out of town, was filled with high school students and their parents. There was low whispering in the church until the ceremony began and Kyle's family walked in behind the casket. Heads were bowed to show respect to the bereaved parents and two young siblings. As the minister approached the casket, he held out his arms to embrace Kyle's mother and father.

Kevin hated to go to funerals, especially when it was a young person. He felt it was a failure on his part for not protecting those who died young or prematurely due to a crime. He sat with his wife and looked carefully around the congregation. He was surprised with the number of students in attendance but saw this as a testament to the strength of the Island. Hopefully, this might continue to remind people about the dangers of crime and drugs that can seep into an unsuspecting community.

Following the service, people were escorted into the church hall for coffee and desserts that had been set up on long tables. People wanted to gather and say something of comfort to the family and relieve themselves of some grief for not knowing what to do. They looked at their children and said a prayer of thanks that they were safe. The mood was somber.

Julia walked over to Kyle's parents and hugged them. She always knew what to do in situations like this, Kevin thought. He knew she had already brought food to both grieving families and planned to do it again. Kevin noticed that Shelly's family was not in attendance. He wondered if they were blaming Kyle for Shelly's drug problem and maybe her death. He understood. He heard they were waiting another two weeks for a funeral, so their extended family had time to arrive.

Kevin and Julia stayed in the hall and listened to people talk about their families and plans for the summer. They also heard stories reminiscing how Kyle scored a soccer goal in the first home game last year. The Islanders loved team sports and encouraged kids at a very young age to become involved with any of the numerous Island teams. Sometimes graduating seniors got scholarships for a sport, but no one went pro, no matter how much money their parents paid for years of lessons and training.

A private ceremony was held at the cemetery, so Kevin drove Julia home before going to see his mother at her job. He had only called her once during the week because of his busy schedule, and at the time, she seemed frustrated with her various worries and wanted to talk with him. As he drove up, he found her sitting at the picnic table in front of the store, having a cigarette.

"I wish you would quit, Mom." Kevin gave her a quick hug and sat on the plastic chair beside her.

"I have quit... several times." Penny took another drag and then put the butt in the old tin on the table that served as an ashtray. She patted Kevin's knee, "I'm glad to see you. How was the funeral?"

"Sad. Lots of people. You know... it's so difficult to understand why these kids were targeted." Kevin stared out onto the horizon where he could see a glimpse of the water. "I wish I could be further along into this investigation."

"Did you talk with that kid I called you about?"

"Yes. Thank you. It was a good lead. If you hear anything else remember to call me. What did you want to talk about? Sorry I didn't get back to you."

Penny took out some envelopes from her store apron. "I can't pay these bills." She had tears in her eyes as she handed the bills over. "I guess I got carried away at the casino. One minute I had the money and the next it was gone." Penny hung her head and looked away from Kevin. He thumbed through the bills and added up the total. He knew he would pay them, but he didn't want this to be easy for his mother. If he got upset, she would become depressed and maybe start drinking. If he let it go, she might think he had enough money on hand to always bail her out.

Putting the bills in his pocket, he said, "Okay. Let me take care of these. Maybe you can ask for more hours at the store and be able to handle things. You know, Mom, I want to help, but I'm not always going to have extra. Julia and I make it work, but with inflation we always try to be smart. What do you think about taking an extra day at work?" Kevin had asked his mother many times to work more days just to keep herself busy and stay out of the casino.

"I'll ask. It's a good idea." She smiled meekly at Kevin and then stood up to go back inside. "I better get busy because I've got some shelving to do." She reached out and gave him a quick hug. Kevin sat for a few seconds more, trying to absorb the situation his mother was in. Maybe he should call his sister and let her know about the money. She had a good job but never offered to help. Looking at his watch, he realized he promised Julia he would take the kids to the park.

Lana spent the day at the precinct instead of attending the funeral. She knew Kevin was personally grieving the deaths of Kyle and Shelly and needed to be with the mourners. She was beginning to understand Kevin's concerns about policing a small community and saw how he addressed each investigation in a timely and sensitive manner. He always took time to listen carefully and then decide the necessary steps to assess risks and conduct further investigation when necessary. She was learning a lot working beside him.

She told Kevin she would stay all day and answer the phone. She also wanted to write up her reports and get everything organized in her mind. Her attention to detail helped in most situations and she knew the importance of making a list of questions that still needed to be answered.

DIANE M. McPHEE

Alan took the 10:00 ferry to Seattle that morning to meet up with his family. As was becoming usual, he wondered if it was going to rain since clouds were beginning to form. Even so, he stood outside on the deck of the ferry enjoying the view. Sailboats were gracing the water and avoiding the ferries that traveled back and forth, like some sort of water dance. Breathing in the fresh air, Alan thought about Maggie. Her exuberance and love of life was rubbing off on him. He felt he might be developing a new lens to see the world. His goal now was to embrace life without the sinking feeling of giving in to aging. Maggie was the perfect example with her upbeat and loving response to life. Things were definitely looking up and Alan was beginning to feel a change in himself, for the better.

The plan today was to stroll along the piers and up to the famous Pike Place Market. More walking, Alan thought, and I'm going to be in the best shape of my life.

When the ferry docked, Kirin and Rani ran up through the crowd to meet their grandfather. As usual, they were both talking at once and were hungry. Alan took each of their hands and reminded them to be aware of other people who were walking beside them. Lindsay came rushing up with a troubled look and frowned at the boys. "I thought I told you to wait! Sorry, Dad, they're just so excited to see you." She gave Alan a quick hug and then took the boys' hands and reminded them, "Let's stay together, now. Your father's waiting on the next block."

Sanjay was all smiles. He loved outings with the boys,

especially when it was summer vacation and Lindsay could come along. They all began walking along the pier smelling the clam chowder and fish cakes cooking at the open stalls. Alan realized he was hungry, too.

"Maybe we should stop for something to eat," Alan suggested, "is it too early for lunch?"

"No, it's not!" Both boys rang out at once.

Lindsay was looking at her phone as she walked. "There's a great restaurant when we reach the market. It's famous for their hamburgers and salads and it's just opening now." She knew that the boys would always want burgers, and she could have salad. "How does that sound to you, Dad?"

"Perfect! I haven't had a burger since I've been here, surprisingly. When I'm working, I usually have fast food every other day!" He was confessing to his bad habits, but he didn't care because he promised himself things would change when he got back to the East Coast.

The day went by smoothly. After viewing the stalls at the market and eating lunch, they decided to visit the Seattle Center and go through the Music Museum called The Museum of Pop (MOPOP). This one-of-a-kind architectural wonder was located next to the Seattle Space Needle and housed some of the world's most legendary pop artifacts. There were award winning exhibitions featuring luminaries in the fields of music, literature, TV, and films. It was founded by Microsoft billionaire Paul Allen in 2000 and designed by Frank Gehry. The amoeba shaped building was inspired by the Fender Stratocaster guitar that Jimi Hendrix was known to destroy after each concert. The bright colors and textures symbolized the power and fluidity of music. Alan looked at the building and said, "It's kind of a mess."

Lindsay laughed and repeated what most Seattleite's said, "But it's our mess."

Alan was beginning to wear down after touring the MOPOP and then taking the elevator to the top of the Space Needle. When Lindsay suggested they return home, he let out a sigh. "I may need a nap."

"No, Grandpa! We want you to watch us play our games!" Alan looked at the boys and smiled. He might be able to watch them with one eye closed.

After a short half hour nap between video games, Alan lingered over dinner with Lindsay and Sanjay. They wanted to know more about the investigation on the Island. Alan told them what little he knew, and that he had dinner at Carson Bowen's house.

"Wow, Dad, that's a big deal. What's he like?"

"He's very nice. Smart. His house is beautiful...you should see the view!" This seemed to impress his daughter and he smiled at the idea. "He's going to defend the guy they arrested."

"What a lucky guy! His family must have money."

"Actually, I think Carson's going to do it pro bono."

"Why? Does he know something that will dismiss the case?"

"Good question. I believe he thinks the guy's innocent and Carson wants to prove the Island has a drug problem that needs to be prioritized and dealt with. But don't let this out. I don't really have all the facts."

They spent the rest of the evening talking about the crime in Boston. Sanjay said that he would love to write a mystery one day and could use the ideas.

SUNDAY, JUNE 18TH

Carson drove to Port Orchard to speak with Leo Spencer, catching him before he left for home. Carson needed to get some personal information about Joel and remind Leo to write a letter. Families had no idea how much a positive letter can help the accused. Judges felt more comfortable giving less punitive sentences when they knew the person in front of them had a family and community supporting them. And it never hurt to remind a judge that they're dealing with a real person and not just another case file.

Leo was packing his car when Carson drove up. He nodded his head and waited for the lawyer to begin.

"Mr. Spencer, I've told Joel I would take his case. We can talk about my fee at some other time, but it will be nominal. Don't worry about it now." Carson continued, "I have all of your information and will keep in touch. It's better if I call you when I know anything, so don't panic if you don't hear from me. Right now, Joel's case will be heard sooner rather than later. The courts put this kind of case on their docket first, so I'll let you know the date. In the meantime, please get your family to write letters. I sent you a form, or guide, to help you know what the judge likes to hear. Send me copies as soon as you can."

Leo kept nodding. "My wife and I can't thank you enough for helping Joel. We'll get those letters written and sent back to you as soon as possible. Right now I'm worrying that Joel isn't eating and may get depressed. There's not much to do in jail. I've given him some books, but he's not really interested. He's never been a reader."

"You'd be surprised what inmates learn to do to keep busy. He may be given a service job of some sort if he keeps his head high. I'll mention that to him today. Maybe he can work in the kitchen, with all his experience."

"That sounds good. I like the idea of keeping him busy." Leo and Carson shook hands.

As Leo drove off, Carson thought how difficult it must be to accept the reality of this situation. Some adult children are abandoned by their families when they get into trouble. Joel was lucky that his family was supportive. Carson hoped he could help as he turned his car around and drove the few blocks to the jail.

Joel was ready to talk with Carson. "I've written down the list of kids I sold to, but you've got to promise me they won't be pressured." Selling the drugs to kids was his crime, not theirs. He wasn't sure how to keep the blame in his court, but he would trust his lawyer. He had to.

Carson had expected Joel to withhold information and was suspicious when he easily gave him the list of names. "You know you'll be charged for dealing?"

"Yes. But I didn't kill anyone."

"And you don't know who else deals on the Island?"

"No. I guess you'll have to ask those kids. Someone has got to talk eventually."

"Okay. This is a good start." Carson slipped the list of names into a folder. "I just saw your father. You're lucky to have his support. I mentioned to him that you may be able to get some kind of a service job in the jail if you stay out of trouble. Maybe working in the kitchen. This kind of thing makes the days go by faster. What do you think?"

"I'll consider it. Thanks."

Carson said he would keep Joel apprised on the case and stood to leave. "Take care, Joel."

MONDAY, JUNE 19TH

Pocket knives were popular gifts on the Island when a boy turned ten. Double digits. The belief was that it was time for young boys to take on new responsibilities and understand about safety issues. The Island was known for encouraging kids to grow up sooner than expected, and a knife was an example of "too much too soon." It wasn't surprising to find a knife at the crime scene.

When Kevin and Lana found a suspicious knife by the scene of the murders, they knew it could have belonged to anyone, or had been dropped sometime after the murders. But forensics found this knife to have a specific history. According to forensics, this was a collector's knife, maybe having been passed down through a family. The report read: *Item 27 - A Keen Kutter swell center whittler knife with a bone handle and a three-and-a-half-inch blade. These knives were made for the EC Simmons Hardware Co. prior to 1940. It could possibly be a K3698 ¾ which was made between 1905 and 1938.*

Depending on its age, it was likely made either by Walden or Winchester.

"Do you know of any knife collectors on the Island?" Lana asked Kevin.

"Not off hand. But someone must be missing this if it's that old. If it wasn't found at the murder scene before, it means they probably lost it recently. This might be a lead, or it could just be a coincidence. You know how people like to wander through crimes scenes, unfortunately."

"I don't understand why people carry knives anyway," Lana questioned, "when there's not much use for them."

"One reason is protection." Kevin himself carried a pocketknife. "Knives can be easily carried and secured with a minimal chance of accidental injury. Around here, they're also used for survival, like if you're stranded or suddenly without power, which the Island is known for. But let's say you're an outdoors person, several Islanders like to think they're country people and will be called on to do something where a knife is required."

"I know they're legal," Lana remarked, "and I understand about personal defense. But why do you think guys carry and women don't?"

"Good question! But I'm beginning to hear that lady's knives are getting popular. They come in bright colors and are even personalized. In fact, the Girl Scouts have offered official knives since 1934. One is a fixed blade with a sheath and the other is a pocketknife."

"Only tough girls in my neighborhood had knives," Lana said, "and we were afraid of them. There's safety and then there's danger...serious injury was something we all feared."

Lana had shared a part of her history with Kevin. She was raised by a single mother in southern California. Her two older brothers had been victims of racial profiling and arrested without cause several times. Lana was more than aware of the unconscious biases that affected Black woman when living in a society built on prejudices. At an early age, she believed her only power was to get an education. Her decision to join the police force was motivated by the challenges related to racism and sexism and her strong desire to change the system.

"I know your background and fears are totally different from people around here. Remember, Lana, you promised to let me know if you're having any problems... especially any issues involving your race or sex. Julia's always on the lookout for abuse of any kind and would be a champion for you, as will I."

Lana appreciated Kevin's concerns and reassured him things were fine. At this point, she had only received welcoming comments from people. But after all these months, she wished she had a friend she could talk things over with. The Island was friendly, but seemed to cater to small groups with shared interests, and didn't seem to readily allow others to join them. At least she had a great boss.

"Where do we go from here on the investigation?" Lana wanted to get back to business.

"On Friday, Joel was arraigned and denied bail. We're going to have to prepare our files for the prosecutor to review. I understand that Carson is also ready to find out what we know but he'll get our reports from the prosecutor. Do you have your reports complete?"

"Just working on the final one now."

Alan was looking forward to having dinner with Maggie. His weekend with Lindsay and family had been pleasantly exhausting. The next big event would be an annual 4th of July party at their house. The boys begged to visit Alan on the Island again and he told them it would have to wait because Sidney was visiting this week. His flight was scheduled for Wednesday.

Just as Alan was about leave for the store, his phone rang. "Alan, it's Kevin. How are you doing?"

"I'm fine, just got back from a weekend in Seattle."

"I was wondering if you had time to interview a few teens with me. We have the names of the kids who have admitted to buying drugs from Joel. I've asked them to come in and speak with us. The bottom line is that someone else is selling on the Island and we need to know who it is."

"Okay, I'm free today until around 4:00. How shall we do this?"

"I have 1:00 and 2:00 meetings set up. Can you make those?"

"I'll be there."

When Alan hung up, he once again wondered how he'd be of any help. In Boston, he'd be searching computer and phone lists, talking with patrol officers, and paying off informants. Here, he wasn't as familiar with the way things were done, but he was interested.

The first two teens who came into the precinct were brothers, one year apart. The oldest, Ryan, shook Kevin and Alan's hands, but the other teen, Jesse, stood back. They explained that they wanted to come together but hoped their parents wouldn't have to be involved.

"Right now, we only need information," Kevin reassured them. "You've told us you were buying drugs from Joel Spencer. Is that correct?"

Both boys nodded.

"What kind of drugs?"

"Weed," said Ryan. Jesse nodded his head.

"How often did you buy?"

The boys looked at each other for a minute and then Ryan said, "About twice a month."

"Where did you buy, at the restaurant?"

"No!" Jesse spoke up at last. "We would never buy there. Joel would meet us somewhere, like at the park or some place. It was no big deal. We know lots of kids who buy weed."

"From Joel?"

"Not only from him. There are other dealers, too."

"Can you give me some names?"

Ryan put a hand on his brother's arm. "We don't know any other dealers."

Kevin looked at Alan to see if he wanted to say something. He had been sitting silently and watching the boys' reactions to being questioned. Alan approached the conversation from another direction. "I know Marijuana is legal in Washington, but you need to be over 21 to buy. You boys are not. This is a risky behavior that can have lasting and harmful effects on your health. Do you boys drive?"

Both boys nodded. Alan continued, "Any substance, like weed, negatively affects several skills required for safe driving, including concentration, coordination, and reaction time. You guys don't want to get into an accident driving high. And driving high, or under the influence, is still a crime."

Kevin let this sink in and then said, "We need names of the other dealers."

Ryan shook his head and said, "We don't know any. But kids all over the Island buy and sell. They get fake IDs or use someone else's ID. I know some kids who buy online from fake pharmacies."

Kevin tried another approach, "Did Joel ever threaten you?"

The teens looked shocked. "Never!" Ryan said. "He's a nice guy. At the restaurant he always helped us out if we got stuck on something or had a problem." Jesse agreed.

All the afternoon's interviews were consistent. The teens only bought weed from Joel and didn't know who else was dealing. They could get drugs anywhere on the Island, though. One of the teens said all you had to do was attend any sports event and look around. Kids bought from other kids. If you wanted alcohol, you only had to sneak it from parents. Cigarettes, too, were easy to buy off someone. Most of the teens complained that the Island was so boring that they needed to get high just to have something to do.

Kevin thanked Alan for being part of the interviews.

Although a bit frustrating, the kids' reluctance to give up their dealers wasn't unexpected. There's nothing worse to a teen than being labeled a "snitch" by talking to adults. Maybe it was all bought online for the most part. Kevin would check this out, too.

Maggie was excited to meet Alan for dinner. She wanted to hear about his weekend, but also hoped to hear about the investigation. Numerous rumors were circulating around the well-known Island gossip mills and Maggie hated this. She remembered, a few years ago, when a few kids had started horrible, false rumors about families to the point where no one knew what to believe. It wasn't until after the damage had been done that some teachers found the rumor group and put them on suspension. The Review had picked up the insidious problem and wrote editorials about dishonesty and false accusations that were only meant to destroy reputations. The small community felt they had been put on notice.

Alan met Maggie at the Thai restaurant in town. Although small, the seating was arranged for privacy, and they were early enough to grab a table by the window. Maggie gave Alan a quick hug and ordered a glass of red wine for both. Alan smiled. He liked this about her.

"First tell me about your weekend." Maggie leaned in close, hoping to share the memories with him. Her bright eyes and unrestrained smile were all Alan needed to begin his litany of adventures he had shared with his family. He also remembered to invite her to the July 4th party. Lindsay had made him promise to do that.

"Sure, I'd love to go to the party," Maggie agreed. "I close my business that day. Over the years I've learned that people aren't always respectful of the Island's no fireworks rule. Of course, there are fireworks...people don't let rules bother them... but I don't want them around my place."

Alan asked Maggie how business was going and if she had heard from her daughter lately. Much to Maggie's chagrin, Carrie had promised to visit but would not be able to now. Catering was a big business during the summer and so Maggie thought she might have to go see her instead. She missed her daughter.

After their dinners were served, Maggie finally asked about the investigation. Alan told her what he knew and confirmed that Carson was taking the case.

Maggie shook her head back and forth, "The rumormongers have already decided that Joel is guilty. It's upsetting that people don't even wait for all the facts, they just condemn the person. They don't want to blame themselves for anything like not paying attention to the drug problem on the Island, and love to have a scapegoat."

Alan put down his chopsticks and looked into Maggie's eyes. "It's more or less the same everywhere, Maggie. Drugs are universal. And teenagers are also universal in their attitudes, arguing with their parents, and acting out. We did it when we were kids. You always hope and pray that everyone grows up without getting hurt or hurting someone else."

"I agree, Alan, but when two kids are shot to death

right down the street where I live, I feel afraid and angry. It makes everything on the news a reality. You know what I mean?"

"Of course," Alan reassured her. "When you read about the number of people getting shot each day, you can't emotionally take it in. But when two are killed, especially in your neighborhood, you grieve. You've lost the sense of safety that you had relied on. I bet more houses are locked these days because of what happened."

"That's one thing driving the rumors. Safety has always been a given on the Island which includes not locking your house or car. Now, people are worried. You can't blame them."

"No, I understand. Are you feeling vulnerable? I thought I saw a security tag on your door when I came over."

"Yes, I have ADT security. I had to have it for insurance coverage since my house is my business. I feel safe if that's what you're asking." Maggie squeezed Alan's hand and nodded.

They changed the subject to Sidney, who would be arriving on Wednesday. Maggie invited them to dinner on Thursday and Alan accepted. Even though this was his vacation, he felt not a minute had gone by where he had nothing to do. He wondered if retirement would be like this.

TUESDAY, JUNE 20TH

L ana's condo was in the Pleasant Beach village. She had a newer two-bedroom unit with hardwood floors and granite counters. She had saved enough for a down payment, but worried that if the HOA increased yearly, she might struggle to keep up with the mortgage. Police jobs paid okay, and she was lucky not to have to pay for extra things like parking or gas mileage, but sometimes her paycheck didn't stretch. She considered getting a roommate, but that would be her last resort. She loved living alone.

As she prepared coffee in her efficient kitchen, she wondered why Kevin wasn't giving as much attention to the gun as he was to the drugs in the investigation. They were getting nowhere with their interviews and forensics had reported no fingerprints on the gun or the knife they found at the crime scene. And what about the knife? If it was a collector's item, someone should have reported it missing. Lana drank her coffee and hurried out the door.

CAPABLE OF MURDER

Kevin was not surprised when Lana posed these questions when she walked into his office. He had decided to go back and interview Jack Richardson again and find out more about his stolen guns. He had also called and asked Alan to ride with him. Lana nodded her agreement and said she would try and follow up on the knife. Somebody must collect knives on the Island.

Alan was getting used to Kevin's calls. He liked being able to give his input without having to write reports or find the answers. All Kevin needed was another set of eyes and ears to flesh out the details and get another perspective on the behavior and body language. Kevin was being methodical in the investigation, and maybe Alan could help him see a bigger picture, if there was one. What was the saying... see the woods... the forest... and not the tree? Or was it the other way around?

When Alan stepped out of his house, he noticed a yellow envelope under the door mat. His name was on the outside and so it was obviously something for him. It just had his name, not an address, which was curious. In Boston, he would be wary of something like this, but he had nothing to fear on the Island and so he opened the envelope. Inside was a typed note that read: *Get away from our Island!* And with the note was a photo of Alan coming out of the police station. Was this a reaction from the editorial?

Kevin drove up to Alan's just in time to see him open the envelope. He then saw the look on Alan's face. Perplexed, Kevin got out of his car and walked up to see what was happening.

"Is there a problem?" Kevin asked.

"I'm not sure." Alan handed Kevin the note and the photo. "Should I be alarmed or is this the way Islanders communicate with outsiders?"

Kevin looked it over and shook his head. "This doesn't seem like a prank to me. Someone has a beef, and I don't like this at all." Kevin carefully put the photo back in the envelope. "Has anyone been pestering or annoying you?"

"No, not that I can think of. But the idea that I'm being followed and filmed is not comfortable. What do you suggest?"

"We need to get a camera on the front door in case this happens again. I know a cop with your experience is more aware than most of their surroundings, but I guess this tells you to be more so. My guess is that it's some disgruntled citizen who cowardly sends this kind of thing. I'll see what I can do about it."

"I have a friend visiting from Boston this week and I was hoping to have him stay with me. I hope this won't happen again."

Just then, Alan's phone rang, and he noticed it was Sidney. Alan took the call immediately. "Hello! How are you doing?"

Sidney sounded frustrated, "I'm afraid I have bad news. My court case has gone long, and I need to be here another week. Can I put off my trip until then? I'm damn sorry this has happened."

Alan understood about his friend's busy docket. "Sure, anytime is good for me. Just let me know the date. I'll be looking forward to hearing about the case."

"Just another fraud. This time with a divorce weighing in to make things complicated. How are you doing?"

"I'm good. But let me call you back later. I'm walking out the door, but I want to fill you in on things around here. Talk later." Alan hung up and looked at Kevin.

"Well, that was timely. My friend had to postpone his arrival. Now I can relax and try to figure out who's following me around. Shall we go?"

"You're still willing to help?"

"Of course! It looks like things are starting to get interesting and I'm not going to be scared off by a note and photo. Where are we going today?"

Kevin was impressed with Alan's appearing unbothered by the contents of the envelope and showing little anxiety about helping with the case. Hopefully, this was a one-off warning and the person who sent it had already backed away. This happens sometimes in small communities. People just want to find a way to get themselves heard. He would have his patrol officers in town pay more attention to who's hanging around when Alan's there. Especially high school kids.

The drive to Kingston was filled with conversation about the various towns and landmarks on the way. Alan was intrigued with how much the area reminded him of New England. Small towns in Vermont and New Hampshire were much older, but the architecture was similar. Shops and restaurants were clustered together in town squares and benches were set along the waterfront. Alan wondered if this was true everywhere around the world.

As they approached the Richardson's house, Alan began to think more about the case. "From my experience, the murder weapon is the quickest path to finding who committed a murder. Since we know where the gun came from, we need to find out all we can from Richardson, about how this theft occurred."

Kevin agreed, although he still felt that everything revolved around drugs. He was pursuing both paths. He wanted Alan to pay attention to Jack Richardson's behavior. "If he had all those guns in a safe, I'm wondering what they were used for. When I was here before, I noticed that Richardson didn't want his son, Sean, involved with the conversation. Maybe we could talk with Sean now."

Jack was surprised to see the police but opened the door and invited the men inside. The house seemed quiet and when Kevin asked, Jack said his kids were on a hike with their mom. "What can I help you with?"

Kevin took out his notebook and asked his first question. "Do you collect knives"

Surprised, Jack replied, "No, I don't. Why?"

"We found one of interest. Because you're a collector, I thought maybe you might collect other items. How many guns do... or did you have?""

"Six. I inherited them from my father and grandfather. I'm not much of a hunter, in fact, the last time I hunted was at the turkey run a couple years ago. I used to go to the gun range to get some lessons, but I haven't been in years."

Kevin looked at his notes and inquired, "Besides the

stolen handgun, you also had a rifle and shot gun taken, is that correct?"

"Right. I can't figure out why they didn't take everything. Maybe they thought they would come back later."

"Do you let your kids take the guns out?"

"Never. Their mother has a big problem with the guns. She's begged me to get rid of them, but I consider them a family heirloom. Right now, I'm waiting for a nearby storage unit to open so I can store the rest of the guns there."

Alan asked the next question. "How did the robbers get in?"

"My son left his bedroom window opened upstairs and it looked like someone climbed up a ladder, maybe, and went through that window. There were footprints outside."

"And as I understand it, the key to the gun vault was kept under your computer."

Jack nodded.

Alan started to put two and two together. If the robber came through the son's window, how did he know about the guns? And who told him about the key and how to get into to the gun vault? "Perhaps it's true that your kids don't know anything about the robbery, but is it possible they talk about your gun collection to their friends?"

"I doubt it. They're like their mom, anti-gun."

Kevin thought for a moment and then asked, "What do you or your kids know about the drug problem in your town?"

Jack shook his head and let out a deep breath. "The ferry brings problems to the town. We're all aware that dealers come and go regularly, delivering drugs and anything else they can offer. There are dog drug patrols on the ferry docks, but I've yet to hear of anyone being arrested."

Alan nodded. He had noticed security guards walking around with these dogs. He also knew that they didn't patrol all day, and someone could easily bring drugs through at odd hours. There was only so much in the state's budget to handle the business of drug dealing.

Alan continued focusing on the guns. "Mr. Richardson, we're seriously concerned about the gun that was used in these murders. Who does your son hang around with?"

Jack was taken aback. "Why? Sean wouldn't know anything. His friends are mostly athletes at school."

"We have to look at every angle. Maybe Sean unintentionally got involved with something he shouldn't. It happens, especially to good kids."

Jack looked worried. "I can't believe Sean would take part in anything to do with drugs or guns."

Alan nodded. "Do you mind if we go upstairs to see the point of entry for the robbery?"

It was a typical teenage boy's room, although it looked neater than most. Alan decided to poke around while Kevin talked with Jack in the doorway. He was surprised to see a plastic bag waded up in the corner of the closet shelf. When he looked closer, he could see the outline of money through the cellophane bag. "Mr. Richardson... can you look at this?"

Jack took a few steps over to the open closet and reached up for the bag Alan was pointing to. Inside was a considerable amount of cash.

Jack looked amazed. "Where did he get this?" He opened the bag and started counting the money. "There're hundreds here!"

Kevin asked Jack, "Where did your son get so much money?"

"I have no idea! He doesn't have a job! I mean he does odd jobs around the neighborhood…but he's just a fifteen-year-old kid."

"It looks like we need to talk with him. When will your wife and kids be back?"

Jack looked at his watch and thought for a minute. "They said around 3:30. Should I call my wife and ask her to hurry?" He was acting nervous, wringing his hands, and blinking rapidly.

Kevin noticed it was 2:45, "No, we'll just wait." He didn't want Jack to warn his son about what they had found. In the meantime, they asked if they could do another search of the bedroom.

Sean Richardson knew he was in trouble when he saw the police car in the driveway. He hoped they hadn't found the money he was keeping for his friend. He would have a difficult time explaining it to his parents who already didn't like Alex.

Sean eyed the two police officers when he walked in the room. He also noticed the bag of money on the table and felt his heart beating rapidly in his chest. Jack motioned to his wife and daughter to walk through to the kitchen, giving each of them a quick hug. He would handle things. Jack picked up the bag and held it out to his son. "Sean, what's this doing in your closet?"

Sean was a big kid who turned out each year for the football team. He had tried to use his talent for sports to stay away from drugs around the school. But the playing field was exactly where he found them. Although he never did drugs, all the other guys did and that put a lot of pressure on him. His father probably thought it was drug money.

"It's not mine," Sean mumbled.

"You better tell us whose it is right now!" His father's voice was uneven, the words sounding forced as his mind raced for explanations. He wanted to disbelieve the evidence as he stared at his son with a pained look that contained hurt and some anger.

Kevin interrupted, "Sean, we're here to help sort this out. Why don't you take a seat, and we can talk it over?" He pointed to the dining room chairs and indicated for everyone to sit down.

"Where did the money come from?"

"I'm keeping it for someone."

"Why?"

"He's in trouble."

"Okay, who's this friend?"

"Alex Peterson, at my school. He's on the football team. He's a junior."

Jack looked at his son with thoughts jumping from the memory of this kid to others on the team. Alan recognized the concerns on his face. When parents encouraged their kids to play sports, they never expected to be putting them in touch with the drug world. He wondered if Sean was scared or feeling guilty.

Kevin wrote down Alex's name. "How did he get the money, Sean?"

"Do I have to say? Or would this be hearsay?"

Smart kid, Alan thought. He was once again watching the disappointment on Jack's face as he took in this new information. Alan decided to say something, "We're not accusing you of anything. If your teammate's in trouble, we'll talk to him. One thing though, Sean, does this have anything to do with who might have stolen your father's guns? We understand your window was left open when your family went away for a few days."

Sean took a deep sigh. He seemed to be mentally berating himself over an action or poor decision on his part. "I left the window open so Alex could get the money. I'd sent him a text telling him I was done covering for him."

Alan looked steadily at Sean, "Covering for what?"

"He wanted to leave…to run away. He's in a bad situation at home and wants out." Sean hung his head, knowing he had betrayed some confidence. Alex was running from an abusive father, and the stories he told Sean about the abuse were horrible.

Alan wanted to know more about the guns. "Did Alex take the guns when he climbed through your window?"

Sean shook his head. "I don't know. He was only supposed to take the money and leave."

"Why do you still have the money?"

"I don't know. I haven't heard from him in weeks."

Kevin had been busy writing down notes. He looked up and asked Sean, "Do you have his address?"

Sean nodded and reluctantly took out his phone. "I don't want to get him in trouble, but I'm worried that something bad's happened to him."

Jack put his hand out to touch his son's arm. "I'm sure you're worried. Thank you for telling us what's happening. Let's hope Alex is okay."

Kevin and Alan left the Richardson's and drove to the address Sean had given them. It appeared to be a newer development in a wealthy neighborhood. When they saw the house, Kevin let out a whistle. "It looks like Alex's family has some money." The house had a three-car garage and looked to be three stories. When they rang the doorbell, a young girl, probably around eight or nine, answered promptly. "Can I help you?"

"Is your father or mother home?" Kevin inquired.

"My parents are both at work. But my grandmother's here. Do you want to talk with her?"

Alan looked at Kevin to decide. At that moment a rather tall older woman came to the door. She reminded Alan of the actress who played on The Golden Girls TV series. In a low demanding voice she asked, "What do you want?" Her mannerism was dominating and bordered on anger. Alan noticed that the girl had stepped back and looked apprehensive. Was she afraid of her grandmother?

Kevin smiled slightly and said, "Is Alex home?"

Looking at the police car outside, the grandmother folded her arms and made a quick decision. "No, he's not. Tell me what this is about."

Kevin stared at her without blinking, "We'd like to talk with him. When will he return?"

The grandmother stared back and didn't say a thing. Finally, the young girl said softly, "We haven't seen Alex. Do you know where he is?"

Alan took a step forward to ward off any consequence the girl may get for speaking out. He watched the older lady's eyes shift to the girl in an annoyed way. He didn't like this scene at all. He could tell there was something very wrong.

"You might as well come in," the grandmother sighed. "We'll probably need your help to find him now." Letting down her guard, Alan noticed that all her bravado was gone, and replaced with concern.

The men were escorted into a formal living room and asked to have a seat. The designer furniture and what appeared to be original art on the walls were impressive. Sitting across from the grandmother, Kevin asked her what was going on.

"We haven't heard from Alex for two weeks now. His father, my son in law, refuses to look for him. They don't get along. But my daughter is beside herself with worry. And so am I." She was wringing her hands and appeared to have tears in her eyes. "He's taken off like this before, but only for a few days. I thought you were here because he'd done something or gotten hurt."

Kevin looked down at his notes. "We heard about Alex from his friend Sean. He's been worried, too. When Alex leaves for a couple of days, do you know where he goes?"

"He never tells me. I've tried to get him to let me know, but he doesn't want to involve me. I told him he could stay with me, but he said no. His father is very demanding, and I know that's the reason Alex leaves." At this point the young girl sat closer to her grandmother and took her hand. Alan noticed sincere affection between the two. He was relieved.

"When will Alex's parents be home?"

"They work in Seattle, so probably around six."

Kevin took out his card and handed it to her. "Please have them give me a call. You can tell them that we're following up on an investigation and that Alex is not in trouble." He hoped by saying this, no one would be blamed harshly for talking with them.

On the drive back to the Island, Alan questioned, "Do you think the local police know anything about this?"

"It appears that Alex's staying away for some days is a regular thing. I'm not sure he's even involved with our investigation, but I still want to talk with him. It sounds like his father's the problem."

Alan thought, in most cases, it's easy to get side-tracked by issues that crop up that aren't relevant to your central investigation. Sometimes you forget the big picture because you become so obsessed by one small area and lose sight of your overall goal. Is that what was happening here? There was now a stolen gun, a runaway kid, drugs, and cash found. The only common denominator were the teens.

WEDNESDAY, JUNE 21TH

Now that Sidney had rescheduled, Alan found he had some free time to himself. He had called Maggie to tell her not to plan dinner on Thursday, and she seemed disappointed. They decided to go to a movie instead and Alan insisted he treat for lunch before a matinee.

Looking around his house, Alan realized things had gotten a bit out of control. He would spend the day doing laundry and generally cleaning up. Later he would call Lindsay and see if they all wanted to come visit on Saturday.

Kevin met with Lana first thing. He needed to talk over the investigation and share what he'd found out. Lana had made several calls the day before about the knife and had written down a few leads. Apparently, there was a group of knife collectors who met a couple times a year. Their focus was selling and networking with each other. She had the name of one of the members.

Kevin called the police chief in Kingston to inquire

about Alex and his family.

"Yeah, we know the family. The father's a hothead, and we've gotten complaints about his screaming at his kids a lot. There's not much we can do, though, because the mother won't press charges and the kids don't want to complain."

"Did you know that Alex has been missing for a couple of weeks?" Kevin was careful not to sound accusing. The grandmother said Alex's disappearances happened a lot, so the police may have just let it go.

"No, I hadn't heard that. Poor kid. He's a great football player and seems friendly enough. When he's checked out a few times before, he'd always returned home. We think he stays with one of the team members. Did you meet the grandmother?"

"Yes, we did."

"Now, she's something else. She's outspoken and can be very demanding. She's nothing like her daughter who's real quiet."

"I left my card for the parents to call, but I haven't heard from them. That's why I'm calling to give you a heads-up. We're in the middle of investigating the two murders on the Island and just trying to follow-up on some leads. It looks like the gun used was the one stolen from Jack Richardson's in June."

"That's a surprise. Richardson's a good guy. Really protective of his family. As far as I know he's never been in any trouble, nor has his son, Sean."

"Good to know. If you hear of anything about the other stolen guns, will you let me know?"

"Sure. And I'll call you when Alex shows up."

Kevin didn't want to let this lead go, but he felt it might be a dead end. Except for the gun. Did Alex steal it? Was he involved with the murders, or did he give the gun to someone who was? Just then he remembered to tell Lana about the note and photo Alan received yesterday.

Lana was surprised to hear that the detective might be followed. "Do you think he's in danger?"

Kevin thought for a minute. "No, I wouldn't say danger, it's probably just harassment. I'm going to have one of the guys keep an eye out when Alan's in town. I just hope I didn't unintentionally get him involved with this case and make someone mad."

"I'll keep a look out, too. Where do we go from here?"

"The dealer in Seattle. This time I want you to go with me."

"What time do we leave? I'm ready to go now."

"I'm going to call Curt, my patrol friend, and see if we can tag along with him and talk to any of his informants who recognize Joel's picture and might know about his activities in Seattle. In the meantime, let's get our reports filled out."

Joel decided to take Carson's advice and asked to be assigned a service job in the jail. He told the guard he was good in the kitchen, and that's where he landed. His job was to bag up the lunches that went out each day to the 275 inmates. They got a peanut butter sandwich, an apple, milk, and a hard-boiled egg delivered to their cells. This job took him most of the morning which helped pass the time. He also got better food choices after a while because the kitchen cook appreciated his good attitude and organization.

In the afternoon, he read for a couple of hours. He preferred non-fiction, but someone had left a Stephen King book lying around and once he started reading it, he was hooked. Maybe he would ask his parents to send him a couple more books by the author. At least it kept his mind off the trial. Carson had promised to call if he had any news, but so far, he'd heard nothing. Joel hoped he didn't get those kids into trouble. What little money he made on sales to them wasn't enough to even put a down payment on a car.

Joel wished he knew who the dealer was in Seattle. If he could give the police a name, maybe he would get a reduced sentence like they did on TV. But every time he bought his drugs, there had been a new person. He figured it was probably a big organization and he was just a wimpy buyer. All he could do now was just worry... and wait.

Carson Bowen had contacted the prosecutor's office with his initial discovery request because the first status hearing court date was set three weeks away, and he needed to know the direction the case was going. The prosecutor was convinced this would be a slam dunk since the gun was found at Joel's apartment and he had spoken with some of the teens who bought drugs regularly from Joel. The problem the prosecutor had, and was working on, was motive. Why would Joel want to murder these two teens?

THURSDAY, JUNE 22ND

Kevin and Lana took the 10:45 ferry to Seattle. Curt met the two Island police at the Seattle precinct and led them to an open conference room. On the table were folders of known dealers who might be of interest. Curt also had photos of local "snitches." These were people who made a few dollars keeping an eye out for shady dealings around the area and selling or trading the info to the police.

"The guy we met a couple weeks ago...the one who owns that little jewelry shop on the lower floor of the market...doesn't know anything. I believe him. But my guys who cover the area were able to come up with a few dealers who your guy may recognize. I made copies of this info for you to take." He pulled a cigarette out of his pocket and lit it. "It's okay to smoke in here," he admitted. "We already work too hard to have to go somewhere else to light up."

"Anyway, my thought is that we can do a walk around today, and if I see one of my guys, maybe we can show him

217

your guy's photo and see what happens."

As they approached the popular farmers market, Lana couldn't help but notice the big cruise ships parked along the waterfront. She knew the vacationers were encouraged to visit the iconic and very popular Pike Place Market, home to a diverse collection of businesses including farmers and crafters. She saw the tourists roaming through the stalls, holding their expensive coffees, and shopping for souvenirs. During the summer months, the sellers enjoyed brisk sales.

Lana hadn't been to Seattle in months. The streets were so clean, compared to her old neighborhood in San Diego. But this was a façade because Seattle had a homeless population that was staggering. The governor and mayor had promised to do something about that, but the city council dithered and bounced between the voters who just wanted the homeless removed or jailed, and those who wanted the city to invest in social services and housing. It was a perennial argument with no solution in site.

Lana heard that groups of homeless people hung out in the public park at the end of the market. As she followed Curt through the crowd, she saw several disheveled and obviously desperate people wandering around the streets. She wondered if the tourists noticed them or just avoided them altogether.

Curt led them through the market and to the sculpture garden on the north side. Trees had been planted years ago and now offered shade along with the ability to hide. Curt knew that drug deals were made here. "Hey, Calvin...over here!" he shouted to a tall skinny man who was wearing a long winter coat. His hair was braided in rows and sunglasses were perched on top of his head.

"Hey... Curt... what do you want?" The man grimaced and walked towards them. Talking with the police was not what people, especially informers, wanted to be seen doing. The man had looked around before approaching.

"What's happening, man?"

Curt brought out Joel's photo and asked if he knew him.

"Yeah, I've seen him. He's some small time amateur who buys things for kids. We all just make fun of him, you know. Why... what's he done?"

"He's in trouble. Have you heard about the murder of two kids on the Island?"

"Yeah... I heard... this guy didn't do it did he?"

"He's in jail. These two cops are looking for leads right now. They believe that if drugs were involved it could be from this side. Maybe someone had a beef with the guy in the photo."

"I'll find out for you. What do I get in return?"

"A free lunch," Curt smiled.

They kept walking and met some other drug informants who didn't recognize Joel's photo. When they stopped to get a hot dog at a vendor, a young kid came up to ask for money. Lana handed him a five-dollar bill and then asked him what he was doing on the street. The kid just shrugged. He seemed too young to be wandering, and Lana hoped he wasn't one of the growing numbers of street kids.

"What happens to these kids on the street?" Lana

wondered out loud.

Curt sighed, "Some of them come from nice homes. They think they're on an adventure, especially in the summer, and plan to return home for school. I don't get it."

Turning to Kevin, Curt asked, "If you found the gun in this guy's apartment, and he says it's not his, who put it there? Any cameras around the building?"

"Good question, but probably not because he lives over a gift shop and the stairs are on the side of the building. But as far as we could tell, the apartment hadn't been broken into and only the lady downstairs has an extra key."

Curt nodded, "Just a thought."

When Lana and Kevin returned to the Island later, they drove to the gift shop first. Kevin asked Della if there was another key to the apartment upstairs. She was happy to show them where she kept the extra key. Her office was in the back of the store, and a locked file cabinet stood beside her oak desk. She used a key from the several she had in her dress pocket to open the cabinet. Rummaging through the files she came to an envelope and pulled out a key. Kevin asked if he could have it for fingerprints. She agreed, wanting to help as much as possible.

"Well," Kevin said as he entered the precinct, "It's a long-shot, but what if someone got into the file cabinet and used this key?"

"Della didn't suspect that the extra key had been taken. Let's think about this. There was no forced entry at the apartment, no window access, so if someone got in and left the gun, they were pretty clever." Lana sat and tried to imagine how that could happen. If not this key, then someone had to have used Joel's key when he wasn't aware of it.

Lana had an idea. "Who rented the apartment before Joel? Maybe they had an extra key made."

Kevin looked up from his desk and smiled just enough to agree with this thought. "You're right. Let's go back and ask."

When they returned to the gift shop, Della was just closing the store. "My last renter was a woman who moved to Idaho. She turned in her key when she left."

"Do you have her forwarding number?" Kevin asked.

"I'll have to find it. Can I give it to you tomorrow?"

Kevin looked at his watch and realized he needed to get home. "Sure. Thanks."

Lana stopped by The Deli to get a sandwich to take home for dinner. The Pleasant Beach Village was busy, as usual, and she enjoyed watching the activity. As her eyes wandered around the crowded area, she noticed Andy Adams waiting on tables. There was something about this guy that creeped her out. It wasn't that he was offish to the customers, it was his overall behavior that suggested he may have been a bully in school. They were always easy to spot. The primary intent of their actions was to make others feel small.

Adams seemed to be the classic attention seeker. Lana noticed his continual effort to get in the spotlight. He laughed too loud and seemed to have some sort of control of his coworkers. Either that, or they were afraid of him or wanted to avoid him. Maybe he liked pranks or jokes at other's expense. When Lana looked around at the other employees, she thought Adams was undermining them by deliberately moving from table to table and subtly promoting himself. What was with this guy?

Andy Adams liked to be in charge. He had grown up on the Island and enjoyed the attention from his customers. He liked the idea of running a small business and being his own boss. As a kid, he was known as the chairman of the classroom, and now at thirty-two that attitude was paying off. He believed people liked being told what to do and he used this to his advantage. He could probably sell a heater in the desert he told his parents. As he checked to make sure his employees were busy, he wondered why the lady cop kept watching him.

FRIDAY, JUNE 23RD

Kevin ran his fingers through his hair in frustration. The investigation was moving slower than he had hoped. But, then again, when was the last time there had been a murder on the Island. Two murders. Shelly's funeral was in a week, and he'd hoped the case would have been solved. He still wondered if they had the right guy.

The prosecutor phoned earlier to ask for an update. At this point, he reminded Kevin, they didn't have enough evidence to prove guilt "beyond a reasonable doubt". They needed to dig deeper.

Della from the gift shop called and gave them the name of the past renter of the apartment, Trina Watson. Kevin called her, left a message, and hoped she would call back. He knew that when the police call, most people wait to call back or don't call at all. To his surprise, his phone lit up with an Idaho number five minutes later.

"Chief Johnson."

"Hello, my name is Trina Watson and someone from your office called me."

"Yes. Thank you for returning my call. I'm calling from the Island, and I understand that you rented an apartment over the gift shop a while back."

"Yes, I did. Is there a problem?"

"Not for you. I just needed to ask if you gave your apartment key to anyone else while you were there. We're following up on an investigation."

"I know there was an extra key, but I didn't make it." Trina paused and waited to hear what Chief Johnson needed to know.

"Do you know who did?"

"The guy I was seeing at the time had one made. I only know because he broke into my apartment one night. That's the reason I left."

"Because he had a key?"

"No. Because of the way he treated me. He was a brute and I decided I had to get far away from him."

"Can you tell me who he was?"

"Andy Adams. He owns the restaurant in Pleasant Beach. The Deli, I mean. If I stayed, he probably would have made my life miserable."

Kevin's interest perked up. "In what way would he do this?"

Trina backed off. "I really don't want to talk about it. I've moved on."

Kevin asked her to call him if she wanted to say or add anything to their conversation later. In the meantime, he needed to talk with Adams about the key.

Carson Bowen also knew Andy Adams. His parents lived next door to him on the Island and considered themselves to be "elite". They believed they deserved this status because they had wealth and personal connections to the state's various politicians. They also socialized regularly with wealthy acquaintances and made large donations to popular causes.

The large estate the Adams owned had been built in the early fifties and had stayed in the family over the years. Sometimes Carson could hear yelling and arguing from across the beach when his windows were open in the summer. He heard the angry voices usually in the evenings, and Carson suspected that drinking was involved. From what he understood from Island sources, the Adams' sons still lived at home and the parents were both controlling and demanding. It was a distraction, but nothing Carson wanted to deal with.

Carson had spent the last few days going over the preliminary discovery evidence he had gathered so far on the murders. He had a lot of questions. So far, nothing reported from the apartment tied Joel to the crime scene. The gun found in Joel's place was confirmed as the murder weapon, but there was little else to tie it to Joel. Carson was waiting to hear more detail from forensics to indicate the height and direction of the person pulling the trigger. Was he/she left-handed, or right? Was there any DNA left at the scene? The first thing Carson needed to do was to look through the lab reports before he started interviewing any witnesses.

CAPABLE OF MURDER

Alan had just returned from a long walk. His stamina had improved to the point where he could walk a couple of hours and feel refreshed rather than exhausted. He'd recently taken to turning his phone off when he walked and so he didn't notice a voicemail from Kevin until around 3:00. "Alan, if you have time later today, I'm going to interview someone at The Deli restaurant at Pleasant Beach around 6:00. Can you make it? Just text me yes or no. Thanks."

Alan didn't hesitate. He texted Kevin that he would meet him in a few hours.

Arriving early to the restaurant, Alan waited in his car and watched the waiters as they made the rounds to lingering customers. There was one guy who seemed genial enough, but there was something odd about his behavior. He appeared to be preoccupied, perhaps waiting for someone or something. Alan noticed how his eyes darted around the outdoor area and the slight nodding of his head. Was this who Kevin was interviewing?

At exactly 6:00 Kevin drove up and waved to Alan to join him. When they entered the restaurant, Andy Adams was speaking with an employee, who appeared anxious, wringing his hands, and shaking his head. Adam's voice was low, but his demeanor was overbearing. Alan realized that this was the guy who was acting so strangely when he drove up.

Kevin spoke first, "Andy, can we have a minute?" He introduced Alan and waited for Andy's reply.

"Sure, let me just take care of this." He reached into

the cash register and put the money into a bank bag. Then he took the bag into another room. When he returned, he invited the two men to have a seat at a nearby table.

"How can I help you?" Adams seemed nervous, rubbing his hands down his pants legs.

"I spoke with you the other day about the two kids who were murdered," Kevin began, "and we're still looking for reasons why Shelly and Kyle were killed. Their stop here was the last one before they died." Kevin took out his notebook to let that sink in. "You said they appeared to be happy and believed it was because of graduation. Is that correct?"

"Yes, as far as I could tell." Andy cleared his throat a couple times.

"Do you know Trina Watson?"

Startled, Andy ran his fingers through his hair and stopped breathing for a second. "Yes, why?"

"Trina says you have a key to her apartment. The one over the gift shop in town. Do you?"

"I might. I used to have one." Andy's eyes darted back and forth, as if trying to remember where the key was or what they knew about his relationship with Trina. "I can look for it. Is there a problem with the place?"

Kevin nodded slightly and said, "Maybe."

Alan leaned into the conversation and asked Andy, "Do you know Joel Spencer?"

"The guy who's been arrested?"

"Yes. Have you met him?"

"No. I don't hang around the Island when I'm not

227

at work."

Alan could tell by Andy's unfocused gaze that he was lying about something. "When was the last time you saw the key?"

"I'm not sure. Let me check my desk in the office, maybe it's there." Andy stood up and rushed across the room. Alan looked at Kevin, "Funny he didn't ask us why we needed the key."

"I'm thinking that, too. He looks nervous."

Andy came back after about five minutes. "I thought it was in my desk, but it's not. Why do you need it?"

Kevin answered cautiously, "We're tying up loose ends for the investigation. Who might have taken it from your office?"

"Anybody can get back there. I don't usually keep any valuables around, I always put the cash in a safe. Am I in trouble?" Andy's eyes were not blinking, and he forced his shoulders to relax, hoping to appear calm.

"No, we just need to find out who has the key. Can you give us the names of your employees?" This was a long shot because nobody would claim to have stolen something. But maybe somebody knew who did.

Andy let out a long breath. "Sure. I'll get the list." A few minutes later he returned and handed a computer printout of his employee's names to Kevin. Alan noticed that Andy's hands were shaking slightly.

"Thank you for this," Kevin said, "we'll probably want to talk with them later."

Alan and Kevin walked back to their cars to talk. "I

know that guy was a problem in school, but I'd like to think he's changed. Since his girlfriend said she had to move out of state to get away from him, I'm wondering if he's still that same brute."

Alan nodded, "His behavior's odd. He appears to be trying to control things and look casual or relaxed, which he isn't. He's tense, almost panicked. I doubt he could pass a lie detector test. I think he knows something. Where does he live?"

"His family owns an estate on the south side. In fact, it's right next to Carson's. They come from family money, and I think that all three of their boys still live at home, if you can believe that. Island gossips say that the father is so controlling they won't or can't leave."

"That's strange, especially now when kids can hardly wait to get away. What do the other two sons do?"

"I don't know. I'll have to ask around. Do you think this is something to pursue? We're looking for how someone got into Joel's apartment to plant the gun and the only thing we've come up with is the missing key."

Alan thought a minute. "It's a good idea to follow up on it. Sometimes the smallest lead fits into the puzzle perfectly and helps solve the case. It's true of witnesses, too. My rule is, don't leave out anyone who may be involved. So, that includes the employees at The Deli."

Kevin looked at the list of employees Adams handed him. Apparently, his younger brother, Cameron, worked at the restaurant a couple days a week. That was interesting. He wondered how they got along.

SATURDAY, JUNE 24TH

L indsay and Sanjay were happy to have an excuse to get away and visit the Island for the day. The Reynolds's family usually avoided their popular town center on weekends. Tourists swarmed the Kirkland streets, especially in the summer, indulging in the restaurants and walks along the water. Although great for business, most locals hated the traffic and the long waits for tables at their favorite eateries.

Lindsay was finally free from school obligations, with all the report cards sent and the classroom locked up. She had a conference to attend in July to keep her accreditation, but otherwise she was free. The boys were signed up for sports camps until August when Sanjay would take his three-week vacation. They usually planned a family camping trip, but this year Lindsay suggested exploring some popular places with her father. He wanted to visit Mt. St. Helen's and Mount Rainier, which she hadn't done in years. He also thought a few days at the ocean would be fun. Lindsay had made a call to her friend who owned a travel agency and hoped to find a hotel by the beach. She was so happy to have this time with her father.

Alan planned to take them to the Botanical Garden today. He had purchased tickets because he knew they limited the visitors because the tours were so popular. The family arrived around 1:00 and for the first time the boys didn't say they were hungry.

"We had a hot dog while we waited for the ferry," Rani said, "It was huge!"

Kirin chimed in, "And we had fries, too. I don't need to eat for a really long time." Alan smiled at this.

Lindsay suggested they take one car and so Alan climbed into their SUV beside the boys. It was more comfortable than he thought. Along the way, the boys told him about their sports programs and bragged about how well they played. Alan didn't mind hearing about their successes because he was their grandfather and thought they were wonderful.

The day was bright and sunny with just enough breeze to enjoy the walk around the gardens. Alan had remembered his camera and stopped several times to take photos of Lindsay and family. He loved watching his daughter as a wife and mother and hoped that their relationship would be stronger now. After two hours of walking, they decided to go to the park and let the boys run around.

Sanjay had brought a basketball and the boys joined him in a game. Pretty soon they had enough players for a three-on-three game. Lindsay sat with Alan and asked him about his time on the Island so far. "What do you do?"

Alan smiled almost sheepishly, "I can't even tell you! The days seem to fly by, and I keep very busy doing nothing much. Maggie and I have had lunch and dinners together, and I take long walks. Oh, I wanted to tell you that I'm reading the first Elizabeth George book you recommended, and I'm totally intrigued. I like Detective Lynley and especially, Barbara."

Lindsay smiled. "What about the murder case? What's been going on with the investigation?"

"Well, it's interesting. I've been on a few interviews with Chief Johnson and the case is more complex than he first thought. He's good at what he does, but he has lots of questions, about motive especially. The guy they have in jail now may not have done it."

"Dad, I hope you don't get involved with this. What happened about the nasty editorial someone wrote about you?"

"Nothing, really. Chief Johnson just told me to let it go." Alan didn't want to worry Lindsay by telling her about the note left at his door and the photo. He hoped it was just a prank but was quietly being very watchful. Lindsay changed the subject and told Alan about the July 4th party they were planning.

Carson was surprised to hear a knock at his door. Standing there was Greta Adams, his next door neighbor. She appeared to be upset and then gave Carson a quick, false smile. "May I come in for a minute, Carson?"

"Sure, Greta. How are you doing?"

She was a small woman, dressed in a simple floral outfit suitable for a garden party. Because of the many beauty treatments available to women of her status, her age was difficult to define. But with three grown children, she had to be in her 50's. She was known to be on several committees around the Island, which gave her a certain amount of influence and recognition, but she also had a peculiar way of interacting with people.

Carson noticed right away that she seemed deeply unsettled or at least more agitated than usual.

Carson invited her in and offered her a glass of iced tea.

"No thank you, Carson. This won't take long. I understand you're defending the restaurant guy who's in jail for the murders." He heard the urgency in her voice.

"That's correct." Carson stared blankly at her.

"Well, I want you to know that my son, Andy, was interviewed by the police yesterday and I'm worried they think he's involved with those awful murders. Do you know if that's true?"

"I can't talk about the case or my client. Any questions about the investigation, you should ask the police."

She let out a slow breath, dragging out the moment. "My son has an upstanding business and doesn't need the police coming around to his restaurant. You know the Island politics... people want to pass judgement all the time. Should I get him a lawyer?"

Carson frowned slightly and narrowed his eyes as if intense concentration would reward him a glimpse of what she really wanted to tell him. So far, not a scrap of evidence pointed to her son or connected him to the crime. So why was she here?

"I appreciate your concerns, Greta. Getting a lawyer would be up to you, but in your son's case, since I have no idea why they questioned him, I really couldn't advise you on whether he needs a lawyer. I do know the investigation is ongoing at this point. I'm not sure why they questioned him in the first place."

"I'm just worried, Carson." Greta turned to leave. But then she stopped at the door and looked back. "I just don't want any trouble for my family."

"Neither do I," he said, and closed the door.

SUNDAY, JUNE 25TH

Andy Adams called a staff meeting early in the morning before the brunch crowd arrived. He wanted his employees to know there was a chance the police would want to talk to them again about the day of the murders. "I know some of you weren't here that day, but as you know, this was the last stop before those two kids, Shelly and Kyle, were killed."

One of the employees spoke up, "I thought they arrested someone…that guy from The Doc Restaurant."

Andy looked sharply at the person, "I don't know anything about the case. But just answer the police questions and don't talk about this to the customers. If you do, you're fired." He glanced around at each person, stopping briefly with his brother. "I mean this. If you're asked about the case, say you know nothing."

Andy didn't trust either of his brothers, especially Cameron. They hadn't experienced the same discipline he had received from their overbearing father. By the time they were teens, corporal punishment had been banned in schools and households. His brothers held this up to their abusive father and threatened to call CPS if he hit them, like he had hit Andy as a child. Mr. Adams still knew how to emotionally threaten them, however, and as a result they often felt insecure and angry.

Watching his youngest brother, now, Andy wondered if he had taken the key to that apartment. Cameron knew about Trina and where she lived. In fact, Cameron liked to hang out at the bookstore where Trina had worked. Should he be worried about him?

Trina Watson was annoyed to hear that her name had been brought up regarding Andy Adams. She hoped that once she escaped his unstable attentions she would never have to look back. At twenty-four, she felt childish having to move back home with her parents. But she needed time to recover from the trauma she felt because of him and was lucky her parents didn't press for details.

Andy Adams was a psycho. At least that was the label Trina put on him. When they had met online, she was more than surprised to find out he lived on the Island, too. At first, she was overly impressed with his restaurant and the guest house on the family property where he lived. After a few months dating him, however, she began to suspect he was stalking her. She'd never forget the night she returned home late after meeting up with girlfriends in Seattle and found Andy in her apartment.

"What are you doing here? How did you get in?"

"I've got my contacts. Where were you?"

"Out. I don't have to tell you where I go. Who let you in my apartment?" Trina knew there were only two keys, hers, and the owner's.

Andy gave her a strange look. Obviously, he'd been drinking and seemed louder and more demanding. "If we're going to continue this relationship, I always need to know where you go if you're not with me." Trina was taken aback with this statement. She had only known him for a couple months.

She took a step to reach for the key that was lying on the table by the sofa. At this point, Andy had grabbed her arm and threw her down to the floor. She struggled to free herself from his grip but was overpowered by his strength. The pain in her back was so intense that her teeth shook. She lay dazed as he jumped up and ran out the apartment, taking the key with him.

That incident wasn't enough for Trina to decide to move. She thought she could avoid him and still live on the Island, but he began phoning her late at night…threatening her if they didn't get back together. She quietly asked around about him and learned of his reputation as a bully. A co-worker at the bookstore mentioned that people who worked for him at the Deli didn't stay long because he was controlling, shouting, and demeaning, and didn't always pay them what they earned.

After another month, when Trina took a long weekend off from work to visit her hometown, she decided not to return to the Island. Her brother drove back to the apartment and loaded up her things. She wrote and told the apartment owner and her boss that she had some personal issues and needed to take some time to recover. Both people were understanding. Trina had escaped a very bad situation.

MONDAY, JUNE 25TH

Once again, Lana came to work on her day off to review the investigation with Kevin. He told her about interviewing Andy Adams on Friday, and that Andy had confirmed he had an extra key to Joel's apartment.

Lana raised her eyebrows, "Where did Adams get it?"

"Well, that's the thing," Kevin tapped his fingers rhythmically on his desk, "he says his former girlfriend who had rented that place gave it to him. She says he had it made because she would never give her key to him or to anyone."

"Who do you believe?"

"We already spoke with the owner of the apartment, and she keeps her keys locked in the cabinet. So, that was supposed to be the only extra key. It seems to make sense that Adams may have 'borrowed' the key from his girlfriend, Trina, when she didn't know it and had one made."

Kevin continued, "It would be easy to do. Let's say that you meet your girlfriend for lunch and then take her back to work. You nab the key somehow, get a copy made, and then surprise her with coffee later that day and sneak the key back. It's possible."

Lana looked amused. "That's a long shot. Let's say that you went to dinner, had a couple of drinks, and when you took her home you insisted on unlocking her door and pocketed the key. All she had to do was lock the door from the inside. Then, in the morning, going along with your coffee idea, you return with a cup of coffee and a bagel, drop the key on the table and voila! Done." Lana smiled with this idea.

"I think I like your idea better than mine. If that's how he did it, then why didn't he throw the key away when she left town?"

"Maybe he forgot about it." Lana sat and stared blankly at her coffee cup. "No, wait. Did he know that Joel rented the apartment next? How soon did Joel move in after Trina left?"

"Let me call Della and find out."

In a few minutes, Kevin had the answer. Apparently, it was only two weeks later that Joel rented the place. Kevin rubbed his hand across his chin, "I don't understand why someone would keep a key to someone's place, but we now have an interesting development. I think we need to talk to Joel again, I'd better give Carson a call."

In a quick conversation, Carson informed Kevin that he was planning to talk with Joel that afternoon to begin prepping him for an upcoming status hearing. Carson had planned a quick visit but agreed to allow Kevin and Lana a short period to ask Joel a few questions. They were limited to the subject of who had access to Joel's apartment. Kevin agreed and arranged to meet the lawyer at the Port Orchard Jail at 2:30 that afternoon.

He told Lana about the agreement. "Do you want to come along?"

"Absolutely." She smiled.

Joel was trying to get used to the monotony of jail life. Because he was given a morning job, he was able to spend the start of his day concentrating on something besides feeling afraid, angry, and overwhelmed. He was lucky that the kitchen crew was friendly and even appreciated his efforts organizing the lunch bags of food. In the afternoons, when he had a lot of time to think, books were his company. He often wondered how Stephen King ever thought of the plots he came up with and considered him a genius. Joel could use someone like King to help him right now.

When the guard announced he had a visitor, Joel expected it to be Carson Bowen. He was surprised to see his lawyer accompanied by Chief Johnson and Deputy Clark. Carson spoke first. "Hi Joel, the Chief has a few questions about your apartment. I agreed to let you speak to him for a few minutes, on the condition that he limit the questions to only that subject. Is that okay with you? I'll be right here so if you have any questions or concerns you can just let me know. I'll stop the interview if I think it's going outside of what we agreed on."

Sitting on the cold seats that were bolted to the floor and laying his notebook on the equally freezing metal table,

Kevin asked, "I have a few questions that have come up in our investigation you might help us with."

Joel stared apprehensively and looked at his lawyer, who nodded reassuringly.

Appreciating his caution, Kevin shook his head. "It's not that kind of a question. We found out there was another key to your apartment circulating around. Did you give anyone an extra key?"

"No. Never."

"Do you know Andy Adams?"

"I know who he is, but I've never spoken with him. His younger brother tried to get a job at the restaurant, but Larry turned him down. He came across as a belligerent kid, like we owed him something."

"Did you speak with him at any point?"

"I don't think so. I probably waited on his table at some point. His family came to dinner occasionally."

"Do you remember anyone being interested in where you lived? Or did you ever feel that someone was watching you for some reason?"

"No and no... what's going on?" Joel looked over at Carson for help.

Kevin and Lana stood to leave. "Joel, we're looking into everything. Right now, we're working on some leads that you can talk over with Carson."

"Okay." Joel sat there, not knowing what to think. Were the police on his side? Lana had smiled when she saw him, which might mean she believed him. He wished he could talk with her alone and find out what's going on. But he knew the Chief wouldn't let this happen. Carson patted his arm in reassurance, then stood and walked the Chief and Deputy to the door. Once the pair had left, Carson turned back to Joel and rubbing his hands together said, "Okay, let's get started."

On the drive back to the Island, Kevin thought out loud. "If Joel didn't have an extra key, that means the only one was Andy's. So, let's say that Andy planted the gun. But why? They don't even know each other. Joel gave us the list of teens he sold drugs to and said he didn't sell to anyone else. Who used the gun on those two kids and why plant it at Joel's?"

Lana watched the road as she thought. "Did Trina say she knew Andy's brothers? One of them would be my guess for taking a key because they would have better access to Andy's office."

"Maybe this time you should call Trina." Kevin wondered how much Trina really knew about the Adams family. Lana may be able to coax some information from her.

That afternoon, Kevin met with the employees from The Deli. They all agreed they had no clue about the missing key. But one of the Adam's brothers, Cameron, objected strongly to being called in to the precinct.

Scowling at Kevin, he demanded to know why he was being questioned. "I can sue you for accusing me of anything!" Cameron rose up out of the chair and waved his arms out. "I know a good lawyer!"

Kevin calmly asked him to sit back down. "I'm not accusing anyone of anything. In fact, you can leave if you want."

Cameron sat down and stared at Kevin. "I don't know anything."

"Fine. You can leave." Kevin picked up some reports on his desk, dismissing this angry and defensive person. He would keep an eye on him.

Lana made a call to Trina Watson and left a voicemail asking her to return the call. She tried to make the message friendly so Trina wouldn't worry. But when Trina listened to the voicemail, she felt her heart palpitating as if she was having a panic attack. Why did the police still want to speak with her? She didn't want to be involved with any investigation, especially if it included that family.

Lana was on her way home after work when Trina called her back. She parked her car before returning the call, wanting to be sure to write down notes of the conversation. "Hello, Trina, thank you for calling me back. We have just a couple questions…do you have a minute?"

Trina softly responded, "I guess. I really don't want to get involved with anything."

"I understand, "Lana tried her best to reassure Trina. "Did you know Cameron Adams?"

Trina let out a deep breath, "Yes. He used to bother me at the bookstore. He would follow me around and even ask me out! When he learned I was dating his brother, he became even more obnoxious. The owner of the store had to ask him to leave at one point."

"How old are you, Trina?"

"I'm 24. Why?"

"Well. Thinking out loud, Cameron is 22 and Andy is 32. You're closer to Cameron's age."

"Does that mean anything? Cameron acts like a teenager…I don't even think he has a job."

"No, it probably means nothing. Did you ever meet Andy's parents?"

"I had lunch at their house one day. It was very uncomfortable."

"Why was that?"

"Mr. Adams was very controlling, I thought, but Mrs. Adams was the annoying one. She didn't seem to have any boundaries."

"Why would you say that?"

"All three of her sons were there and she kept asking them if they needed money. I guess they all get allowances if you can believe it! She talked to them like they were still young children…not motherly, but weirdly…like babytalk."

"How did they respond?"

"I guess it was normal because they answered her, you know, like 'yes, I can use some cash' and 'can you make me a hair appointment'."

"What about the father?"

"He didn't say much until Cameron criticized the food. And then he exploded! He told him to go to his room and stay there. The funny thing was, Cameron jumped up and ran out of the room. It's as if something had been thrown at him."

"It must have been very uncomfortable. What was Andy's reaction?"

"He just smirked. Later I asked him if that was a typical

meal, with all the drama, and he just laughed at me. I couldn't tell if he was embarrassed or wanted to annoy me."

"When was the last time you saw Cameron?"

"Right before I left the Island. He must have found out I was leaving because he dropped by the store and gave me something."

"What was that?"

"It was a bracelet. It looked expensive so I didn't take it. He got really upset and stormed out of the store. Let me tell you, I'm so glad to have nothing to do with that family."

"Okay, thanks, I appreciate what you've told me, Trina. I don't want you to worry about getting involved. I have everything I need. You take care."

"Thank you, deputy."

Lana wrote down some pertinent information and wondered if this was going to impact their case at all. It highlighted the dysfunction in the Adam's household, but nothing tied it to the murders. They still had to find a motive.

TUESDAY, JUNE 26TH

Alan hadn't heard from Kevin since Friday and hoped it was because the case was moving along. Usually, unless you got lucky, it took months or even years to resolve a murder case, even when you had someone in custody. He then wondered about the photo that someone had taken of him. He wasn't worried but knew from experience it was best to be cautious. He decided to call Maggie and talk this over with her.

"Alan! So nice to hear from you." Maggie was her usual effervescent self, always offering a warm and inviting conversation.

"Hi, Maggie. Do you have time for lunch?"

"Can you come here? I have so many leftovers from the party my guests had over the weekend. Please let me fix something."

Alan smiled into his phone and agreed. He would be there in an hour.

Maggie had hoped Alan would have time to talk this week. She was bothered, once again, with the gossip going around. Now some people were criticizing the police for continuing the investigation. They had already tried the case in their minds and found Joel guilty. She knew it was just a small group of naysayers, but it upset her when they got away with it.

By the time Alan arrived, Maggie had soup, salad, and sandwiches already on the table.

"How did you do this in such a short time?" Alan looked astonished.

"It's my special gift," beamed Maggie. "Now, sit and let's eat and talk."

Alan told her about Lindsay, Sanjay and the boys' visit while showing her the dozens of photos he took while they were here. "I was hoping you might have joined us, but you're always busy on the weekends. Lindsay's really pleased you'll be coming to the July 4th party."

Maggie told him some funny stories about her visitors and their party. She didn't take photos, but after seeing Alan's she thought maybe it was time to try to get some good ones for advertising. After lunch they sat on the porch with iced tea and Alan was ready to tell Maggie about the note and photo left on his doorstep.

"Alan, I don't like this at all. What did Kevin say?"

"He wasn't too worried. He said he would have his patrol officers keep an eye on my place and try to drive by more at irregular times. I guess they'll be watching for anyone carrying a camera." Alan laughed at this, knowing that everyone took cell phone pictures these days. "Can you think of why someone would want to follow me?"

"No, but I'll ask around. Don't worry, I won't tell anyone it was you. If there's a prankster around town, somebody will have heard about it. What else do you know about the case?"

"Kevin and I interviewed Andy Adams at The Deli. It was the last place the two teens were seen before the murders. Adams's kind of strange."

"The whole Adams family is strange! The mother has no boundaries. She treats her three sons like a mother hen, always organizing their movements. Maybe it's to counter the father who's a brute. He controlled those boys all throughout school and now continues to demand their attention. You know he bought The Deli for Andy, and his own accountant watches over the money. He's paranoid that his sons will steal from him. Maybe they should..." Maggie smirked. "I've always felt sorry for those boys."

"Any talk around town about them being involved with drugs?"

"Cameron and Andy were both picked up for dealing when they were teens. Their father got the family lawyer to get the charges dropped to a misdemeanor and have the records sealed."

Alan shrugged, "Well, that figures...wealthy parents helping their kids get out of things. Lucky kids. Did the boys go to college away or locally?"

"Andy went to Northwest, but Cameron only went to junior college for half a year. He has a behavior problem that probably needs medication and a great deal of therapy."

"What about the middle boy? What's his deal?"

"Brent is a nice kid as far as I know. He went to WSU, as far away as he could get from his family and still be in state. He has a veterinarian degree and works somewhere off the Island. I think it's Belfair. The strange thing to me, is that all three boys still live at home."

"That's odd. Is there a guest house on the property perhaps?"

"I heard that Andy stays there. It's small, like a studio apartment, but it has plumbing."

Alan decided to change the subject. He wanted to know about the history of the Island and the surrounding towns. They made plans to drive to Port Angeles the following week.

Kevin and Lana were once again at a loss. If they couldn't prove that someone had stolen the key to Joel's apartment, they had no leads. Kevin decided to visit Kyle's parents and see how they were holding up. He liked Kyle's father, Cody, and had known him mostly as the soccer coach and ref for the Island teams. Cody Smith was a great coach and teacher for all the young players.

When Kevin drove up to the Smith house, he noticed flowers and plants spilling out onto the yard. He imagined they had received many remembrances from their Island friends, and their farmhouse couldn't hold them all. Cody answered the door and asked Kevin inside.

"I wanted to stop by and see how you and the family

are doing."

Cody lowered his head and quietly responded, "As good as can be expected. Do you have any news for us?"

"I'm afraid not. You heard that someone's been arrested, I'm sure. But so far, it's all circumstantial and we're searching for more evidence."

"I know the guy you arrested. Kyle worked with him at the restaurant. As far as I've heard on the grapevine, this guy sold drugs to kids. Is that right?"

"We're looking into everything, Cody. We've interviewed several people and we're trying to put together a case. How's Marilyn doing? And the kids?"

"They all went to Marilyn's mother's house for a while. We thought it was best to take the kids off the Island and let them grieve. Marilyn is doing okay. We're all just sad."

Kevin understood. This was one of the worst parts of his job, watching the grief. Especially when it's a child who's killed. He shook hands with Cody and promised to call him if anything of interest came up. As Kevin drove away, he thought he'd better go check in on his mother. She wasn't working today so he hoped to catch her at home.

"Kevin! What a surprise!" Penny Johnson was still in a caftan she wore around the house to hide her weight. Her wispy hair was damp from a late morning shower, and she apologized to her son for being in such a state. "I overslept this morning. Can I get you a cup of coffee?"

Kevin agreed to coffee because his mother had a new Keurig Coffee maker that she loved to use. "How are you doing, Mom? How's work?"

Penny laughed a little, "Boring. I try to keep busy, but we have so few customers lately that I find myself just sitting outside."

"It's because people are on vacations."

"Probably." Penny handed her son the steaming cup along with some sugar. "How's your case coming along?"

"Okay. You heard we've arrested someone. Do you know who this guy Joel is?"

"I don't, but some of my friends at the casino talk about him. They say he's been selling some drugs to kids, is that right?"

"I can't say, mom. You know that. What else are they saying?"

"Oh... one of the gals says she knows someone who has stolen guns. She said it's her neighbor who always complains about the raccoons and coyotes. He's bought some guns at a good price off a young guy. She's sure they're illegal."

"How does she know the guns are illegal?"

"He's a felon. He can't have guns." Penny looked pleased to have figured this out.

Kevin asked for the name and number of her friend and finished his coffee. His mother always surprised him with what she learned at the casino and the small store. Maybe this was something and maybe not.

Driving back to the precinct, Kevin felt a sense of despair. He couldn't imagine how much pain both Shelly and Kyle's families were feeling. Even when the case was finally closed, their loved ones would still be gone. He decided he would call Ted Macdonald, the prosecutor, and find out if he had updates on a possible trial schedule or thoughts on the evidence needed to charge the murders.

Macdonald was on the ferry back to the Island when Kevin called and agreed to meet him at the precinct. Besides working on Joel's case, the busy prosecutor also had Island offenders who were jailed in Seattle and needed his attention. Hopefully, Kevin was calling to say he had found something new. It frustrated him how slowly everything moved when cases were held up and waiting for additional evidence.

"Thanks for dropping by Ted." Kevin pulled up a chair for the lawyer. "Do you have any information about the pending trial schedule? Do you know which judge will be assigned?

"Not yet... but it will be assigned soon and then the judge will want to know about discovery. Joel's lawyer will no doubt start filing motions as soon as we have a judge. I would."

Kevin told him about the missing key and Trina Watson's impression of the Adams family. "It sounds like the father has quite a hold on his sons."

Ted nodded. "I know who he is... he's a bully of a man. Any leads on the key?"

"No. We interviewed the employees, and no one wants to say anything. I believe Andy warned them to keep quiet. I don't trust him."

"He's got years of deceiving if he's anything like his father. Did you hear why Trina left the Island?"

Kevin reached for his notes. "To get away from him.

That's all she said at first. But later she told Lana that Andy was a brute and that the youngest brother, Cameron, pestered her at work. I think he liked her. She said he tried to give her a bracelet before she left and wanted her phone number."

"Well. Let's keep an eye on the two brothers. Anything else?"

"I just got the name of a woman whose neighbor has some illegal guns. He's a felon so he shouldn't be around firearms. I thought I'd check it out."

The prosecutor got up to leave. "We have enough time to keep looking for answers. Keep in touch."

When Ted left, Kevin got busy writing up his reports. He stopped for a minute to call the number his mother had given him about the guns. Mrs. Teague didn't answer and so he left a voice message. Fifteen minutes later she called back.

"Chief Johnson, this is Mabel Teague. How can I help you?"

Kevin was amused with the energy the older lady seemed to have. She was almost breathless with her eagerness to talk. "Mrs. Teague, my mother gave me your number because you were concerned that your neighbor had illegal guns. Is this correct?"

"Yes! And I'm worried about the animals that roam around behind my place. I live right up against a woody area, and I know the animals are safe there. But this man wants to shoot them!"

"Where do you live, Mrs. Teague?"

"Here's my address. Are you going to come to

my house?"

"No, but give me the name of your neighbor. I don't want to let him know you were the one who called."

Mabel Teague took a deep breath, "Oh... of course! I didn't think of that!" She gave Kevin the name of her neighbor. He ended the call and promised to call Mabel back later. When Kevin looked the guy up for his police record, he saw he had been in jail a couple of times for possession and DUI. He decided to pay him a visit.

Lana looked up from her desk when Kevin walked out of his office. "Something come up?"

"Maybe, do you want to come with me? I'll brief you in the car."

Lana was intrigued when she learned about this new lead but was also wary that it was another false one. When they got to the house and knocked on the door, a very small man in his fifties answered, and a look of astonishment shown on his face. "Whatever it is, I didn't do it," were the first words out of his mouth.

Kevin asked him if he had any firearms on the premises. The man shook his head and asked if they had a search warrant. Kevin said no, but he would call for one right now. He reached for his phone when the man stopped him. "All right! I have a couple guns because I'm sick and tired of the damn animals that run all over the place around here. The coyotes keep me awake all night with their howling, and the raccoons are always getting into the trash bins and scattering trash all over the place."

"We need to take the guns, sir." Kevin reached for his

citation book to write up a ticket. The man let out a yelp, thinking that he would be arrested.

Kevin understood his anxiety and explained, "Sir, I'm only going to write you up a ticket and you can deal with your parole officer about it. I need to take the guns."

Lana was confused why Kevin didn't arrest the man. But she followed his lead and walked through the unkempt house to a tiny bedroom where they found two guns in the closet.

Kevin took photos of the guns and asked, "Where did you get the guns?"

"Some kid was selling online. I paid good money for them."

"Do you have his name?"

"No, I paid in cash."

"Okay. I need you to come with us to make a statement. I want a description of the kid who sold them to you."

Now Lana understood what Kevin was doing. He only wanted the name of the seller, and if he convinced this guy he wasn't in trouble, he would be cooperative.

At the precinct, and after looking through photos of teens on the Island, the man said he didn't recognize the kid who sold him the guns. Lana had an idea. Scrolling through her computer, she finally found what she was looking for. When she turned the screen to the man and showed him a school photo, the man cried out, "That's him!"

Kevin and Lana both looked at each other with the same astonished reactions. The photo was of Alex Peterson,

Sean Richardson's friend who was missing. Lana asked, "When did you purchase the guns?"

"Around the end of May, or the first week in June. He had a couple more guns to sell, but I wanted the shotguns."

"Did he have a 9mm handgun for sale?"

The man looked more uncomfortable and darted his eyes between the two police. "I'm not sure. It was all online." He reached up and rubbed his head, pulling at what little hair he had left. "I think there was one, but don't quote me on that."

Kevin brought out a statement form and had the man fill it out with whatever he remembered about the sale. Lana left the room and called the number of Alex's grandmother. She answered on the first ring, "Hello, who is this?"

"Hello, ma'am, this is Deputy Clark from the Island. We spoke to you last week about Alex. Has he returned home yet?"

"No, he's not home. I'm worried beyond belief! Do you know anything?"

"Alex's parents never returned our calls, and we're wondering if they could help us find Alex."

"Well, I'm not surprised by his parents' reluctance to call you. They're hardly attentive parents and I think they've given up on Alex. Is there something I could do?"

"If you hear from Alex, please let us know. In the meantime, I'd advise you to call the police in Kingston and report that he's still missing."

"I'll do that right now. And can I call you if I hear anything?"

"Please call us, even if it's something small."

Lana returned to Kevin's office and shook her head. "Still missing," she reported.

WEDNESDAY, JUNE 27TH

Online gun sales could be generated from anywhere. The fact that Kevin and Lana had a person who bought one might make the search easier, but they had to get Alex's computer first. Lana tried to make some sense out of this new development in the case.

"If Alex stole the guns, sold them, and then hid the money in Sean's room, how come he didn't come back to get it?"

"Well, let's think," Kevin answered. "If it's true he was planning to run away, he would need a lot of money. So maybe this isn't his first robbery. Let's talk with Sean Peterson again about when he first started to get the money from Alex."

Kevin had another thought. He called the Kingston police station and asked to speak with the Sheriff. He found out that since last year there had been several small burglaries reported in the area. People were complaining that even though the stolen items were minor, like outdoor equipment, they still needed to be replaced. Others had their cars broken into and had installed security lights to ward off intruders. Kevin appreciated the information and rang off.

Looking at Lana with a smirk, he said, "It looks like Alex may have been busy this year. If it is him, stealing and then probably selling the stuff, he must have an outlet somewhere. Kingston police don't have the staffing to do any real investigations on break-ins involving small property thefts. They just take a report and keep it on file in case they get lucky and catch someone in the act."

Lana started to search her computer while she spoke, "You can always sell stolen property online, it's like eBay or the neighborhood sites. But a few sites can only be accessed through a third party."

"What do you mean?"

"It's an anonymous site. Money changes hands through different sources. Let's say you're looking for a specific part for your car. It's expensive if you go to a dealer, so you search online for it. Someone has probably stolen the part and it's up for sale. You go to this site, find the part, and send the money by cashier's check."

"But where do you pick it up?"

"It's sent to you."

"Why would anyone get involved with this sort of thing?"

"Because some of the things are hard to find, or too expensive or are collector's items. It's how coins and stamps are traded."

"Why don't they get caught?"

"It's too big an operation. It's like money laundering. Nobody's talking."

"So how would a kid like Alex find out about it?"

"Probably word of mouth, but you know kids are all over the internet sites. And it only takes one mention on Instagram for the word to spread. We should probably talk to his parents." Lana's smile turned up in the corners, thinking that they may have just stumbled onto something. "Do you want me to call them?"

Mr. and Mrs. Peterson were difficult to reach. All the calls Lana made were sent to voicemail, so Kevin decided to visit them that afternoon at their business in Seattle. They owned an investment firm near the new stadium that had been built for Seattle's popular NFL football team, the Seahawks. As Kevin drove past the stadium, he marveled at the pricey new construction in the area and wondered how much the property was worth now. He knew that the cost of parking was at an all-time high in the Seattle area, and was surprised to see most of the spaces filled. People must be earning big bucks to be able to afford a car in the city.

The Peterson's building was a modern brick building next to the train depot. The lobby was filled with colorful abstract art on the walls and leather furniture. The dark wood floors added to the atmosphere of money and the receptionist behind the desk was dressed in designer clothes. She raised her long lashes and asked Kevin who he was here to see.

"I'd like to speak with Mr. and Mrs. Peterson."

"Do you have an appointment?"

Kevin took out his badge, "No, please let them know I'm here."

Mary and Lyle Peterson were younger than Kevin expected. Lyle Peterson was a tall man, probably 6'4" and looked like he worked out. His hair was professionally styed and probably dyed because it looked a shade too black. His wife, Mary, was also tall, and Kevin wondered if they had been on basketball teams in school. She was blonde, dyed a frosty blonde, and dressed in a linen suit that matched her blue eyes. She appeared cold and remained silent.

Kevin noticed they were tanned and exceptionally healthy as they held out their hands to greet him. Neither one asked if their children were okay. Kevin was led into a conference room.

Declining a beverage, Kevin began his questioning, "Do you know where your son is?"

The parents looked at each other, perplexed, and shook their heads in unison. "What do you know about Alex?" Lyle asked.

"We know he's been missing and may be involved with a case we're investigating. I understand that he's taken off before."

Mr. Peterson stared directly at Kevin, expressionless, "Alex has taken off a few times before. He usually returns in a couple of days. We're getting used to it. Have you found him?"

"No. Do you own any guns, by the way?"

They looked at each other and shook their heads, again in unison. "We're anti-gun. Why?"

Kevin took a moment to reflect on this. "Do you know Sean Richardson?"

Mary Peterson finally spoke up; her voice was low and steady. "I believe he's one of Alex's friends. They play football at school together."

Well, thought Kevin, at least she knows something about her son. "Did you know of any cash that Alex earned lately? Did he have a job or access to money?"

Lyle raised his eyebrows and held his head back in surprise. "We give him an allowance, but it's only for things he needs for school. Why?"

"How much does he get for allowance?"

They looked at each other and finally Mary said, "Fifty dollars a week. As far as we know, it goes for books and school supplies."

"Is it possible that he just saved it and didn't use it for that purpose"

Once again, they looked at each other perplexed. Lyle shook his head and said, "He might have saved some of it, but he paid for his school supplies and occasionally for food when he was out with his friends. Why are you asking us these questions? Is Alex in trouble with the law?"

"We're following up on some thefts that have occurred in your town. Several guns were stolen from Jack Richardson's house in early June, and one is part of our investigation. Apparently, Alex had access to this house because he's friends with Sean. He also stored some cash in Sean's bedroom. We want to find out where the money came from."

Mary looked confused and started to say something when Lyle put a hand on her arm. "We're done speaking with you." He stood and escorted Kevin out the door.

Kevin understood the Peterson's reluctance to give him more information. But were they protecting their son or their reputation? He didn't appreciate people like this who lived for money instead of family. On his way back to the ferry, Kevin called Curt to see if any more information was discovered about the Seattle drug dealer they were looking for.

"No, sorry Kevin. We have so many things in the fire right now and we're overloaded with burglaries because the cruise ships are docking regularly. People on vacations aren't very cautious and are easy victims for thieves." Kevin thanked him and thought how lucky he was to be working on the Island where things were usually calm.

On the ferry ride home, Kevin ran through all the leads they had covered. He started writing down a list of questions.

Who had access to the Apartment?

Who bought the gun?

Who was selling drugs to kids on the Island?

Where is Alex Peterson? What does he know about guns or drugs?

By the time Kevin arrived at the office he was determined to find the answers to these questions. Lana greeted him with news. "I talked with Della at the gift store, and she doesn't have security cameras on the back stairs. She said the cameras for all the shops are pointed to the front entrances because most of them don't have access from the back."

"Did she have any more comments about Joel?"

"Just that he was a nice guy. Didn't cause any trouble."

Kevin related what he found out from the Peterson's. He also wrote on the white board the questions he had thought about. "Let's think about possible suspects. We haven't done this because Joel was arrested, and we thought it was over. But let's think." He started to write names on the board.

Andy Adams. Had a key to Joel's apartment. Known to be controlling. Last to see Shelly and Kyle alive.

Cameron Adams. Probably knew where the key was in the Deli. Bad temper. May have seen Shelly and Kyle before they were murdered.

Jack Richardson. Owned the gun.

Alex Peterson. Missing. Stole the gun for cash?

David Waters. Drama teacher. Worked with both teens.

Ryan and Jesse (waiters at The Doc). Seemed nervous about being interviewed.

Mira Connelly. Friend of Shelly's. Seems to be holding something back.

Kevin and Lana agreed this list of people gave them some direction and, maybe, insight. Alan had suggested to Kevin that interviewing a person twice would only work if it was by another officer. He explained how a second person's point of view might see the evidence or statement from a different perspective or pick up on something the first interviewer missed. Kevin and Lana divided up the list of people to interview.

Lana was pleased that she had the Adams brothers on her list. After talking with Trina, she had a better idea of how insidious their behavior could be. She decided to find Cameron first thing in the morning.

THURSDAY, JUNE 28TH

Cameron was just leaving home when his phone rang. When he answered, he cursed himself for not letting it ring through. That woman police officer wanted to talk with him. He knew who she was, just about the only Black face in the community, and still new to the Island. What did she want from him?

Lana arranged to meet with Cameron at the Lynnwood Coffee shop. His attitude defined him as he sat sulking in a chair when she entered the shop. She took a seat next to him, introduced herself, and began her questioning without preliminaries. "Cameron, I understand you work at the Deli. Were you working the day of the murders?" She wanted to see his reaction to the word "murder".

Cameron raised his head and stared at her. "Do I have to answer this?"

"Well, no. But I will ask you to come to the station and do a formal interview if you want. This is just a chat."

"Okay. Yes, I was working that day." Cameron fidgeted in his chair.

"Did you speak to Shelly Mann and Kyle Smith?"

"I don't... didn't... know them that well and so no." Cameron took a deep breath as if he was already bored.

Lana wrote something down and then continued, "Do you know Trina Watson?"

Cameron's eyes opened wide, and he seemed to be gritting his teeth as he held his breath. "Why?"

"I understand you bothered her at work. Do you remember being asked to leave where she worked on occasion?"

"Yeah... so what?"

"At the time, she was dating your brother."

"He was too old for her!" At this point he stood up to stop the conversation.

Lana stood also. "Where were you when the murders happened, Cameron?"

"I don't have to tell you. You'll have to talk to my father's lawyer next time you want to question me." Lana watched him stomp out of the café. Noting his demeanor, she wondered why he was so anxious and why he was lying. She already knew he wasn't working on the day of the murders.

Looking at her watch, Lana decided to drive over to the Deli and talk with Andy Adams. She wanted to get to him before he heard from his brother or, maybe, his father if Cameron kept his threat.

Andy was busy checking his staff records when Lana

walked in. He let out a loud sigh, cocked his head, and smirked. "What do you want?"

Lana looked around the restaurant to see if customers were present. It was still early in the day and only a table outside seemed to be occupied, so she walked up to Andy and handed him her card. "I have a few questions."

Andy led her into his office and shut the door. There was just enough room for an oak desk and two wicker chairs. Andy sat casually behind his desk and motioned to Lana to take a chair. When she sat down, she took out her notebook and pen. She decided to review his previous statements to see if anything had changed.

"You told us you saw Shelly and Kyle here on the day they were murdered." She glanced at Andy before continuing. He nodded.

"And you said they were in great moods, maybe even high. Is that right?"

"Well, I can't be certain if they were high, officer, I just said they seemed like they were celebrating."

"Yes, well, did you notice drugs at all on them?"

"No, of course not!"

"Why do you say that? Are you not aware of drugs on the Island?"

"Why are you asking me? I don't watch my customers for drugs or any sign of drugging. I'm selling food, not babysitting!"

"Chief Johnson noted that you didn't hear them mention what they were doing after they left here. Now that you've had more time, do you remember anything at all?"

Andy shook his head. "I wish I did, but we were very busy that day because of graduation. I had my whole staff on board, working."

Lana nodded, knowing this was a lie. Several of the staff they interviewed said they didn't work that day because they wanted to attend the graduation. "Do you know the place where Shelly and Kyle were killed? It's just down the road and we understand that kids go there to hang out, or drink and drug."

"Listen, officer, I'm a bit too old to care about where high school kids hang out. I don't have a clue where or what they do these days."

"One more question, Andy, where's the key to Trina's apartment?"

Andy stopped breathing. He turned his head to the file cabinet behind Lana and then back to her. "I told Chief Johnson it must have been stolen. I kept it here and then forgot about it. I don't have a clue where it is."

"What do you keep in the cabinets?"

"Oh... just receipts and tax information. Files on employees and insurance papers. Nothing personal."

Lana stood up and looked carefully around. She hoped this made Andy nervous. He was hiding something. From what Trina had said about his parents, she wouldn't be surprised if he was stealing money. Maybe he was planning on an escape.

Kevin had a busy morning. He had called David Waters and planned to meet him when he found out he was still at school, organizing the theater equipment. He had never met David, but he had been to several plays and thought they were almost professional.

David shook hands with Kevin and led him to the auditorium. It was the one place that wasn't filled with clutter.

"How can I help you officer?"

"I understand you saw quite a lot of Shelly and Kyle because of the work they did on the sets."

"Yes, I did. They were great kids. I hear you've arrested the guy who did this horrible crime."

"We're still tying up some loose ends in our investigation. Apparently, both kids were into drugs. Have you heard any of the kids talk about who's giving or selling them drugs?"

"I wish I could help. I have a freshman daughter and the drug dealing worries me. You hear stories off and on about this kid or that. I always thought it was some Seattle dealer who sold here. You know how easy it is to get on the Island."

"Do kids talk to you about this?"

"Sometimes. Usually, it's the ones who are worried about their friends. I always advise them to go talk with the counselors. I try and stay out of it."

"Are the counselors around now? I should speak with them, too."

"The most popular one just quit. She was young and probably transferred to a bigger district. It's quiet for singles here."

"What's her name?"

"Ashley Philips. The principal knows more about

where she is now."

"Can you think of anyone who wanted to hurt those kids?"

"I have thought about it and can't think of anyone. Kyle was a bit of a showoff, but everyone was used to him. Shelly was going places. She had a knack for creating space and color that made our sets amazing."

Kevin left the drama teacher and wondered if he should find Ashley Philips and see if she knew anything. If the teens confided in her, maybe she heard the name of the dealer. He sat in his car for a while and wondered if they were going too far afield with their inquiries. Maybe it was time to speak with the principal and discuss the investigation. But first, he had to go talk with Mira Connelly.

Mira was just entering the bookstore when Chief Johnson drove up. When he called her name, she was surprised.

"Can I speak with you for a minute, Mira?"

Mira's eyes darted back and forth as she tried to think. "Here?"

"If you have a few minutes." Kevin repeated. "I only have a couple questions about your friend Shelly. Can we go inside? I know there's an office in the back because the owner's my friend."

Mira led him through to the back of the store. The small office was comfortable, filled with bookshelves and two lazy boy chairs. They both sat and Kevin began his inquiry. "Did you know Shelly was taking drugs?"

"Maybe. I guess so. Everyone does." Mira looked

nervous as she wrung her hands together.

"Do you know who she was getting her drugs from?"

"No. Probably Kyle."

"Did you notice anyone who had a grudge or didn't like Shelly? Maybe someone in the drama group?"

"No. We all liked her. She was amazing with the sets."

"When was the last time you saw her?"

"Graduation."

Kevin knew that Mira was nervous, but he also knew she had a friendlier side. Her acting ability was well-known, and she was popular around the Island. "Mira, we don't want to get anyone in trouble. Anything you know about Shelly, or Kyle, that will help us find their killer is appreciated. Did either of them seem worried or upset about anything? Did you notice a change in your friend's behavior?"

Mira lowered her eyes and seemed to consider these questions. "Well, I heard that Shelly went to see the counselor a couple of times. I think she was having trouble at home. Her parents were overly protective."

"In what way were they protective?"

"She had strict hours and they were always on her to get good grades. Shelly studied all the time, especially for the SAT test. She got lower scores than she expected and didn't get into the college she wanted. I heard this upset her parents. She was going to the community college this fall to take classes."

Kevin nodded his head. "Thank you for sharing that. It helps to get a clearer picture of Shelly. Remember Mira, I'm just up the street if you need to talk about anything. Our job is to keep everyone safe."

Mira gave Kevin a nervous smile and stood to go. Kevin sat for a minute to consider what she had told him. If Shelly was pressured by her parents, maybe that's why she took drugs, as an escape. Now he had another direction to go. He needed to talk with the counselor at the school.

Lana and Kevin returned to the office and shared the new information they'd gathered from the interviews. Lana was impressed with what Kevin had learned from Mira and the drama teacher. "Do you want me to follow up with the counselor?"

"Let me talk with the principal first and find out more. If it's true that the kids were confiding in her and she knows something, we should tread lightly. She may have confidentiality issues."

Lana needed some direction on how to proceed. "What about the Adams brothers? They're both lying and probably think they're protecting each other besides themselves."

"I'm now more interested in the stolen gun. Who got a hold of the key and planted it at Joel's? Was it the killer or someone protecting the killer? Let's say it's the Adam's father who found the gun and feared that one of his sons killed the teenagers. So, he decided to frame Joel. If he got the key from the restaurant, he would have the opportunity to plant the gun."

"Wow... that's pretty far-fetched... but possible. How could we find that out?"

"Time to go talk with the Adams."

"Do you want me to come with you?"

"No, I need you to call Jack Richardson again and see if his son Sean knows anything about who Alex sells his stolen goods to. Maybe all the kids have secret sources or something. Even if it's a rumor, tell him it would help us."

Kevin was leaving the office when he saw Alan walking down the street. Kevin hailed him and had an idea.

"Alan, how are you doing? Any more problems?"

Alan shook his head and smiled. "Nothing lately. The note and photo must have been a prank of some sort. Where are you off to?"

"As a matter of fact, I'm on my way to talk with Mr. Adams about his sons. I have a suspicion he knows more about the missing key and who planted the gun. His sons are clever, but he rules the house. Do you have time to go with me?"

"Sure. I like these ride a-longs. The best part is I don't have to write up a report."

On the way, Kevin brought Alan up to date. He reviewed his conversation with the Petersons in Seattle and the lead he got from the drama teacher. "I hope the high school counselor wasn't involved with this. I need to call the principal to get her number because she's transferred out of the district. I also talked with one of Shelly's friends and she said Shelly was pressured by her parents to excel. I don't doubt it because she was an only child, and they wanted the best for her. The problem might be that Shelly couldn't always match their expectations. This Island suffers from overzealous parents."

When they reached the Adams house, Alan was impressed with the size. The three-story brick home was surrounded by lawn and garden that was at least a full acre. The house featured high windows and stately columns that flanked the entrance. The beveled glass on the front door gave view to the large chandelier that hung gloriously in the entrance. The door was opened by a young woman who appeared to be out of breath.

"May I help you, gentlemen."

"We'd like to speak with Mr. Adams." Kevin showed her his badge.

"I'm his secretary. Please come in and have a seat. I'll tell him you're here."

She escorted them into a living room which was filled with light. An elegant grand piano dominated an enclave, surrounded by windows looking out into a garden. Floor to ceiling mahogany bookcases took up space on the far wall, and a marble fireplace the other. Linen sofas were arranged by the fireplace and Kevin and Alan took a seat. Alan noticed that several arrangements of fresh flowers were spread around the room, and he wondered who took care of them. Probably a maid or someone who took care of everything, since it appeared that money was not a problem.

Drew Adams walked confidently into the room and shook hands with the men. "Chief Johnson, how can I help you?" Adams sat in a wingback chair and crossed his legs. He wasn't a tall man, but because of his bravado he appeared to dominate the room. He was dressed in beige golf clothes, belted tight around his middle. Alan wondered how much golf he played since his skin tone seemed to match the color of his clothes.

"We have a few questions about the Deli and a certain key that might have been taken from the office there."

"Well, you would have to ask my son about that since he runs the place."

"We have spoken to Andy. He claims the key was in his desk and he doesn't have a clue who took it. How often do you visit the restaurant?"

At this point in the conversation, Mrs. Adams entered the room. She appeared startled by the men and absentmindedly put her hand to her hair and took a short breath. "Oh, I didn't know we had guests."

The men stood at once and her husband introduced her. Greta Adams extended her hand to Alan and Kevin and then excused herself from the room. Alan noted she didn't ask why they were there.

"Getting back to your question about the restaurant... I never go there. It's for young people and I prefer to keep out of my son's business. But I will warn you, chief, I don't appreciate how you've been questioning him lately. If it's about the murders, I assure you he knows nothing about them."

"Your other son, Cameron, doesn't seem to want to talk with us. He says he was working the day of the murders, but he's not on the list of employees for that day. Do you have any idea why that is?"

"I hope you're not implying that my boys have something to do with that brutal killing. I will have my lawyer on you in a minute if you go near them with accusations."

"We're only here for a friendly conversation. It's just standard procedure to try to eliminate any potential witnesses or suspects from our list as we try to narrow in on the perpetrator."

"But you've arrested someone already! That guy from The Doc!"

"It's an ongoing investigation."

Adams stood and put his hands in his pockets. "I'll have to ask you to leave now. I have some important phone calls to make."

Kevin thanked Adams for his time and looked once more around the beautiful room. He wanted to remember as much as possible so he could describe it to Julia when he got home.

"Well. What did you think?" Kevin asked Alan on the drive back.

"I wonder what it's like to have so much money. Do you think anyone plays the piano?" Both men laughed.

Kevin tapped his fingers on the steering wheel and thought out loud. "I wanted to put him on notice. If his sons are involved with any of this, he'll be raving mad. He'll also lawyer up in a heartbeat to protect them."

"Do you really think they're involved?"

"It's a possibility. Someone had to buy that gun. And with the key missing and the connection with Andy's former girlfriend living in that apartment, it makes sense they know something."

"What do you know about Mrs. Adams? She seems to

be nervous or very timid."

"Julia says she 'mother hens' the boys. Does their wash and cleans their rooms…or has someone do it. She belongs to several lady's clubs and charities that donate money to local causes, especially to improve outdoor spaces. The Island is full of those kinds of groups."

"I wonder how she survives with a house full of men."

Cameron was always a "mommy's boy." He relied on his mother to do everything for him. Because he was the youngest, she worshiped him and insisted he stay as close to the family unit as possible. He reveled in her attention. His father hated how his mother doted on him, and thought his son was lazy. They argued constantly about his lack of direction. When Cameron announced he wasn't going to college, his father yelled and told him to get a job or get out of the house. Because he was already working part time in the Deli for Andy, he decided to up his hours and hope that would get his father off his back. Cameron hated his father.

Cameron had begun using drugs in middle school. He despised being compared to his brothers throughout the years and used drugs to mellow out his anxieties. At first it was just weed. He could get that easily. Kids on the Island had multiple sources, including some parents who dealt on the side. By the time he got into high school he was into speed and ecstasy and a little cocaine.

His need for a reliable source for his drug habit had spurred Cameron to hang out with a rowdy gang of users who always had a ready supply of drugs. They were clever and posed a low but growing threat to the community by breaking into empty houses and cars to get drug money. Even though they were petty criminals, whatever they managed to steal was quickly sold on an anonymous internet site. Most Islanders were ignorant of the dark side of the internet and never located their stolen items again. The money the gang made was kept in a stash to fund their drug buys.

Rick Knowles was the gang's leader, and, like Cameron's older brother Andy, was brash, bullying and demanding. Cameron was in awe of him and frightened by him at the same time. Knowles ran the gang almost like a cult, you either went along or you were out, and he demanded loyalty.

In the past few months, Knowles had let his gang know he was tired of only doing small-time burglaries for small time money. He had bigger ambitions. There was more money to be had by selling drugs to the willing market of kids on the Island. He had a source off the Island for supplying any drug he wanted, and knew it was time to stake out a territory and get in on the action.

Knowles instructed the gang to be more discriminating in their robbery efforts and to look for things like high end cameras and guns, which were easy to sell and brought in more cash. So far, they had been successful and had several thousand dollars on hand from sales, as well as a small armory of weapons. Knowles found a site where he could sell guns anonymously to anyone, including underage buyers. Money was starting to roll in.

Cameron didn't understand why guns were so prized,

but he didn't want to question it. He stayed away from that part of the activity, and only got involved with buying and selling drugs. The day of the murders, Cameron had been hanging out with the gang. He heard that Knowles had successfully arranged for a drug delivery from a source in Seattle who was able to deal in bulk. The plan that day was simply to meet the courier on the south side of the Island, pay him or her in cash and bring the drugs back to Knowles. It sounded like an easy run. They needed at least three guys to make it happen.

When Knowles looked around at the gang, he made a quick decision. "Sonny, you and Terry take the cash and make the pickup. And take Cam with you." Both lead guys nodded but were a little stoned and seemed anxious about being a part of such a big deal. They talked it over and decided to take a gun in case things got tricky. Terry picked up a 9mm handgun that Knowles had planned to fence and put it in his coat pocket.

Cameron wasn't really interested in tagging along because he had spent the day drinking, smoking weed and snorting ecstasy. By the time they took off to meet the courier he had enough drugs in his system not to care what he was doing or where they were going. He sank into the backseat of the car and dozed off.

The guys followed directions along an old Island road and stopped beside an aging red farmhouse. Hiding their car in a densely wooded area, Cameron was told to wake up and get out of the car. They led the way through a path to a campsite. This was to be the meeting place. They sat and waited for over an hour. Sonny got worried and constantly looked toward the road where he expected the courier to appear. Terry, by this time was high on Molly, and casually examined the gun he had taken out of his jacket. He began pointing it randomly and pretending to shoot at made up targets like he was in a video game. Suddenly, two figures appeared on the path behind them, as if out of nowhere. Their unexpected appearance startled Cameron... and Terry, who was still pointing the gun jumped up in a panic. Before anyone could say anything, Terry pulled the trigger three times, hitting both figures... They fell where they stood as blood drained from their wounds.

Cameron remembered being in shock and then breathing rapidly in a panic. He stood up shaking and shouted at Terry. "What did you do?"

Terry looked down at the gun in his hand, amazed that it had gone off, and then flung the gun toward Cameron as if it was on fire and took off running with Sonny right behind him. Cameron froze, and then bent over and picked up the gun. Becoming aware that he was suddenly alone he turned, took a glance in the direction of the fallen intruders, then ran after his friends. By the time he reached the car all he saw were taillights receding in the distance. Sonny and Terry were nowhere to be seen. Dizzy with anxiety, Cameron took out his phone and called his mother.

When her son had called in a panic that day, Greta was able to leave the house immediately and rush to him. Cameron had sounded so unreasonably upset on the phone that he didn't make any sense. She could only figure out where he was located and so she quickly advised him to walk to the elementary school up the road and wait for her.

When she arrived at the school, Greta was shocked to see Cameron. He was pale and shaken, and in his hand was a gun. "Get in the car!" she demanded.

"I'm sorry, Mom. I'm just so sorry…"

"Put that thing in the glove compartment. We're going to drive to Jackson Park and talk." As they drove away, the road was suddenly filled with police and a Medic unit, with flashing lights and sirens blaring, heading in the opposite direction.

Realizing Cameron's distress, Greta put her hand on his shoulder to try and calm him. "It can't be that bad. I just don't understand why you would have a gun, though."

They arrived at the park three miles away and found a sheltered table off to one side. Cameron continued to shake and then started to cry. "I can't believe it happened! I was just sitting there, and he shot them!"

Greta sprang up off the bench. "Shot who?!"

"Two kids! They were only walking down the path and he shot them!"

"Cameron, what kids? Who shot them? When?"

Cameron had his face in his hands, trembling with fear. "We were supposed to meet someone to buy some drugs and…Should I even tell you what happened? Will this make you a part of it?"

Greta thought for a minute. Although she was a quiet

person, she was also very clever. She would get her son out of this. "Listen, Cameron, I'm going to need to know how you got this gun and then we need to get rid of it. You didn't shoot the gun, right?"

"Right! The other guy just threw it at me after he shot them and then he ran away. When I went after him, he was gone."

"Okay. We're going to go back home, and I'll get rid of the gun. In the meantime, I want you to go to your room. I'll send up some food and say you're not well." Greta hugged her troubled son and then walked him back to the car.

Greta had kept her promise to Cameron and had gotten rid of the gun. Her plan was to divert any attention away from her family and not take a chance that the gun might be found if she just threw it away. She finally decided to put it somewhere that, when found, would implicate someone other than her boys.

People never thought Greta was listening, but she knew more than anyone suspected. Weeks ago, Greta had found the key to Trina Watson's apartment when she was looking through Andy's office desk for a pen to remind him of an appointment. The key was in an envelope with an address on it and Greta knew it was Trina's. Andy had mentioned where Trina lived because he knew his mother liked the gift shop. Greta took the key out of the envelope and put it in her pocket, mainly to get it away from Andy. She knew he was still upset that Trina had left town.

When Greta was shopping one day later, the gift shop

lady mentioned that Joel, the waiter at The Doc Restaurant, had rented the apartment upstairs. Everyone seemed to like the waiter, and Greta had met him once at a social gathering where he was catering. But the last time Greta was in Seattle looking for a new carpet, she had spotted Joel standing in a semi-secluded doorway off First Ave. talking with an odd stranger and then exchanging what looked like a wad of cash for some small packets. Greta had kept what she saw and suspected to herself. He was obviously buying drugs.

When it became clear that she needed to dispose of the gun to protect Cameron, she knew exactly where she would put it.

Greta was worried when she walked in and saw the police talking with Drew. She had to act quickly. Greta's only mission now was to keep Cameron safe. Her plan would involve getting him off the Island and away from the investigation. She knew her son was impulsive and always suspected he was on drugs so maybe it was time for rehab.

After the detectives left the house, Greta heard Cameron's voice from downstairs. She needed to convince him to move quickly. "Cameron, can you come upstairs?"

Worried that he was deeper in trouble; Cameron entered his mother's study reluctantly. "What's going on?"

"The police were just here. I don't like this."

"I don't either. That lady cop tried to question me this morning. Do you think they suspect anything?"

"We'll have to wait and see. In the meantime, I want

you off the Island."

"What do you mean? Like a vacation?"

"No, like rehab." Greta stared at her son. She was serious.

Cameron stared back. "Why? I'll stop the drugs if that's what you want."

"No, Cameron, I need you away from here and from the investigation. The only safe place I can think of is rehab. Everyone will understand and even feel sorry for you."

"Do you mean a place to stay for a couple of months while they turn me into a loser?"

"Would you rather go to jail?"

The thought made both their hearts beat quickly.

FRIDAY, JUNE 29ᵀᴴ

It was a busy morning at the precinct. Kevin had called the principal of the high school and they agreed to meet in the afternoon. In the meantime, Lana was on her way to Kingston to speak with Sean Richardson one more time. She hoped he knew more about where his friend Alex hung out when he decided to stay away from home.

Kevin was on his way to lunch when his phone rang. "Johnson. How can I help you?"

It was Lana. "I have Alex. What would you like me to do?" She was prepared for anything at this point.

"Bring him in."

Alex had been hiding in a small hotel just off the Valley Road in Kingston. Sean Richardson had found his friend there when he followed him from a nearby Chevron station where Alex was buying supplies. Sean didn't know if Alex had possession of any guns, but he wasn't going to take the chance by approaching him. He had two choices, let the police know where Alex was, or forget he even saw him.

Sean was trying to decide what to do when he heard that an Island officer was coming to talk with him again. He surprised Lana with the address of the hotel.

Alex lifted his hands up in the air when he opened the door and saw Lana standing there. He then let his arms fall to his sides in a show of complete surrender. The pitiful state Lana found Alex in was enough to break her heart. He appeared to be exhausted and there was food scattered around the room and clothes everywhere. Lana thought he looked much younger than his seventeen years.

Lana phoned Alex's parents to tell them she had located their son and would be taking him in to the precinct for some questions. She left a voicemail for each of them. She then called his grandmother.

"Do you have time to come to the station?" Lana hoped for Alex's sake that she would agree.

"Yes, of course. I can be there in an hour."

This was the best possible answer. Alex's grandmother was obviously worried about her grandson and would be sympathetic and understanding.

That morning Alan had decided to take a few days and do some sight-seeing. Before he left, he called Kevin to see if he could lend an ear on the investigation. Talking things through always helped when he was on a big case in Boston.

"Alan, I'm glad you called. Do you have some time? We have a lead on the gun now. Lana just found Alex."

Alan delayed his travel plans.

Kevin and Alan had time before Lana returned to discuss what they needed to learn from Alex. If he was involved with drugs and selling guns, he might be the connection they needed for knowing who killed Shelly and Kyle.

"Lana says that he's scared. She doesn't think he was involved or even knew about the murders on the Island. He was just planning to get away from his father."

Alan shook his head. "It sounds like Alex was caught up in some emotional abuse and neglect. Sometimes abuse points the finger to all kinds of criminal practices and types of aggression. Hopefully, he'll be honest with us."

Lana stayed with Alex in the interview room while waiting for his grandmother to arrive. She tried to reassure him that things would be okay if he just told the truth, but he looked like he wanted to flee, expecting the worse. When his grandmother walked into the room, she immediately gave him a hug. Alex leaned into her.

Five minutes later, Kevin and Alan quietly entered the interview room. Lana introduced Alan to Alex and his grandmother and explained his position as advisor to the investigation. They both nodded briefly and looked worried.

Lana began the questioning. "Alex, we need to ask if you stole any guns from the Richardson's house."

Hanging his head, Alex nodded.

"Okay. We found one person you sold a rifle to, but

now we need the name of who you sold the 9mm handgun to."

Looking wearily to his grandmother, Alex admitted, "There was this guy I always bought a little weed from and so I asked him if he was interested in a gun. I sold him that gun."

Kevin took out his notebook and prepared to write down names. "I need the name of that guy. Do you have any other contact with gangs or kids involved with burglaries on this side of the water?"

"I know a few. But just their first names."

"I'll need those names."

Alex's grandmother spoke up, "What were you doing stealing? You know I would help you if you needed something."

Alex raised his head and looked sorrowfully at her. "Grandma, I just need to leave. I can't take it anymore."

She nodded her head. "Come stay with me, then."

Kevin thanked Alex and then said he would have to call the Kingston police and report all of this. He imagined they would want to talk with Alex. Kevin let Alex leave with his grandmother.

Alan stayed for a while longer to review the case. "It's a step forward... now that you have a connection with the drugs and the guns. Things may be falling into place." Alan shook his head. "Sometimes it's beyond me to understand why teenagers think they'll never be caught. They believe they can do virtually anything if they get their hands on a gun and have a partner in crime."

Kevin nodded and responded, "And I know that most

kids need to get high on something before the time of the robbery. It gives them courage or maybe lack of conscience. Unfortunately, nearly half of juvenile robbers experience some kind of violence in their homes, like Alex admits to."

"It's a terrible cycle." Alan immediately thought about his two grandsons.

SATURDAY, JUNE 30TH

Kevin got a hold of the Kingston precinct the next morning to collect information about the names Alex gave him. "Do you recognize any of these names?" he asked the Sheriff.

"Yes, I do. One of the kids has been in trouble before. His name is Rick Knowles. My guess is that he's one of the gang members, if not the leader. He's twenty and probably bullies the younger kids into going along with his robberies. Do you want to meet him? I know where he lives."

"I'll be there in an hour."

Kevin called Lana and asked her to join him. He liked how good she was at moving from general to specific questions and getting to the heart of what they needed answered.

Cameron Adams was busy packing for his interview with a rehab facility in eastern Washington. His father had finally gone along with the idea of rehab, especially after Cameron produced the drugs he had hidden in his room. Instead of arguing with his father, Cameron had played the obedient and regretful son, promising to follow the agenda of the treatment. Before he left on the bus to the facility, his mother handed him a phone where he could reach her in an emergency.

"Why do I need this?"

"Try and hide it before you get there. They'll be taking your phone and I want to be able to reach you in case something happens. You're not out of the woods yet."

Cameron slipped the phone in his pocket and hugged his mother. She always thought of everything, and he needed her on his side.

Lana and Kevin met the Kingston Police Chief and headed out for Rick Knowles's apartment. He had been living outside of town in a strip mall community close to the main road. The apartment house was old but seemed to be surviving because of the upgraded shingles that never appeared to weather. When they knocked on the door, an older lady answered.

"We're looking for Rick, madam, is he home?" Kevin smiled briefly.

"He's not here. Why do you want him?"

"He may be able to help us with a case and we just

have a few questions..." Kevin was cut off when he heard a voice.

"Who is it grandma?" When the person saw the police, a panicked look came over his face. He looked around for an escape, and of course there wasn't one.

All three police entered the house and asked Rick to have a seat. Lana was the first to question him. "Do you know Alex Peterson?"

"No. I mean maybe."

"We understand that you may have purchased a gun from him. What can you tell us about this?"

"No comment."

Kevin stood up and said, "Okay. Get your things and we'll complete this interview at the station."

He followed Rick to get his coat and shoes and noticed that the bedroom he slept in was set up with a forty-inch computer screen and a detailed map on the wall of the surrounding area. Curious, Kevin asked, "Why do you need such a big screen?"

"I don't have to tell you anything." Rick yelled. "I want a lawyer."

Kevin reached for his phone and called to get a warrant.

When they arrived at the precinct on the Island, a local public defender was already there. Rick Knowles was not ready to talk. In the meantime, Kevin had a voicemail from the high school principal and decided to return the call while Knowles met with his lawyer.

"Thank you for getting back to me," Kevin began, "I understand you employed a counselor, Ashley Philips. I need to speak with Ashley."

"Can I ask what this is about?"

"We're still following leads on the murders of Shelly and Kyle, and I understand that Ashley may have spent time with Shelly Mann. Any information she can give us would help."

The principal offered to call Ashley and see if it was possible for her to meet with the Chief to talk about a student she had counseled. Kevin appreciated the help. When he hung up, Lana was shaking her head. "Knowles is refusing to talk. The lawyer said he would be back to speak with him again."

"There's got to be a connection here. It's all about the key, the drugs, and the gun."

Carson Bowen met with Joel earlier in the day and was concerned with his listlessness. Joel confessed that being in jail was depressing and the lack of freedom was finally affecting him. He had lost his appetite and sleeping was difficult because of all the noise. Carson tried to boost his confidence, but he had little news about the investigation.

"Are you reaching out to your family?"

"Yeah, but they are just as worried as I am."

"Do you want them to visit? I could call them."

"No, don't even suggest it to them. They've already done too much for me."

"Is there anyone else you want to talk to?"

"No. Well, maybe that detective from Boston. I need

to talk with someone who isn't connected to the Island."

Carson called Alan and it was arranged that he would meet with Joel on Sunday.

SUNDAY, JULY 1ST

Alan wondered why Joel wanted to speak with him, but maybe it was true what Carson said about his being someone without ties to the Island. On the drive there, he called Kevin to see what was happening with the case.

"Well, Alan, we've had some interesting turn of events. We have one guy in custody as of yesterday and we're getting a warrant for his house. From what I can tell, he has a sophisticated system set up of areas to case and burglarize. Alex sold the gun to this guy."

"Good work. So now the gun purchase is solved. What about the drug dealing?"

"That's the interesting thing... this guy in custody also sells drugs. This is the dealer we have been looking for... or one of them. We're still working on Island dealers. I'm hoping a counselor at the high school can give us some leads."

"Joel asked to speak with me. Carson says that his

spirits are down. Hopefully I can be of some help."

"I really appreciate that, Alan. I just don't think he's involved in the murders."

On the drive to the jail, Alan reviewed what Kevin told him about the case. Unfortunately, he couldn't mention any of this to Joel because that was his attorney's job. Alan decided all he would do is offer support and listen. If Joel was depressed, the best Alan could do was to let him know he understood and maybe suggest some survival strategies.

When Joel was brought into the conference room, Alan immediately noticed he had lost weight. His shoulders dragged low, and his arms seemed to lose all tension. He slumped into the metal chair and looked at Alan. "Thanks for coming."

Alan nodded, "What can I do for you?"

"I feel like I'm failing at everything right now." Joel hung his head.

Realizing that Joel needed emotional support and aiming to show empathy, Alan paused and then said, "Joel, you're probably very confused about things right now and don't know how to sort everything out. I'm here to listen if that will help. I'll keep anything you say between you and me."

Joel raised his head and looked cautiously at Alan. "I've done some stupid shit, but I didn't kill anyone. I've been set up and might even go to prison for something I would never do." He hung his head again.

Alan could see how despondent Joel was and didn't want to add to the pressure, but he was concerned about his mental state. "Joel, I'm certain you know all about depression. This is a tough environment to be in and I suspect you're probably scared. It's common for people in jail to lose hope and blame themselves for something that may not be their fault. I can't imagine how lonely you must be feeling."

"My parents have been supportive, but I don't want them to feel responsible. They don't have a lot of money and I'm worried they'll burn through their savings trying to help me. And I've already damaged my reputation on the Island." He tearfully heaved a heavy sigh.

Alan listened. "I have a son a few years younger than you. Last year I found out he had a drug problem and, even though he didn't want help, I still supported him. He had the courage to face the truth about his addiction and go to treatment. Perhaps your parents feel the same way I do, by attempting to understand what you're going through and offering what they can."

"I've messed up before. That's why I'm so depressed. If I'd just taken rehab seriously, I probably wouldn't be here."

"You have plenty of time to begin again. Look, let's be honest here, you've made some bad choices, but you can't change that now. What you can do is try to help your lawyer and the police find out the truth." Alan paused and let that thought sink in.

"Meanwhile, try to take it a day at a time and not spend your time imagining the future. None of us know what's going to happen. I think Chief Johnson is good guy and I know he's still looking for the truth. I don't think he's going to railroad you and you've got a good lawyer from what I hear.

Trust him."

Alan then started with another tactic. "I want to talk with the guards about getting you on some medication to increase your appetite. It's important you stay healthy. How are you sleeping?"

"I sleep as much as I can. I guess that's not a good sign either."

"How about reading material? I know some people like crossword puzzles and word games to keep them occupied. I'll have some sent over."

"Thanks. Can you tell me anything about how the investigation is going? Anything at all?"

"Chief Johnson and deputy Clark are still working on the case. I can't give you details but your attorney can keep you informed."

Joel nodded his head and then very quietly asked, "How's your son doing now?"

Alan smiled. "Sam's got a good job helping teens with addictions. He also coaches an inter-mural coed basketball team with a number of those kids on his team." Alan was proud of the changes that Sam had made over the past year. "Right now, he's staying with me and saving money to get his own apartment. Boston rents are unbelievably high. He's taking care of my dog while I'm away."

Joel almost smiled at the thought. "What kind of dog?"

"A golden. Harry's old but still likes to run. Do you like dogs?"

"We had a couple when I grew up. One was an

annoying pug and the other a very patient husky. They were funny to watch."

Alan liked to see Joel lighten up with this thought. "I heard you grew up in the country. Did you have a horse?"

Joel smiled widely. "Yes, we did. How did you know?"

Alan laughed out loud. "Everyone on the East Coast thinks people out here own horses and ride daily. It's an image we get from watching all the westerns."

"Are all the people on the East Coast uptight and stressed out?"

Alan laughed, "Probably."

After an hour of conversation, Joel thanked Alan for coming to see him. Alan urged him to reach out to his parents and told him to call again if he needed to talk.

Before he left the facility, Alan spoke with the director and asked him to have Joel evaluated for depression. He would call later to see if Joel got the attention he needed.

MONDAY, JULY 2ND

Kevin was in the office earlier than usual. He had spoken with Alan the night before and appreciated the support he had given Joel. It was a bonus for the Island to have a reliable professional who could be unbiased.

Ashley Philips had left her number with a message that she was free to talk that morning. After checking in with Lana, Kevin called Ashley, hoping she might be able to help.

"I'm not asking you to break the rules or breach any confidentiality, Ashley, but I know you had conversations with Shelly Mann and hoped you might be able to give us some information."

"I'll do my best, Chief Johnson. Some things I really can't discuss but tell me what you need."

"Shelly was into drugs. Did you know this?"

"Yes. She was thinking about going to Narcotics Anonymous meetings and we were looking for one off the Island. Her parents were not aware of her habits, and she wanted it to stay that way."

"Did she get the drugs from Kyle?"

"Yes. As far as she told me."

Kevin asked a few more questions and then rang off. If Kyle was only buying from Joel, then there would be no other direction to go. Frustrated, Kevin yelled out, "Lana? We need to talk!"

Lana rushed into Kevin's office. He never raised his voice and so this was important. "What?!"

"What are we missing here? Knowles isn't talking. Someone else could be dealing drugs and knows who pulled the trigger. Any guesses?"

"Cameron Adams is my first choice." Lana was certain he was involved in more ways than one.

"Let's go talk with Rick Knowles and see if Cameron is one of his gang members."

Rick Knowles had been dealing for years. His father was in prison for the third time on assault with a deadly weapon, and his mother had left years ago and was probably homeless. His grandmother was his only support and she hardly spoke to him. All he had to do was give her some money for his room and she let him do what he liked. And he liked making money... and drugs. He almost had enough money put aside to escape the small town and see the world. That was his dream.

The guys he hung out with were getting too crazy. He knew something had happened when two of the guys never returned that night. Had they been involved with the murders? The 9mm was gone along with some drugs from the stash they kept locked up. Was that the gun used to kill those kids? He didn't trust anyone right now and needed to keep a low profile. But he would not take the rap for any murder.

When he heard the police wanted to talk with him again, Rick just laughed. They couldn't hold him for anything because as far as he knew they had no proof. Rick sat in the uncomfortable jail cell, and hoped to speak with his public defender again and get out.

Knowles was led into an interview room that was windowless and cold. The metal table and chairs were in the center of the room, remaining impartial. Kevin had rung the public defender earlier and he was there in minutes. It wasn't often that he was involved with a murder case, and he advised his client to listen and wait for his instruction to answer.

Kevin began, "Do you know Cameron Adams?"

"Who?" Knowles sneered his answer.

"We understand that you have a group of teens who you pal with. Right now, we have a search warrant for your grandmother's house, and we'll be examining your computer's hard drive, as well as your phone. We'll be looking through your computer to see what you've been doing lately. Now... do you know Cameron Adams?"

"Yeah."

"When was the last time you spoke with him?"

"I don't know! He comes and goes like the other guys. He likes to party."

"I need the names of your group members."

Knowles looked at his attorney for direction. They

spoke briefly and then Knowles said, "Okay. If I give you some names, can I go?"

"It depends on what we find on your computer. I'll be honest with you, Rick, we have information that you've bought some guns on the internet. These guns are illegal, many have been stolen, and one was used in a double murder. If we tie that gun to you, you could take the rap. How does this sound so far?"

Knowles squirmed in his seat and put his hands in his pockets. When he started tapping his shoes on the floor, Kevin knew he might have something to tell them. They both waited.

"Okay," Knowles began, "Cameron was one of my guys. He was older than most, but he seemed careless and full of himself."

"Did he do drugs?"

Knowles looked at his attorney who nodded. "Yeah. He liked Molly, ice, Ecstasy, and coke, mostly, but always had some weed on him."

"This is important, Rick, what were you and your guys doing on the night of the murders?"

"What?! I didn't have anything to do with those kids getting killed!"

"I didn't say you did. I just want to know where you were."

"I can't remember. Maybe just hanging out."

"Who was with you?"

"I don't know."

"Where did you get the 9mm semi-automatic?"

Knowles looked at his attorney and then said, "No comment."

Kevin looked at Lana to see if she had any questions. She turned to Knowles and asked him, "What do you know about the robberies that have happened in the area?"

"No comment."

"Why do you have a detailed map on your wall that circles wealthy areas in Kitsap County?"

"No comment."

Kevin and Lana stood to leave the room. Walking back to his office, Kevin said they needed to talk with Cameron again.

When Kevin and Lana arrived at the Adams's house, they had to wait over three minutes before someone came to the door. It was Andy and he seemed perplexed. "What do you want?"

"Is Cameron here?"

"No."

"Where is he?"

Andy hesitated and then turned his head and called for his father.

"What's going on here?" Drew Adams came to the door to confront the officers.

Kevin nodded and smiled briefly, "We'd like to speak with Cameron."

"What for?"

"We have some questions to ask him."

"Well, you'll have to wait. He's on his way to rehab

and won't be out for a month."

"Where?"

"I don't think I have to tell you that." Drew started to close the door and then hesitated. "What's this about?"

"I'll let you know." Kevin and Lana turned to go without another word.

When they got to the car, Kevin pulled out his cell phone and called Ted Macdonald. He told him what they knew about Rick Knowles and Cameron's association with him.

"We just found out that Cameron Adams has checked in to some re-hab. Can you find out where it is?"

"I'll look around and let you know. My guess is that Adams made sure Cameron was out of the way because he knows something. What else is happening?"

Kevin listed the interviews he and Lana had with various people. It seemed they were narrowing in on the key and the gun. They both wondered why Joel had been targeted when he had no contact with any of these people.

By the time Kevin returned to the office, Rick Knowles had been let go pending any charges that might come his way. They had retrieved his computer and other evidence of potential robberies he may have been involved with, but they didn't have enough to charge him yet. It made Kevin nervous to think he might run, but maybe Knowles was smart enough to know it would only make him look guilty.

Just as he was gathering up his reports, Alan walked in. "Thought you might want to go to lunch." Alan hoped he was right because he wanted to talk some more about the investigation.

"Sure, sounds good. How about the diner?"

Alan already liked this little eatery. Since he kept his walking routine, he considered it to be okay to indulge in the high calorie waffles and scones they offered. Today he planned to order homemade taco soup.

On the walk to the diner, Kevin thanked Alan again for going to see Joel.

Alan nodded. "By the way, I spoke with the director at the jail, and he arranged for Joel to see the nurse so, hopefully, he'll get some medication for his depression."

"If it's true that he wasn't involved, I hope he gets his drug dealing sentence reduced."

"What's going on now?" Alan was curious but was still thinking about Joel and hoping to let him know things were looking up.

"Right now, we need to talk with Cameron Adams. Apparently, he was sent to rehab by his parents. I don't know if it's because they think he was involved with this case, or because he's scared of the gang he's been hanging out with. Anyway, I need to talk with him."

"Do you think he killed those kids?"

"Truthfully, no. I don't think he's capable of murder. He's weak and depends on his mother too much to do something stupid. But he may know who did."

When Alan and Kevin reached the diner, they decided it was best to stop discussing the investigation. Talking about such things in public was never a good idea. They ordered their meals and then Kevin wanted to know what Alan had planned for the coming weeks.

"My friend Sidney will arrive this Friday. I have a list of places I want to take him, but I know he wants to relax, too. So, we'll do both. I want you to meet him. Maybe we could have dinner one night."

"I'll tell you what. Why don't you bring him to our house for a real NW barbecue? My wife would love to meet Sidney and get a chance to know you, too. She's a real people person."

W hen Kevin and Alan returned to the precinct, Lana was quick to tell them that Cameron was in treatment at an expensive rehab in Yakima.

"Ted just called and said the treatment center was evaluating Cameron today."

Being cautious, Kevin reviewed his next move. "We don't want to get in the way of his progress if it's true he's there for rehab and not hiding. We'll let them know we just need some clear answers to help us with an investigation. What do you think, Alan? Do you want to drive over with me?"

"Sure, when do we leave?"

Looking at his watch, Kevin said, "Now."

The three-hour drive to the east side of the state was relaxing. There were fields and fields of crop planting that farmers had cleverly labeled for passing cars to identify. Also along the way were farmers markets that seemed to be bustling with business. Once they passed through Vantage, the halfway point, the grounds got drier, and the surrounding hills looked like a cowboy could ride for hours, just like in the movies. This part of the state appeared far different from the west side, and Alan guessed this was true politically and economically as well.

"I'm glad I came along," Alan remarked. "This side of the state seems to have lower mountain ranges and wide-open views. I bet it's warmer in the summer here."

Kevin nodded, "And more snow in the winter. There's a great resort in Chelan with a 55-mile-long lake. Julia and I take the kids there in the summer. It always feels like we've gone to another state because it's such a change, in the weather especially."

Kevin had called the director of the rehab ahead of time to inform him of their visit and to set up a room for them to speak with Cameron. By the time the men arrived, they were informed that the clients were at dinner. Kevin and Alan were led into a typical conference room and were offered dinner which they both accepted. They waited for over an hour before the door opened again.

Cameron was shocked to see the two officers. He stood at the door to the room and thought about running. But where? The door closed behind him as the two men stood up and asked him to take a seat. Cameron slowly sat and rubbed his hands together.

"We have a few questions," Kevin began. "And I'm sure you can help us out. To begin with, do you know Rick Knowles?"

Cameron stared at Kevin. "Yes."

"Good. He knows you too. Did you belong to his gang, or group, of guys?"

"Yes."

"Thank you. Now, we understand that this gang, or group, likes to party. You know, do drugs, and possibly drink. Do you know if they also get a hold of guns?"

Cameron sank back in his chair. His heart was pounding in his chest, and he thought he might pass out. What should he say? "I'm not sure."

"Well, let me ask you this... did any of them have a 9mm semi-automatic handgun in their possession?"

Cameron looked around the room for a way out. Kevin was aware that he was considering escape and said, "You know, we're not accusing you of anything. We just want to find out who killed Shelly Mann and Kyle Smith and not let them get away with it. If you know something, we don't want you to be in danger, too."

Cameron had already thought about this. He lost sleep being terrified that the two guys who murdered the teens would come after him. He began to shake and felt tears start exploding in his eyes. Kevin stood up and went to sit beside him, putting his hand on his shoulder for comfort. "It's okay, Cameron."

"Can I call my mother?"

Surprised by this question Kevin asked, "Does your mother know about something, Cameron? Is she trying to protect you?"

Cameron looked stunned. What had he done? Now they will question his mother. "No... no... I just wanted to ask her if I needed a lawyer."

Both men looked at each other skeptically. Kevin turned to Cameron and asked, "Was it your decision to go to rehab or your mother's?"

"Both, I guess."

"Where were you at the time of the murders?"

Cameron shook his head over and over. "I didn't do it! I didn't do it!"

"But maybe you know who did. And if you do, we need to protect you."

Cameron knew it was over. He had to tell them everything that happened.

TUESDAY, JULY 3RD

Kevin made the decision to leave Cameron at the rehab center as long as there was 24-hour supervision. He had given up the names of the two fugitives and an all-out alert had gone out to locate them. At least they now knew that Joel was not involved.

Alan was up early and decided to go visit Joel and give him the books and games he had promised. When he reached the facility, he was surprised to see Kevin. "I guess we have the same thing in mind."

"Carson's already been here to fill Joel in with the discovery."

"So how did the gun get to Joel's apartment?"

"Greta Adams did that. Can you believe that? She was protecting her son and wanted everything to point another direction. We've talked with her, but she's lawyered up quickly."

"Now that you have the names of the shooters, what

are the chances of finding them?"

"They're amateurs. I think they'll do something stupid, and we'll get them. I'm just sick to know that if they weren't high on drugs, they might not have shot those kids."

"Is that what Cameron said?"

"Yeah. He said one of the guys was fooling around with the gun and getting crazy. Cameron was almost out of it himself until the gun went off. It appears that Shelly and Kyle were merely at the wrong place."

"Their poor families. It reminds me how drugs and impulsivity are tied so closely together."

"I'm going to have the charges dropped for Joel. At least about the murders. He'll still have to face the drug dealing charges."

"Can I go with you to see him?"

"Of course. Hearing it from both of us will probably give him the support he needs."

L indsay hadn't heard from her father for a week. She was concerned but didn't want to pressure him by following his every move. The boys had been begging to visit the Island again and had big plans to go fishing with their grandfather. Lindsay left a message on her father's phone in the hopes that he would like this idea, too.

Alan looked at his daughter's message and called back. "Hey, I was going to call you today."

"What have you been up to? We haven't spoken for a while."

Alan loved the fact that his daughter was keeping up

on him. "Chief Johnson and I took a drive over to the eastern side of the state. He wanted to interview someone, and I tagged along."

Lindsay had given up worrying that her father would want to get involved with the case. "How's the investigation going?"

"It's okay. We know that Joel was not involved in the murders, so that's one good thing."

"I'm sure my friend Tessa will be pleased to know that. She really likes the guy and was shocked when he was arrested."

"From everything I've learned, the Island seems to have some problems with identifying the main reason why bad things happen. There needs to be a better understanding about drugs for one thing."

"Please tell me that you're not going to start some committee and get involved."

Alan laughed at the thought. "Absolutely not! From now on it's all about you and the kids. I still have another month here."

Lindsay laughed. "What are you doing this weekend?"

"My friend Sidney is arriving on Friday. I want you to meet him, so how about coming over on Saturday and we can make a day of it?"

"Sure. The boys have been hoping you would take them fishing, so I'll tell them this will have to wait."

TUESDAY, JULY 10TH
(ONE WEEK LATER)

A lan's phone rang just as he was having his second cup of coffee.

"Alan... did you see *The Review* this morning?"

Alan put down the newspaper and replied, "I'm just reading it now. It looks like they caught the two guys who killed those kids."

Kitsap County Sheriff's Office detectives have charged Sonny Cramer and Terry Volts with the murders of Shelly Mann and Kyle Smith. Surveillance cameras captured the two hiding in an abandoned warehouse on Kitsap Way near Gorst. Both men are being held in jail on first-degree murder charges with bail set at $1million. Both claim that it was a drug deal gone bad.

Maggie sighed, "I wish it never happened. Those two poor kids... their whole futures were just starting. I hope the Island pays attention to how quickly a life can change when you get caught up with drugs."

Alan agreed. Changing the subject, he asked Maggie what her plans were for the week.

"I'm free until Friday. Do you want to do something?"

"You promised to show me around. How about another Bed and Breakfast? Or is that like a busman's holiday for you?"

"No! I love seeing how others run their business. I know of a wonderful place I've been wanting to visit. How soon can you be ready?"

Made in the USA
Middletown, DE
10 September 2022

73506276R00181